SEE HOW THEY RUN

ALLY CARTER

SEE HOW THEY RUN

BOOK TWO OF EMBASSY ROW

SCHOLASTIC PRESS | NEW YORK

Library of Congress Cataloging-in-Publication Data available

ISBN 978-0-545-65484-5

10 9 8 7 6 5 4 3 2 1   16 17 18 19 20

Printed in the U.S.A.   23
First edition, January 2016

Book design by Yaffa Jaskoll

FOR JOAN BENNETT, SUSAN WILLIS, ROSE BROCK, AND ALL LIBRARIANS. EVERYWHERE. (ESPECIALLY THE ONES WHO ARE ALSO ASSASSINS.)

CHAPTER ONE

I don't know where I am. I don't know why I'm here. And as I study the woman who stands two feet away from me, staring, I realize I don't know her either.

Not even a little bit.

Sure, she is my grandfather's chief of staff. She says she was my mother's friend. I've seen her every day for weeks now, but she is a stranger. For a second, I have to wonder if this might all be a nightmare. But not a nightmare, really. A hallucination. A fantasy. An . . . episode. That's what the doctors call it when my mind drifts to places that aren't real and aren't here and aren't now.

I've been doing it for years, they tell me.

Ever since my mom died.

Ever since I —

No. I don't let myself think about what I did. There are some things that, once remembered, you can never quite forget.

"Grace, it's okay," Ms. Chancellor says. "You're safe here."

I know she's afraid I'm going to turn around and run down the tunnel from which we've just emerged. Or, worse, that I'm going to lash out — that I'm going to fight. With her. With the truth. With reality, because reality keeps trying to kill me, and one day it might just succeed.

"Grace?" Ms. Chancellor's hand is on my arm, and only then do I realize I've started to shake. Then again, I'm always shaking.

Unlike Ms. Chancellor. I look at her hand — at how steady it is — and I think about how it held the gun. She didn't waver. She didn't tremble. She just took aim at the most powerful man in Adria and pulled the trigger.

That was a week ago. Now she's looking at me as if nothing happened at all.

"Will he die?" I ask before I even realize how much the answer matters.

"Who?" Ms. Chancellor asks.

"The prime minister. He's in a coma, right? Will he die? Or will he wake up?"

I want him to die so that he can never hurt anyone again — so that he will never be able to tell the world it was the US ambassador's chief of staff who sent him to his grave.

But I also want him to live so he can tell me why he wanted my mother dead and exactly who first gave the order. I need him to give me a list of all the people that I have to destroy.

2

I wonder which fate Ms. Chancellor would prefer for the prime minister. As usual, she's not saying. Instead she eyes me over the rim of her dark glasses and answers, "Oh. It's not clear whether or not the prime minister will ever recover. It was a very serious heart attack, after all."

For a second, I'm certain I've misheard her. But then I realize that she's smiling like someone who is three moves away from checkmate and there's no way anyone can stop her.

"You can't be serious," I say.

"Oh, I'm quite serious. Heart trouble runs in the prime minister's family. The attack was very sudden, you know. Almost lethal."

I saw Ms. Chancellor shoot him. I saw the bullet wound and the blood that covered his chest. I saw it!

Didn't I?

I don't know anymore, so I shake harder.

"No." My voice is quiet even though I want to scream. "It wasn't a heart attack. He was shot. You —"

"Of course it was a heart attack, Grace. What else would it have been?" Ms. Chancellor gives me a knowing look, and I'm pretty sure this is her way of telling me I'm not crazy. But she will never, ever say so.

Heart attack.

Now I know why the streets have been so calm, the city so normal. I've been alone in my room for a week, but even so I should have recognized the signs of a country not at all concerned about an attempt on the life of its primary leader. If Adria thinks the prime minister was brought down by natural causes — not an American bullet from an American gun — then . . . "No. That can't be. People can't actually believe that his heart failure had nothing to do with the bullet in his chest."

Ms. Chancellor cocks an eyebrow. "What bullet?"

There would have been paramedics and doctors, the Adrian equivalent of the Secret Service. And reports — so many reports. My mind can't fathom the amount of power that this kind of cover-up would take — the scope and scale of a lie of this magnitude. But I know by looking at her that it isn't just possible — it *happened.*

I'll never look at this woman the same way again. It's one thing to mortally wound a man, but then to make it look as if it never happened at all? Who is she? *What* is she?

Nothing is as it seems.

After all, the room we're in isn't supposed to exist. I'm not supposed to be alive. My mom was supposed to be an antiques dealer.

No one was supposed to want her dead.

Slowly, Ms. Chancellor steps away and I stop focusing on her and start focusing on where I am, in a passageway deep beneath the city of Valancia, standing on the threshold of a secret.

"What is this place?" I sound almost feral, I know. And I shake harder.

"We shouldn't have come here," Ms. Chancellor says, worried now. "You're not ready yet. It's okay. We can come back another time."

4

I shake my head. "No. I want to know everything. I want to know everything *now*."

I'm too thin, they tell me. Too frail and tired and broken. I can see it in her eyes. The lies I've been living with for years have all fallen away, leaving me with nothing but pain and anger and a deep, deep sadness that this woman would give anything to fix. She's kind enough to try, but smart enough to know she should know better. So Ms. Chancellor pats my arm.

"Very well, dear. Come along."

Ms. Chancellor walks ahead of me then turns back, holds her arms out wide, and sweeps them across the massive space that sprawls before us.

"What do you think?"

I think I'm still in a nightmare. A very elaborate nightmare. But I don't dare tell her that.

I just follow her onto a balcony that is old — no, *ancient*. But it doesn't creak beneath my weight. The walls are solid stone. Below us, the floor is composed of glossy white tiles that gleam beneath the massive gaslight chandeliers hanging overhead. A huge stained-glass window shines from high on the wall to my left, its light slicing through the cavernous space, showing the symbol that I have been seeing for days but never really stopped to study until now. We are at least a hundred feet beneath the streets of Valancia. How the light reaches that piece of stained glass I do not know and do not ask. There are far more important questions on my mind.

"What is this place?" I ask, knowing the answer must matter but having no idea exactly how.

5

"It is the headquarters," Ms. Chancellor says.

"Headquarters for what?"

But Ms. Chancellor doesn't answer. Instead, she starts for the steps that spiral down to the floor below. "Come with me, Grace. There is a lot for you to see."

When we reach the bottom of the stairs, I touch the heavy wooden tables that sit in the center of the room. They're covered with books that are so old their pages have actually grown thin. I think I could probably see through them if I held them up against a light.

"It's like a library," I say, reaching out for one of the old books.

"Not without gloves, dear," Ms. Chancellor chides. I pull my hand back. "And it's not *like* a library, Grace. It *is* a library. Of a sort."

That's when Ms. Chancellor walks by the weapons — rows and rows of them lining one wall. There are spears and swords, daggers and arrows — bows so large they look like they must have been wielded by giants. It makes me think of empires and gladiators and the battle between good and evil. I've lived on army bases my whole life, but I've never seen anything like this.

"Are those real?" I ask.

"Of course."

"How old are they?"

"How old is Valancia?" Ms. Chancellor glances over her shoulder and eyes me. She doesn't wink, but she looks like she might want to. "Come now. There is something in particular you need to see."

I follow Ms. Chancellor through an arching doorway, down a stone corridor that twists and curves. The ceiling is low, and gaslights burn at even intervals, but even so, the light is dim as it bounces off the old white stone.

There is no sound here, a hundred feet beneath the city. No honking buses or ringing trolley bells. No tourist has ever set foot in these hallowed halls — I'm sure of that. I'm walking in important footsteps, but I have absolutely no idea whose.

Finally, the corridor opens into a large circular room. The ceiling rises, dome-like, above us. And in the center of the room stands a woman, carved from wood. She looks toward a sky that she can't see, reaches out for a sun that she can't touch. One wing is unfurled behind her, its tip long since rotted away. Her other wing is broken. And I know this poor angel will never fly again.

"What is this?"

I hold my hand out tentatively, asking for permission, and Ms. Chancellor nods.

"Go ahead, dear," she says as I touch the old, smooth wood. "It was the masthead of a ship a very long time ago. One of seven ships, to be precise. This is the angel that guided the *Grace*."

I spin on her. "The what?"

Ms. Chancellor grins as if to say *You heard me*. Then she just brings her hands together and asks, "Do you know the story of Adria, dear?"

My grandmother was Adrian. My mother was born here — raised here. I came here every summer for the first twelve years of my life. I'm fluent in Adria's language, but I don't know this country, I'm starting to realize. It's my home, but I still feel like an invader, someone who should be cast outside its walls.

"Mom used to tell us the story," I say. "But somehow I think it was the wrong one."

Ms. Chancellor chuckles. "What you and most of the world have been told *is* true. It is simply a tad bit *incomplete*. As much of history is wont to be."

My blood is pounding harder now, like I've been running. But am I running to or from? I honestly don't know.

A chandelier hangs overhead, but the gaslight is dim — a fluttering, flickering thing. So Ms. Chancellor lights a candle and holds it up, walking toward the wall that circles around us.

In the glow, I realize that the wall is covered in canvas. A mural stretches all the way around. Several arching doorways stand at regular intervals, breaking up the scenes.

When Ms. Chancellor raises her hand, her light shines upon sand and ancient strongholds and a scorching sun that reflects off the shining armor of an army riding into battle.

"At the end of the twelfth century, the Third Crusade was coming to an end," Ms. Chancellor says, beginning the story that every child in Adria learns in the cradle.

On the next panel, sand blends into sea as seven white sails set out for the horizon.

"Sir Fredrick and his knights left the holy land. They took their seven fastest ships and made for England, but a massive storm blew them terribly off course. They couldn't see the stars. They had long since lost sight of land. Day after day the storm

8

beat on, until these men who had survived years of battle began to fear that they would die there, swallowed by the sea. But then — as the story goes — on the seventh morning, Sir Fredrick saw it."

When Ms. Chancellor moves to the third painting, I have to step back to fully realize what I'm seeing. A man. It is a painting of a man, a *giant*, standing in the clear blue waters I know well.

"As you know, Grace, the Romans founded Valancia. Even two thousand years ago it was the crossroads of the world, and to mark the entrance to the bay they erected a monument, something to announce to the world that this was their land. Of course, eventually, the Roman Empire gave way to the Byzantines, and the Byzantines eventually lost Adria to the Turks, and the Turks to the Mongols, but the point is that for a thousand years a great stone idol stood, guarding Adria's shores."

"What is it?" I ask, gesturing to the painting.

"It's Neptune. Roman god of the sea. Some say the angel led Sir Fredrick and his knights through the storm, kept them safe until Sir Fredrick could see Neptune on the horizon like a beacon, calling them home."

I watch Ms. Chancellor's light play over the scene as seven ships sail though the long, dark shadow of Neptune's outstretched hand.

"Was there really a statue?" I ask.

"Oh yes. I'm told it was the height of two football fields."

"Why haven't I ever seen it?"

"Oh, it fell and eroded away ages ago," Ms. Chancellor says with a wave of her hand. "The important thing is that it still stood when Sir Fredrick and his men battled that storm. Because of it, they found Adria. And safety."

It's easy to imagine ships full of war-torn knights coming here to outrun their demons. I don't stop to consider the irony that this is where mine found me.

In the next painting, Adria looks like Eden. The seven ships bob on peaceful waters while the knights make their way onto the land. They fall to their knees and kiss the ground.

"When Sir Fredrick's men climbed onto our shores they were greeted by people who had never known anything but war and unrest — people who had been mere pieces on a chessboard for centuries. They were greeted by people who took them in. Of course, at the time, Adria was ruled by the Mongols." Ms. Chancellor points to the painting, at the warriors who watch Sir Fredrick's knights from the hills in the distance. "But the knights quickly formed an alliance with Adria's people, and together they fought until this new land was their own."

When Ms. Chancellor turns to me again, there is a new twinkle in her eye. "Seven knights came to Adria, my dear. What the stories never say is that this is where they found and married seven women."

When she reaches the next-to-last picture, Ms. Chancellor shines her light upon the beautiful faces of the brides who stand behind their husbands, smiling knowing smiles.

"These women had been born here, raised here. They knew every tunnel the Romans had carved beneath the city, every cave high in the hills. What the history books never say, Grace, is that

Sir Fredrick and his knights won Adria because their wives showed them how to do it."

She says this like it's important, and I have to remind myself that once upon a time, my mother came to this room and heard this story.

A part of me has to wonder if this is what killed her.

Ms. Chancellor lowers her candle. "Now, it's important to understand that Adria had never known peace. Not really. It was too important, too pivotal — every great empire wanted it for its own. And so as the knights of Adria ruled, their wives watched and listened and whispered in their husbands' ears ways to keep their homeland from being pulled once more into war and chaos."

She takes another step and lets her light fall upon the image of a great stone wall beginning to rise around the city.

"They told their husbands they would feel safer behind a wall. They suggested who the new country should trade with and why. And, most of all, these women remembered what their mothers and grandmothers had learned from the Romans, the Byzantines, the Turks, and the Mongols: that history almost always repeats itself. And it is almost always written by men."

She's right, of course. There's a loop in my life — a pattern of violence and death and heartbreaking sorrow that I would give anything to stop. To rewrite. To end. But my walls are not yet high enough, not strong enough. What Ms. Chancellor doesn't know is that I never will stop building.

"So that is how Adria was born, Grace. Sir Fredrick became King Fredrick the First. The knights who led the other six ships were given lands and riches and a place at the king's side as his most trusted advisors. Years passed, and their sons became princes and lords and the leaders of Europe."

She pulls the candle farther from the wall. Its gentle glow lights her face, and somehow I know this moment matters. My heart is pounding, my hands sweating as Ms. Chancellor turns to me.

"We are what became of their daughters."

CHAPTER TWO

Three years ago the prime minister of Adria called his chief of security into his office and ordered him to kill my mother.

I don't know why.

When I started asking questions, the same prime minister ordered the same man to kill me.

And now the prime minister is in a coma and my mother is dead, but the mystery lives on. The look on Ms. Chancellor's face tells me that she thinks the answers are here, in this dimly lit alcove and centuries-old story. But I don't see it. So I look up at the angel, willing her to guide me to the truth.

"What did the daughters do?" I ask. I can't meet Ms. Chancellor's gaze.

"They did the only thing women could do a thousand years ago: They stayed in the shadows. But shadows are the perfect place from which to watch, to see. And make no mistake, my dear, the women who founded Adria saw everything. We *still* see everything."

"My mother was a part of this?"

Ms. Chancellor nods. "And your grandmother. And your grandmother's mother, and so on for a thousand years. Every girl born to one of the Society's members was observed and, if she seemed an appropriate fit, she was introduced to the Society in her sixteenth year. In time, we grew. Our reach expanded. And through it all we watched and recorded history, gently guiding it on occasion."

I think about the gunshot wound that miraculously became a heart attack. I remember the room full of dusty, ancient books and weapons.

"So you're a secret society . . . of librarians?"

Ms. Chancellor laughs. "Among other things," she says. But in my mind I'm remembering how she held the gun, how calm she was when she fired. "Every army in the world knows that knowledge is power — information, the world's most lethal weapon. The women keep the secrets, my dear. We have always kept the secrets."

"Did one of these secrets kill my mother?"

The lights are flickering, off and on. Ms. Chancellor glances behind us then reaches for me. "Come along, dear. I'm afraid our time is up."

When Ms. Chancellor takes my arm and leads me away, I realize we're going back the way we came.

"Stop," I snap, jerking free of her grasp. I know how I look, how I sound. Ancient secret societies don't have room for petulant children, but it's too much, too fast. And it isn't nearly enough. I want to stomp my foot, to scream, to cry. I need to curse my predecessors for their club and their secrets because they led to what happened to my mother. I hate this Society and every one of its members. Even the one who is standing right in front of me.

"You said someone wanted my mom dead because of her job."

"I did say that."

"So what was her job?"

"She was an antiques dealer," Ms. Chancellor says.

"What was her job *here*?" I ask, my frustration boiling over.

"She was an archivist, Grace. *An antiques dealer.* Her job was collecting and retrieving rare and valuable artifacts that pertain to Adria or the Society."

"Were these artifacts valuable?"

"Yes."

"Were they dangerous?"

Ms. Chancellor brings her hands together. "Anything of value can be dangerous if given the right conditions."

"What did she find?"

Ms. Chancellor studies me, as if weighing which will harm me more, the truth or yet another lie. She's too calm, too poised as she studies me. I have no idea whether or not to believe her when she says, "Honestly, I have no idea."

"No!" I howl — rage and fear and dread bubbling up inside me and spilling over. "You have to know something! You have to."

Instinctively, Ms. Chancellor steps closer, but she doesn't put her arms around me. She knows better than to try to hold a wild thing.

"We will find it, Grace," she says.

I'm weaker than I'd like to admit, because I find myself wanting to believe her.

She leads me back into the first big room. As we're passing by the weapons, she says, "Making yourself sick won't help matters. You both have a lot to learn, and you're going to need to be at your best when we begin."

"I don't care. I want . . . Wait." I stop. "Did you say *both*?"

The stained-glass window is overhead. Dust dances in the inexplicable beam of light, and that is where she's standing.

I see the outline of her silhouette, and when she moves slowly forward, I know immediately who it is.

"Hello, Grace," Lila says. "Haven't you heard? We're going to be sisters."

I am my own worst enemy. But if there were to be a second place, it would go to this girl. Lila's black hair is glossy and straight. Her nails perfectly polished, her back perfectly straight. She's my Brazilian-Israeli best friend's twin sister, but there is nothing of Noah in the girl in front of me.

Lila is the anti-Noah, which means she's also the anti-me.

I spin on Ms. Chancellor. "Yes, Grace," she says to my unasked question. "You and Lila will be joining us at the same time. Isn't that wonderful? Learning about the Society is so much better with a friend."

Lila is not my friend.

One look at the girl tells me she is thinking the same thing, but Ms. Chancellor practically beams. "I'm so excited for you both. Now go on. I'm sure you two have a lot to talk about."

No, I want to say, but somehow I manage to bite back the word.

"I'm afraid I'm needed at the embassy. We will continue this soon," Ms. Chancellor says before hurrying ahead of us.

Lila and I follow in silence, climbing the spiral steps to the door Ms. Chancellor showed me just an hour ago. But even if we're quiet, my thoughts are loud. I can't even try to hide my disappointment. My mom was supposed to make more sense to me now. This was her big secret. I am where she once was, on the verge of learning the things that she once knew. But as Lila and I start down the tunnel that will take us outside, I can't help but feel my mother slipping further and further away. The woman I remember now simply feels like a lie, and there's nothing new to replace it.

"Weird, right?"

It takes a moment to realize Lila is talking, a moment more to realize she's talking to *me*.

"You're in the shocked-and-confused phase right now. It's okay. I get it. The shock goes away after a few days, but the awe . . . the awe hasn't gone away for me yet."

"So you didn't know . . ."

17

"What?" Lila looks at me. "That my mother belongs to an ancient league of secret lady assassins or whatever?"

"They aren't assassins," I say. Then I think about it. "Are they?"

"Oh, certainly." Lila rolls her eyes. "Did you think their battle-ax collection is for when the librarians want to collect late fees?" She doesn't wait for me to answer before she shrugs and says, "In answer to your question, no. I didn't know. My mother told me a few weeks ago. Did yours tell you?" It takes Lila a moment to realize what she's said. "I mean, before she died?"

She doesn't sound embarrassed. After all, Lila is the kind of person who isn't afraid of the truth and doesn't have time for regrets.

I shouldn't either, I realize, but all I can say is, "No. I never knew."

Maybe my mom died too soon. Maybe she didn't think I belonged here. Maybe it's just too hard to work something like an ancient family legacy in over breakfast. But no matter why, the fact remains that my mother never told me, and my mother never will. There was a time that would have made me cry, but that's the good thing about being dead inside, I guess. Dead people don't feel pain.

Then something occurs to me — something that has nothing to do with my mother.

"Does Noah know?" I ask, and Lila laughs.

"Noah doesn't have a clue. About anything. Ever. It is safe to assume that Noah is perpetually clueless."

"I'm worried."

I don't know where the words come from or why I say them now. Aloud. To Lila. But I can't take them back, and it's too late. Lila's already looking at me like I'm even crazier than she'd been led to believe.

"What do *you* have to worry about?"

"Well, let's see . . . Three years ago the prime minister ordered my mom's death, but I accidentally killed her instead. Didn't remember it, though. And then a few weeks ago the prime minister tried to have *me* killed, but he ended up in a coma, so we have absolutely no idea who else wanted my mother dead. Or why. Or how it might all tie into the shadowy secret society that my ancestors evidently founded a thousand years ago. So I have worries, Lila. I have plenty."

The look Lila gives me is so cold it's like maybe I didn't say a thing. And maybe I didn't. I'm starting to wonder when Lila shrugs.

"Fine. Evade my question." She reaches for the ladder and climbs outside.

I want to yell at her and pull her glossy black hair or force her to break a nail. Most of all, I want to go to Noah and tell him how annoyed I am that his twin sister and I are going to be in the same secret society. But I can't do that, of course. Because . . . *secret society*. I have one more secret now. One more mystery. One more set of lies. But I'm not lying to myself anymore, and that has to count for something.

The sun seems too bright once we make it to the street. I'm still standing, squinting, when Lila says "Don't look behind you," which means, of course, I start to turn, but Lila grabs my arm. "Keep walking."

Lila loops her arm through mine. It's the way the fashionable women always walk together down the chic streets near the palace. *This feels so European*, I think before realizing that we *are* in Europe. We probably look like confidantes. Friends.

Looks can be deceiving.

"What is it?" I ask.

"There's a big guy with a scar on his face watching us. I think he's . . ." She makes a quick glance back. "Yes. He *is* following us."

How many times in my life have I thought I saw the Scarred Man? Too many to count. For years, it was just another by-product of my messed-up mind, my fear. My crazy.

Now it's just one more thing I have to feel guilty about.

After all, the Scarred Man is no longer the Scarred Man. Now he's . . .

"Dominic." I force out the word.

"What?" Lila asks.

"His name is Dominic. He used to be the prime minister's head of security."

"Do you think he saw us leave the tunnel?"

I *know* he saw us leave the tunnel, but that's not something I can tell Lila. I jerk to a stop and turn around. Dominic is across the street, standing perfectly still. Watching. He doesn't smile and doesn't wave. He doesn't even try to hide or act natural. There's no denying what he's doing. He is tracking me.

Lila says something in Hebrew I don't understand. Or maybe it's the Portuguese equivalent of *creepy*.

I should tell her that I know him. Sort of. I should let her know that he and I are . . . something. Not friends. Not family. We have whatever bond forms when you spend three years shouting from rooftops that the Scarred Man killed your mother. We are bound by whatever it is that lives on long after someone saves your life. Or maybe he's here because my mother was his first — and maybe only — love.

I killed the love of his life, I realize with a start. And, suddenly, Dominic's glare has an entirely new meaning.

"Sorry, Lila. I've got to —"

Go.

Run.

Scream.

I have to get away from here before the guilt makes me throw up all over Lila and her perfectly polished toes.

"Where are you —"

"Bye, Lila. Just tell Noah I said . . . bye."

Then, before my new sister can see through me, I'm gone.

CHAPTER THREE

I run until my lungs want to burst and my legs turn to noodles. I hear nothing but the pounding of my feet against the hard-packed dirt. I feel nothing but the stinging slap of the tree branches and thorny vines that swipe against my face and scratch my legs. But I can't stop. I have to go faster, higher, stronger.

I have to outrun the past.

Even after I break free from the brush that covers the path I keep running until I literally cannot run anymore. I skid to a stop, kicking at pebbles that tumble down the cliff and splash into the sea. Only then can I let myself breathe.

At the top of the cliffs, the air that blows off the Mediterranean is warm and wet. It pushes my hair from my face as I stand here, hands outstretched, desperate to fly. But I can't fly. And I won't jump. No matter how much I want to, regardless of how deep I know the water off the shoreline is.

I am not supposed to jump off the cliffs anymore. I'm not supposed to take chances or tempt fate. Besides, my grandfather and Ms. Chancellor have been watching my every move for days. If I come back to the embassy with bruises, they'll see them. If I pick at my food they'll ask why. And so I stand on this ridge, high above the city, hiding in plain sight, pretending to be an ordinary girl.

Just your average teenager who recently learned she shot and killed her own mother.

"Grace!" My name comes flying on a breeze that smells like smoke. When I close my eyes I hear glass shatter, a woman scream.

"Grace! No!"

The cries haven't changed in years, but now I know what they mean. Now I know she's not trying to make me run. She's trying to make me *stop* — to put down the gun I'm holding. She is trying to tell me that it's okay and that the Scarred Man — that *Dominic* — isn't trying to hurt her. But it's too late. In every sense of the word.

I shake my head, try to clear away the smoky haze. But the words come again.

"Grace, no!"

I clench my hands together so tightly that my nails almost draw blood.

"Grace, stop!"

The voice is too deep, too close. Too real. And that's what makes me spin. As I do, the rocks beneath my feet shift. I've ventured too close to the edge and I can feel the ground beneath me giving way, crumbling, and soon I, too, am falling. The wind rushes up to greet me, and for one split second, I am free.

But then a hand reaches me. It grasps my arm and I'm jerked back. Instead of stone, I slam against a hard, broad chest, and then we topple to the ground. Arms come up to hold me, squeezing me so tightly I can't fight. I am frozen. Trapped. Then the boy beneath me rolls, forcing my back to the ground as he looms overhead, making certain there is no place left for me to fall.

I don't understand what Noah says next, but I'm pretty sure it's in Portuguese and probably vulgar. He's breathing so hard and we're so close that I can actually feel his chest rise and fall. Even though we're lying on the ground, it's like he's run a marathon — like he's still running. Chasing after me.

He curses again and then spits out, "What were you doing, Grace? What were you *thinking*?"

He isn't angry, I can tell. He's terrified. Even after he leans back and lets me go, his hands are still shaking.

"You told me you'd never jump off of here again. You *promised*!"

"I wasn't jumping," I say — but Noah doesn't believe me. He wants to, but he can't.

It's not his fault that he's not stupid.

I try again. "I wasn't going to jump, Noah. I swear."

When he leans toward me, I can't help myself; I scoot away.

"You're lying," he says.

"No. I'm not. I just come up here sometimes. To think."

"To think about what? Jumping?"

"No!" I stand, and the wind blows in my face again. There are no more traces of smoke. The air is salty and brisk, slapping me awake. Still, it's almost like a dream when I say, "My mom, okay? Sometimes I come up here and think about my mom."

"Oh." Noah eases back.

"What are you doing here, Noah?" I ask, suddenly worried that maybe Dominic isn't the only person who has been watching my every move. Maybe I've just been too sloppy to notice.

"What am *I* doing here?" Noah throws his hands out wide then rests his elbows on his bent knees. "Well, I haven't seen you in a week. You are my best friend. And sometimes I like to check and make sure my friends aren't dead. There. Did I cover it all? I think I got it all."

It sounds good, but I'm not buying it, so I ask again, *"What are you doing here?"*

Noah pushes to his feet and hastily brushes the dust off of his khaki shorts and dark T-shirt.

"What am I doing here?" he snaps. "What do you think I'm doing? I followed you! I saw you running down the street like a madwoman, so I followed you, because . . ."

He trails off, unwilling or unable to go on, so I finish for him.

"I'm a madwoman."

"Because I was worried about you, okay?" Noah looks at the sea then back to where I stand, dusty and wind-blown. My arms and legs are scratched and probably bleeding. "Can you blame me?" he asks.

I can't, but I don't dare say so.

"I'm not going to leave, you know," Noah says when my silence is too much. "You can't run me off. It's too late for that. We've done international espionage together. We're bonded for life."

I laugh in spite of myself, because even though Noah can't make me happy, every now and then he makes me forget to be sad. And sometimes I try to tell myself that it's enough.

Then he looks at me again, joking aside. "What is up with you?"

"Nothing."

"Where were you? What made you so upset?"

I want to tell him — I really do. Noah is good and kind and safe — a diary in human form — and I want to pour out all of my secrets. But they're secrets for a reason, and Noah can never, ever know. Not about Lila or the Society or the Scarred Man or me. Especially me. It's taken sixteen years for me to find a best friend; I can't risk losing him now.

"Nothing, Noah. I'm fine. Really."

I turn from the cliffs and start toward the rough path that leads to the street below. But before I get far, Noah reaches out and grabs my hand. As he spins me toward him, he is heartbreakingly serious.

"Just don't jump, Grace. Okay? Please don't jump."

"Yeah. Okay," I say, and move again toward the path, but Noah keeps my hand too tight in his own and pulls me closer.

"I mean it. Don't get yourself . . . hurt. Okay?"

I've only lived on Embassy Row for a few weeks, and already Noah knows this about me — that I'm reckless, that I'm dangerous. That I can never be trusted. And that's the problem.

"I'm not going to jump, Noah," I say, but even I don't really believe me.

He doesn't question my word, though, as we start down the path that is even wilder and more overgrown in the heat of summer. He doesn't even question my sanity.

He just says, "I saw the Scarred Man today."

"His name is Dominic," I say, repeating the words I have told myself over and over since that fateful night.

"Yeah, *Dominic*. I saw him. And I don't trust him."

But I'm already shaking my head. "He's just a man with a scar. Not all people with scars are evil."

Noah gives me a look. "Of course not. But think about it. You say Dominic killed your mom —"

"He didn't," I blurt. But Noah doesn't hear my tone. He doesn't read the pain that lives behind my eyes.

"Yeah." Noah waves my concern away. "But he's supposed to be the prime minister's head of security, right? And then the prime minister's heart mysteriously gives out right in the middle of the G-20 Summit? On the Scarred Man's watch? The prime minister is in a coma, Grace."

"I am aware, Noah."

"Don't joke. And don't tell me that's a coincidence," Noah finishes strong.

It's not, but I don't dare say so.

"I was wrong," I tell him. "Okay? Dominic didn't kill my mother. My mother's death was an *accident*."

I don't choke on the word — and for that, at least, I'm grateful. But Noah still hears a little of what I don't say.

"There's something you're not telling me."

Noah has been my designated best friend since my first night on Embassy Row. But he wasn't there the night the prime minister finally cornered me. He didn't see the way Dominic put himself in danger. And he can never, ever know that the prime minister was shot and Ms. Chancellor was the one who picked up the gun and pulled the trigger. Noah may be my best friend and all, but I'm pretty sure he's not ready for the international implications of a high-ranking diplomat from one country actually shooting and seriously wounding the prime minister of another. Wars have started for less. And if Noah knew the truth . . . if *anyone* knew the truth . . .

I think about Grandpa and the president and the diplomatic implications.

And then I think about the Society and wonder what they've already done to keep the truth a secret. I don't want to know how far they might go to make sure it stays that way.

"Grace. Gracie!" Slowly, Noah's voice brings me back. Then he smiles and squeezes my hand.

"You okay?" Noah is a good enough friend that he actually cares about the answer to that question. Which means he's too good a friend for me to actually give it.

Instead, I kick a small stone that sits on the path, watch it tumble down the hill, and say, "Come on."

A few minutes later we're stepping back onto Embassy Row. The sun has started to set across the Mediterranean, and the flags of the embassies all blow in the salty breeze, like soldiers standing guard against the massive wall that has held Valancia safe against intruders for at least a thousand years.

Wordlessly, Noah falls into step beside me, his long legs eating up the ground, two of my strides matching one of his.

"So," he says, spinning around and walking backward, "what are we going to do now?"

"Now, Noah, I go home."

"Okay. Good plan. First stop, USA. We'll tell your grandfather and Ms. Chancellor that you're going to spend the evening with me. I'll give them my best responsible-role-model smile, and they'll be putty in my hands. Then what? A movie?"

"No, thank you," I say, trying out my best good-girl voice.

"No movies. Check. Hey, Lila's planning a thing later. We should go."

Lila. The realization almost stops me. Noah doesn't know the truth about Lila.

"Grace?"

"Oh, right." I shake my head. "That's a great idea, because your twin sister is such a fan of mine."

"No. It's a great idea because you are my aforementioned best friend and it is summer in one of the most beautiful cities in the world."

Noah is grinning at me, teasing, mocking just a little. He doesn't know that he should hate me. Fear me. Pity me. I should like him for that, but in the end I can't respect anyone who could be foolish enough to be sucked into all of my lies.

As the sun dips lower, shadows descend on Embassy Row. Noah stops, and I have no choice but to turn and face him.

I can't help but notice he's stopped smiling.

"What's going on with you?"

"Nothing."

"You're up to something. And you're not telling me, and that offends me. Just a little. It hurts." Noah motions to his heart. "Right here, Grace. Right here."

I'm almost certain he's joking. Almost. He laughs, but then, in a flash, he's serious again.

"You're scaring me, Gracie. Just tell me what it is. Tell me and let me help you."

But no one can help me. Not anymore. Not ever again.

"I'm sorry, Noah," I say as we reach the US embassy's gates. The marine on duty nods to us but doesn't speak. He's almost invisible, and Noah and I are almost alone.

"I will see you later, Grace."

"Yeah. I'll see you later."

He points at me. "At Lila's shindig, right? I'll meet you right here. In this spot. Nine o'clock. Because you are going to go with

30

me. We are going to be typical teenagers for a brief, three-to-six-hour window this evening."

I can't help myself. I laugh a little as I ease toward the gates. "Take care, Noah."

"I'm taking that as a yes. You heard that, Martin." Noah points to the marine. "She said yes."

Martin opens the gates and I step onto US soil, but Noah is still calling at me through the fence.

"I will be here, Grace. And you'd better be here, too, or else I'm storming the fences. Or" — he looks up at the imposing iron bars that surround the embassy's grounds — "I'm going next door to Germany and getting Rosie to storm the fences! Don't make me cause an international incident."

Martin is laughing as I step toward the doors. When I glance back I can't help but notice that Noah's grin is wide and honest. He doesn't see the truth about me because he doesn't know where to look for it. Buried deep. Paved over. If he knew me better he might see through my facade, so I swear that Noah can *never* know me better. I am safe in my mother's homeland, my grandfather's house. Embassy Row is my new home, and I'll be fine here as long as I'm surrounded by strangers.

I'm just starting to tell myself that it's okay, that no one here will ever guess the truth about my mother's society or my terrible secret, when I see the doors of the residence open and I hear a familiar voice say, "Hello, Gracie."

CHAPTER FOUR

The boy in front of me is not a stranger, and yet he feels like one. His hair is shorter, practically shaved. His arms are leaner, his posture better. But the hardest thing to realize is that he isn't looking at me like he used to.

He called me Gracie.

But I am not his little sister. Not really. Not anymore. I'm the monster who killed his mother, and now both of us know it.

I knew I'd have to see Jamie eventually, but I'd assumed I'd have time to prepare, to brace myself for him lashing out, fighting back against the thing that killed his mother. I knew I was going to have to deal with this someday. I just never guessed that *someday* would be *now*.

Before I can blink, Jamie lunges for me. He's faster than he used to be, stronger. In a flash, his arms are around my waist and my feet are off the ground. I close my eyes and feel his harder-than-I-remember shoulders beneath my hands as he spins me around and around. For a split second, I let myself forget that I'm not little — that I'm not safe. This is my big brother, the boy who slayed all my monsters. But just as soon as I'm back on the ground, I remember: The monster is me.

Guilt makes my eyes burn. I want to run and hide, but I just stand there, looking at my big brother.

"What . . . what are you doing here?"

Something happens when the sun sets in Adria. There comes a moment every day when the sky is clearer, the water is bluer, and the entire city looks as if it's made of gold. It actually *glows*, and when my brother smiles, the honey-colored light hits him and he looks like he's wearing a halo.

"Surprise!" On anyone else, Jamie's smile would be cocky. But on him it's so natural and easy that it makes me want to cry.

"What are you doing here?" I ask again.

"Do I need a reason to come visit my favorite sister?"

I'm his only sister, and that's what I'm supposed to say. It's my line, my joke. But I can only ask, "What about West Point?"

I can't even imagine my father's response should Jamie wash out. But of course that thought is preposterous. Jamie doesn't fail. Not at anything. Not ever.

"West Point is still there," he tells me, trying to tease, but I don't laugh anymore. My brother, of all people, should know that.

"Why aren't *you* there, Jamie?"

"Relax, Gracie. I'm on leave. We're finished with basic, and we had a few days, so we —"

"We?" I ask just as another boy steps through the embassy's door. It's the one used for the ambassador and senior staff. For family. But I have never seen this boy before in my life. And yet, instantly, I know him.

He is like every boy on every military base in America. At least from a distance. Even in civilian clothes, boys like him are always *uniform*, with their nearly shaved heads, muscular shoulders, and bulging biceps. He is caught in that space between man and child. A little baby fat is still in his cheeks, but he has the body of an adult male.

I know without asking that he was some kind of high school sports stud. Football? No . . . wrestling. The boy takes a step; I watch him move, and I know he was some kind of hotshot high school wrestler just as surely as I know my own name. He carries himself like someone who hasn't yet been beaten. But high school — and even West Point — are not like the world at large. He doesn't know what I know: that, eventually, everybody gets taken down.

"Gracie, I'd like you to meet John Spencer," Jamie says. "Spence, this is my sister, Gracie."

I hold out my hand. "Grace." I glare at my brother. "He's the only one who gets to call me Gracie."

Spence takes my hand and tips the cap that he wears over his too-short hair. "It's nice to meet you, ma'am," he says.

This makes me laugh. *Ma'am?*

34

"Yeah, don't you know, Gracie?" Jamie puts an arm around me. "We're in training to become both officers and gentlemen."

Jamie thinks he's funny. He's trying to make me laugh again, but I just look at John Spencer. Spence.

"You go to West Point, too?" I ask him.

"Yes, ma'am."

"And you're both on leave so you just happened to pop across the Atlantic Ocean?" I say.

I don't ask how many phone calls Jamie has shared with Grandpa. With Dad. I don't want to know how many hours they have worked and worried behind my back, strategizing how to pull me back from all the metaphorical cliffs — and all the real ones, too.

Was this Jamie's idea?

And does anyone really think this can do anything but go terribly, horribly wrong?

Spence and Jamie share a glance before Spence answers, "My grandmother was from Adria. I've never been, and when Blake said he was coming this way, I decided to tag along."

"Blake?" I ask.

"Blakely." Jamie says our last name as if that should explain it all. "Blake. You get called by your last name a lot at West Point, and . . ."

"Oh, I get it. Spence. Blake. Very cute. Very fun. You guys are adorable." My brother is looking at me. No, I realize with a start — my brother is *seeing* me. He's not like Noah. He's known me longer — better. And I'm afraid that Jamie is going to see all of my new secrets, read them in my eyes. It's the one thing I can't ever let happen. Not again.

Suddenly, I step back. I feel my brother's arm fall away. "It was nice meeting you, Spence. And, Jamie, I'll see you soon, but I've got . . . things to do."

"I'll go with you."

"No, Jamie. It's okay."

"It's not okay. I came a long way to see you. Now let me see you. I miss you."

When I pull away again, Jamie moves in front of me, blocking my path. This isn't some maneuver they teach at West Point. It is Sibling 101, and Jamie's always been a natural.

"Wait," he says.

"Don't," I tell him.

"Don't what?" He is using his Big Brother tone, daring me to deny that he is taller, stronger, faster. Older. But he has spent two semesters already at West Point, and I'm no longer the girl he left behind. The *me* who lives in Adria feels more like an only child.

"Don't lie to me," I say, my voice too low for Spence to hear it.

Jamie is facing me, away from his friend. Maybe that's why he allows a look to cross his face, almost like I've slapped him.

"I'd never lie to you, Gracie."

Except you have, I want to say. *You lied to me every day for three years. You are still lying if you dare to stand there, looking like a part of you doesn't hate a part of me.*

But I don't say a single word.

"Gracie —"

"West Point cadets don't get leave, Jamie. And if they do, they don't leave the country."

"Well, actually," he says, sidling closer, "we do have a break between terms. And we *are* allowed to leave the country if we miss our kid sisters."

He wants us to pretend, to act like nothing's wrong and nothing happened. But I am so, so tired of making believe. I have been living a lie for three years. My mind is having a hard enough time remembering the true version of events; I can't bear another fake one.

"Don't you mean, if your kid sisters have nervous breakdowns? West Point cadets get to go on big international trips then?"

I wait for Jamie to joke again, to laugh. Or, better yet, to walk away. Yes, walking away would be so much better than standing in the fading light, pity filling his eyes.

"I'm fine, Jamie. You didn't have to come check up on me."

But he just shakes his head slowly, side to side. He sees right through me.

"Now who's lying?"

Spence has drifted back inside, and for once, Embassy Row is quiet and still.

"Do you have a good therapist?" Jamie asks, slipping from brother to father to mother. My role is still the same.

"Yes."

"Are you going?" he demands.

"Yes."

"Do you *want* to get better?"

"Yes!" *I don't know.*

When a pair of women pass by on the sidewalk, Jamie takes my arm and pulls me deeper into the shadows of the embassy's yard. The women speak in rapid Adrian, the language of our mother. And for a second I swear I can almost see her standing on the other side of the fence, calling out that it's time for us to come home.

"I know you know." Jamie's voice shakes. "I know you remember what happened, so don't tell me you're okay."

I'm supposed to say something now. Something good or kind or clever. Something to show just how sorry I am and just how much progress I've made. I'm supposed to make my brother stop worrying.

But the truth is, if my brother was smart he wouldn't be worried. He'd be terrified.

"Grace —" Jamie starts, but I can't listen to any more — I can't take any more. The guilt and shame have been weighing on me for three years, and the only thing I can do is pave over them with rage.

I deserve my guilt, but I shouldn't have to live with Jamie's betrayal, with all of their lies.

"You *knew*!" I can't help but shout. "All those years, you knew the truth and you never told me!"

I expect Jamie to lash back, to fight. He's a soldier now, isn't he? But he's just shaking his head.

"You're my little sister. Protecting you is my job, so I'm not going to apologize for not telling you the truth. You can yell at me all you want, but I'm not sorry."

"You had no right to keep that from me!"

"I had every right!" Jamie shakes his head, almost like he's locked in a nightmare, trying to wake up. "It was better when you didn't know, Gracie. I'd make you forget all over again if I could."

"You lied. Everyone lied. Grandpa and Dad and . . . them, I understand. But not you, Jamie. Never you."

"You didn't see you, Gracie. Mom was dead and you were dying. Really. I'm not exaggerating. The guilt was *killing* you! I hated seeing you in that place. I don't know how much longer Dad and I could have taken it — watching you scream and shake and yell about the *Scarred Man*. You just couldn't take it anymore. *I* couldn't take it anymore. So when they decided to stop fighting and let you think what you wanted to think, I didn't care. I wanted to lie. I wanted to forget about everything as much as you did. About Mom. And you. And the intruder, and how —"

"The *intruder*?" For a moment, I'm sure that I've misheard him.

"The burglar. The intruder. Whatever. The man who was there. The reason why you . . ." My brother can't say *pulled the trigger*, and despite the setting sun, some new light dawns.

Jamie doesn't know.

Not the whole truth. Not really.

They lied to him, too.

No one ever told him the truth about the Scarred Man. He doesn't know about the Society or the prime minister or Ms.

Chancellor. He only knows that his kid sister fired the shot that killed his mother. He has no idea why.

It should anger me, infuriate me. I should charge into my grandfather's office and call him out on all of his lies. But then I realize that Grandpa might not even know the truth. Maybe Ms. Chancellor and her Society have been manipulating him, too. Their cover-ups could go back at least three years. They could go back a thousand.

I should end it all right here and now, but for once I am on the inside. For once, Jamie is the person left behind.

I must stay silent long enough for Jamie to soften, because he smiles.

"Are you at least a little bit glad to see me?" he asks.

I shrug, play along. "The jury is still out."

Hearing him tease me, love me, I come to realize that he *doesn't* hate me. Not at all. And I guess that means I have to hate myself even more to make up for his bad judgment.

CHAPTER FIVE

Grandpa's meetings run late, and goodness knows we aren't allowed to eat without him. Not since Ms. Chancellor decreed that tonight's meal is to be a family affair. Which is a little ironic, since she's not family. Neither is Spence. But Ms. Chancellor took me into the tunnels. She told me something about my mother. And, most of all, she saved my life. We might not have the same blood, but we are bonded now, and I won't even try to deny it. Even if sometimes I'm pretty sure she'd like to.

By the time we gather around the big, formal dining room table it's dark outside and my stomach is growling, but I don't say a thing.

"And how do you like West Point, young man?"

I can hear Grandpa talking from his place at the head of the table, but he's so far away I have to strain to listen. Ms. Chancellor tried to force me into a dress, but we compromised on shorts that don't have rips in them and a nice sweater. I can feel her watching me as I pick at my salad. It's like she's the only one who can see that Jamie is a time bomb that has landed back in our lives. It's just a matter of time until the truth slips out and we all go boom.

"Is your father a military man?" Grandpa asks.

Spence wipes his mouth before speaking. "My mother, sir. She's in the Air Force."

"Excellent." Grandpa takes a sip of his water. "Just excellent. And your father, what does he do?"

The conversation goes on like this through two more courses.

What classes are their favorites? What sites should Jamie show Spence in Adria? Will they be here for the Festival of the Fortnight?

And, through it all, I want to turn to my brother and scream. *Did you know Mom was involved in some kind of secret society? Did you know someone ordered her death? Did you know that even though I pulled the trigger, someone else sent an assassin to her door?*

Did you know it might not be over?

"The potatoes." It takes a moment to realize that Spence is whispering to me. "If you don't want to eat they make a great hiding place for the rest of your food."

I look down at my plate, which is almost full. I haven't taken a bite in a long time, I realize. My fork just dangles in midair.

"Or you could always slip whatever you don't want under the table and give it to me. Like a dog," Spence says, then grins. "I'm

42

not joking. The food here is a lot better than what we get at school, and I'm always hungry. It would be an honor." He takes a big bite and gives me a wink, but I can't help thinking about what John Spencer *doesn't* do.

He doesn't ask me how I'm doing. He doesn't wonder what is wrong. He isn't watching as if waiting for me to implode or explode or just turn into a puddle of mashed potatoes. Spence is the only total stranger at this table. So he's the only one I really trust.

"Well, John." Grandpa's never been a fan of nicknames. "Jamie tells me that you have family ties to Adria."

"Yes, sir," Spence says. "My grandmother on my father's side was Adrian. Her family immigrated to the US after the Second World War."

Grandpa considers this. "Yes. A lot of people left then. Those were dark days for Adria. But they passed, I'm happy to say. The dark days . . . they always pass." Grandpa doesn't look at me as he says this last sentence, but I can feel everyone at the table *not* staring at me as the words reverberate around the room.

The silence is too much. All I hear is the sound of Spence chewing his asparagus. I'm allergic to asparagus, but right now I would welcome the feeling of my throat closing up, an excuse to go to the emergency room — anything to leave here. Now.

"So, I hear you've made friends."

It takes a moment to realize that Jamie is talking to me. It isn't his teasing older-brother voice, though. It's his I'm-trying-to-hide-how-worried-I-really-am voice. And I don't like it.

43

"A few." I would tell him about Noah and Rosie and Megan, but I don't think my brother wants to hear about the hours we spent in the basement of the Iranian embassy or the time we broke into the Scarred Man's house. There are a dozen lies I could give him, but suddenly I remember one essential truth. "Alexei's gone."

I wait for Jamie to react, to say something or make some kind of sign that he's heard me, but nothing comes, so I go on, "Did you know that? His dad had to go back to Russia a few days ago. Alexei is gone, Jamie. I mean *gone* gone. I don't think he's coming back."

"I heard" is all Jamie says.

"So have you talked to him? Did he tell you why he left or —"

"It's for the best," Grandpa says. He doesn't look up from his potatoes.

"What's that supposed to mean?" I snap, but Grandpa spears me with a look.

"Our relationship with the neighbors is hard enough without the two of you gallivanting around the city. You should have stayed away from that boy, Gracie."

"Alexei running around with *me* was a problem? He and Jamie have been best friends for forever," I say with typical younger-sibling outrage.

Grandpa cuts his steak. "And your brother is now a cadet at West Point. Jamie should not be gallivanting around with Russians either."

My retort is on my tongue. Jamie, I can tell, is trying to decide whether or not to argue. But before anyone can say a thing, Spence turns to Jamie and asks, "You're friends with a *Russian?*"

"Embassy Row." My brother shrugs. "It's a crazy place to grow up. The Russian embassy is next door. Alexei's dad was the Russian ambassador's chief of staff. We used to play together when we were kids. We kept in touch."

I can't believe what I'm hearing — what Jamie isn't saying.

"Alexei is your *best* friend," I remind my brother, but Jamie only grins.

"In fact, I left Alexei in charge of Gracie here." He gives me a wink. "No wonder he had to leave the country."

Jamie is trying to tease, to take the awkward out. But Spence is staring at him, trying to process what he's just learned. James Blakely, Jr. — Blake — is friends with a Russian. He's looking at Jamie as if he never really knew him at all.

"Where in Adria was your mother's family from, John?" Ms. Chancellor asks Spence. He takes a moment before turning to her.

"Valancia, ma'am."

"And what was her name?"

Carefully, Ms. Chancellor draws Spence into a discussion of family trees and Adrian history, but I don't listen. I just sit, staring at my peas.

After a while, Jamie leans closer. "You're not eating."

"I'm not hungry."

45

I don't look up, but I know Grandpa and Jamie share a look. I'm starting to regret not taking Spence up on his offer to help me smuggle food off my plate.

"She's never hungry," Grandpa says.

At the other end of the table, Ms. Chancellor uses her best posture and smiles her brightest smile. "Now, Jamie, how long will you boys be able to stay?"

"Three weeks, I think. The new term starts about then."

"How lovely. You have certainly come at the right time of year. Jamie, you'll have to be sure you show Spence all of the festivities."

"I'm looking forward to it, ma'am," Spence says.

For a second, I have to wonder how I've ended up here — at this table. It's all so polite, so serene. So normal.

So fake.

I look at Ms. Chancellor. "May I be excused?"

"We have your favorite dessert coming, Grace. Don't you want —"

"No." I push my chair away and drop my napkin on the table. "I mean, no thank you. I have . . . plans."

When I start to rise, Spence is already up and holding out my chair — not yet an officer, but maybe a gentleman. As I leave, he smiles at me and whispers, "I promise not to check your potatoes." But I don't stop and I don't laugh. I just hurry toward the door.

•   •   •

46

I'm almost to the gates when I hear the heavy steps that pound behind me.

"Gracie! Wait up!"

I don't even slow down.

"Grace, I said wait." Jamie doesn't sound mad. No. He sounds like someone trying very hard to sound like nothing is wrong at all. "What are you doing?"

I don't know.

"Where are you going?"

I stop and face him. "Out."

"Out where? Are we gonna go climb the wall for old times' sake? Get gelato? Hey, I know. We can —"

"No," I say, harder than I should. When I look at Jamie, I can see how much he wants us to be who we *were* instead of who we *are*. I hate him for pretending nothing's wrong and I hate myself for knowing that it's not true. I'd give anything for that not to be true.

"I mean, I'm sorry, Jamie. I can't. I have plans."

"What kind of plans?"

Hiding from you. Beating myself up. Wandering the city by myself for hours and hours, hoping to find a portal back in time. All of these things are true. But I just say, "I'm doing something with Noah."

Jamie steps back and eyes me skeptically. "Who's Noah?"

My initial reaction is shock. How is it possible he doesn't know? Then I remember that Jamie lives on another continent now. He goes to another school and is living in another world. My big brother has gone to some place I can't follow. It was inevitable,

I know, but a part of me can't help but mourn the fact that I will never chase him and Alexei over the wall again.

"Noah's my friend." I sound almost defensive. As if maybe I'm not allowed to have any friend that he hasn't preapproved.

Jamie bristles. "Boyfriend?"

I almost laugh. Suddenly, Jamie's protective posture makes sense.

"Friend who is a *boy*," I tell him, but Jamie doesn't look so certain. He isn't going to take my word for it. Not on this.

"I think I need to meet this Noah."

"No need. I assure you, Grandpa and Ms. Chancellor both like him. He's adequately safe — almost boring. A stickler for the rules."

"But is he good enough for you?"

Is it Jamie's question or the earnest look on his face that makes me laugh? I don't know. And I suppose it doesn't matter, because I just throw back my head and howl. Not a chuckle. A full-throated laugh like I haven't had in ages. It's the kind of laugh that, three years ago, might have gotten me tied down, my meds changed.

I know that I sound crazy, but the difference is, now, I no longer try to stop it.

"Gracie —"

"Don't you know, Jamie?" I cut him off, and, suddenly, I'm not laughing anymore. I shake my head. "Your kid sister? The murderer? Maybe she's the one who isn't good enough."

A darkness crosses my brother's face, and I know I've finally

48

done it. I've mentioned the unmentionable thing, and I couldn't take the words back even if I wanted to.

"Don't say that," he scolds me. "Don't make jokes."

"Do you really think I'm joking?"

Does he hear my voice crack? Does he see the tears that are welling in my eyes? He's an expert on battle strategy and discipline and making things straight and clean and even. But he will never, ever know how to fix me. And it hurts him. Turns out, hurting him is one of the few things that can still hurt me.

"I gotta go, Jamie."

"I flew across an ocean to see you, Gracie. To help you."

"Don't you know? I'm too far gone to help. Besides, my shrink says I'm supposed to socialize and partake in activities that will cement my relationships with my social peers." I put on my most serene smile. "Socialization is incredibly important for those of us who are emotionally unbalanced."

"Hey. That's my sister you're talking about."

"I'm sorry," I say. And I am. Not because I said it, but because it's true. Jamie deserves so much better than me. "Really, Jamie. I can't . . . I can't do this right now. Please. Just let me go. Please."

"No," Jamie says, suddenly the boss of me. "I'm not going to let you hightail it out of here and go to a party with a bunch of strange kids."

"Kids? You're nineteen!" I snap, but it's like Jamie doesn't hear me.

"Do you really think that's a good idea?"

"Better than staying here," I mumble to myself.

"Let me help you, Gracie. Let me in."

Jamie wants me to get better. He wants his kid sister to come back. He doesn't quite know that his sister is dead — that she died the moment she murdered his mother and then, again, the moment she remembered.

"I love you, Jamie," I say, and I mean it. I really do. I mean it far more than I can bring myself to say. "And I'm sorry."

Then I hug my brother, who is so shocked that he lets me past him and out the gate without a word. Before he can quite realize what has happened, I am already gone.

CHAPTER SIX

I knew you'd come back." Noah hops down off the stone ledge that runs around the German embassy. There's a cocky bounce in his step as he tells me, "The ladies . . . they always come back."

That is when Noah notices the new boy standing by the US gate, watching me through the wrought-iron fence. I know how it must look, my tall, handsome brother scowling after me, watching my every move.

For a second, Noah pauses. "New man in your life?"

"Not a man," I tell him. "A brother."

Instantly, Noah changes. "That's the infamous Jamie? Come on. Introduce me."

"No."

When Noah stops cold, his expression is somewhere between amused and angry. I can't read his tone when he asks, "Are you ashamed of me or ashamed of him?"

"Both," I say, and start walking up the street.

A moment later, I feel Noah fall into step beside me. For a while, we walk along in silence.

"I will meet him eventually, you know."

"I know."

"He hasn't seen you in months."

"I know."

"*I've* barely seen you in days."

I stop. "You saw me a few hours ago."

"You know what I mean. A week ago you disappeared into your room, and then today you finally came out and I saw you running toward the cliff like wild dogs were on your heels, so" — Noah pauses — "talk to me."

When I stop and spin, I try to keep my voice calm, but the exasperation comes out anyway. "I don't want to talk anymore, okay? My brother wants to talk. Ms. Chancellor wants to talk. My grandfather . . . well, he never wants to talk, but that doesn't stop him from looking at me disapprovingly. So please don't make me talk anymore. I'll go to Lila's stupid party as long as we don't have to talk. Okay? Please, just one talk-free night — that's all I'm asking. Please, Noah. Can you do that for me?"

"I was going to say that we're walking the wrong direction." Noah points both thumbs behind us and takes a step back. "Lila is branching out."

As we start down the sloping street of Embassy Row, Noah is silent. He doesn't ask me why Jamie's here. He doesn't even start to mention my mom. An easy, comfortable peace settles around us as we walk through the glow of the gaslights and under the arch of the city gates. We make our way outside the safety of Valancia's wall, closer to the ocean.

I glance up at Noah's strong profile. "Party on the beach?"

"Something like that." Noah shoves his hands into his pockets. "So, Jamie . . ."

So much for peace . . .

"I said I don't want to talk."

"I know. I'm not asking about *you* and Jamie. I'm asking about Jamie. What's his story?"

"He's on break from West Point — that's our big military academy for the army. It's a big deal. He's a big deal. He's probably going to be a general someday. He might even be president. Everybody loves him."

"Why is he here?"

"I told you. He's on break, and —"

Noah stops. "Why is he here, Grace?"

For a split second, I actually want to tell him the truth. I want to pour out all the things I know or remember or would give anything to forget. But Noah doesn't know what happened to my mother. When Noah looks at me he doesn't see the girl I used to be or the monster I've become. He only sees a tiny bit of my crazy. And that's more than enough.

"I was wrong, you know. About the Scarred Man. I was

53

wrong for years, and Jamie knows it. He knows that finding out the truth has been hard on me. He's worried about me."

Noah takes a slow step back. There's nothing but moonlight and the sound of the waves and this boy who could be at home almost anywhere on Embassy Row and yet has chosen to be here with me.

"Just so you know," Noah says, "he's not the only one."

I'm just about to speak when Noah points to the darkness and I see a long pier. A tiny girl stands on the very end of it, her blond hair catching the light of the full moon that is rising over the city. She waves wildly in our direction. For a second, I think she might jump off the pier and swim toward us. As it is, she just runs.

"Grace! I haven't seen you in ages!"

"I saw you a week ago," I say, but Rosie barely registers the sound.

"But you missed my birthday! I'm a teenager now. Do I look like a teenager?" Rosie smiles and laughs, so happy she's practically bouncing, and I'm suddenly reminded of the fact that she's thirteen now.

The age I was when Mom died.

The age I was when everything went wrong.

This is supposed to mean something, a part of me registers. I'm supposed to forgive that thirteen-year-old version of me because she was young and scared and she was just doing the best that she could at the time. I'm supposed to be kind to thirteen-year-old

Grace, and seeing thirteen-year-old Rosie is supposed to remind me of that.

But it doesn't.

"I'm sorry, Rosie. Happy birthday. What else did I miss?"

Rosie shrugs. "Nothing. I find there is a lack of international intrigue at the moment." For a second, her German accent is so heavy that she sounds like a spy in a black-and-white movie. "The prime minister is still in a coma, you know."

"I know."

"So . . ."

"So what?"

"So it seems more than a little coincidental that the Scarred Man is supposed to be the prime minister's head of security. And you think the Scarred Man killed your mother. And then the prime minister has a 'heart attack'" — she makes air quotes around the words as she says them — "and ends up in a coma!"

It's not a coincidence. But it's not the truth either. And no matter how much I care for Noah and Rosie, that's the last thing I can tell them.

"I know you're thinking that it's Dominic's fault. But you're wrong. I was wrong. I'm sorry."

"For what?" Noah asks, genuinely confused.

For lying to you.

For lying to me.

For ruining your lives.

But I can't say any of that, so I just ask, "Where's the party?"

55

There should be music and lights and the not-so-hushed voices of people scurrying through the darkness, but Noah and Rosie and I are virtually alone in the moonlight. It feels like we're the only people in Adria as Noah raises a finger and points to the inky darkness of the Mediterranean.

"There."

I look, but I see nothing but stars and sky and salty water reaching all the way to the Italian coast. The moon is rising behind us, and the water looks so dark, so bleak. Once upon a time they thought the world was flat, and sometimes I still do. I want to swim out there, farther and farther until I reach the edge.

But then I see it.

There is a fire flickering in the distance, a tiny dot in the ocean of black sea and starry sky. It takes a moment for my eyes to adjust and make out the dark outline of trees, for me to remember the island that rests three or four miles offshore. As kids, Jamie used to tell me it was filled with monsters — dragons and minotaurs and the ghosts of the people who, a thousand years ago, let the city fall. And right now I'd prefer any of those creatures to the beasts I know are gathering on the island's shores.

I want to run away, to tell Noah and Rosie I'm sick or afraid of water or just plain afraid. But that's the thing about being the girl who's spent years convincing the world she's not afraid of anything: At some point, someone is going to find out you're afraid of everything.

I'm just starting to open my mouth, to protest or turn away, when Noah points to the motorboat that has appeared on the horizon and is coming toward us fast. "Here's our ride."

I'm pretty sure my jaw drops. My excuses fade away. The moonlight catches the long black hair that blows behind the girl who stands at the controls of the boat that's pulling up to the end of the pier.

I'm fresh out of excuses when Megan looks at us and says, "Get in."

"They say the island is bigger than the city, but I don't think it looks that big. Do you think it looks that big?" Rosie has been talking nonstop since we left the pier. I'm starting to think she might be afraid of water. She's in a puffy orange life vest and clinging to the side of the boat. "I guess maybe it could be that big, but . . . Everyone says it's haunted, but I don't believe it."

"Why?" Noah asks, teasing. He nudges her gently with his shoulder. "Don't you believe in ghosts, Rosie?"

"Oh, no." Rosie sounds serious. "Of course I believe in ghosts. I just don't think they'd waste their time haunting an island where no one ever goes."

"But if people didn't think it was haunted then they might go there . . . and give ghosts a reason to haunt it," Noah tries.

But Megan shakes her head. "No one goes there because it is three-point-six miles from shore; there are no docks and no bathrooms, not to mention no Wi-Fi, cell signals, or running water."

Noah shrugs. "That too."

"There are dragons." I don't realize I've said the words aloud until Rosie spins on me.

"Really?"

Her eyes are impossibly big and blue.

"No."

At that, Rosie looks incredibly disappointed, but recovers quickly.

"So, Grace . . ." she starts slowly. "I was thinking that now that you're feeling better, we should probably start —"

"No," I say again, cutting her off.

"You don't even know what I was going to say!"

I don't need to hear what she has to say to know my answer. "Dominic is just a man with a scar, Rosie. The prime minister had a bad heart and Dominic didn't kill my mom. He didn't."

The last words I say only for myself. I lean closer to the edge of the speedboat and let the mist hit me in my face. It makes me feel alive. Behind us, the lights of Valancia grow dimmer, and on the horizon the island looms larger.

A few minutes later Megan is pulling up among dozens of other boats that float not far from the island's shore. She drops anchor just as Noah pulls a small inflatable lifeboat from somewhere and jerks a cord, causing the raft to burst to life, inflating in less than a minute. Before Megan can step down into it, though, Noah swings her off her feet.

"Allow me, my lady," he says while easing her effortlessly over the side of the big boat and placing her gently into the raft. Megan laughs and hits him playfully on the arm.

58

"Noah!" She giggles. "Put me down, silly."

I stand for a second, too stunned to speak. Then I look at Rosie. "Are they . . ."

Rosie shrugs. "Your guess is as good as mine," she says, then jumps into the little boat beside Megan.

A second later, Noah and I follow.

CHAPTER SEVEN

When we finally reach the island, I pull off my shoes and wade through the waves, heading toward the beach. The Mediterranean is cool as it laps against my ankles, and the shoreline is rocky beneath my bare feet. Someone has built a bonfire, and its flames lap up at an inky sky that, here, so far from the city, seems impossibly full of stars. There is music playing, a pounding bass that's keeping beat like the lapping waves. And all around me, there are people.

Beautiful people.

Awkward people.

People who are so engrossed with the person beside them that I highly doubt they even remember where they are.

People who want to be anywhere but here.

But as Noah and Megan and Rosie and I walk into their midst, no one notices, no one stares. At the beginning of the summer I was an anomaly, a mystery. A new girl. There are even more reasons for people to stare at me now, but no one here seems to know them. I vow to do whatever it takes to keep it that way.

"I wonder if Alexei made it home okay." There's a wistfulness to Rosie's voice. "It would be weird, don't you think? Going home. I mean . . . *this* is home. Isn't it?"

I have no home, I think, and then she looks at me.

"Have you talked to him?" she asks.

Even though there are probably fifty people on the beach, no one hears. We are anonymous, hidden by the island's shadows and our peers' complete lack of interest.

"No. Why?"

Rosie shakes her head. I think I see some meaning in her eyes, but I can't decipher it. The beach is too dark, and I'm too bad at this — at *having friends*. So I just keep walking, following in Noah's footsteps.

From a distance, the party looks the same. There's a bonfire raging in the center of the beach. Big pieces of driftwood circle around it and a few people gather in clusters, sitting on the wood or scattered across blankets and a few boulders. The beach stretches from the water to the big trees and dense forest that no doubt dominates the center of the island, growing untamed and untouched by man.

It feels like Megan has brought us to the far side of the earth, some uncharted territory or unknown land — like maybe we are our own civilization, if only for tonight.

We curve around the beach and, for a moment, the mainland is blocked by rocks and trees, and it feels like we've gone back in time. There are no roads, no lights, no signs of the twenty-first century. We've come to a place where even teenagers look different. Our phones won't work here. There is nothing but the music and the fire and the night.

"Come on," Noah says, looking back to make sure Rosie and I are still following.

A low stone wall stretches across part of the beach, crumbling and overgrown by vines and weeds, and I know we aren't the first people to set foot here. We are just the first in a very long time.

"Don't wander off, okay?" he says. A moment later, he looks right at me and repeats, "Okay?"

"Yeah. Right. I'm not going anywhere," I tell him.

He doesn't look convinced.

As we walk closer to the fire, I feel the heat of it, pulsing toward me like the music. Through the lapping flames I see Noah's sister chatting with some English girls known as the three Cs: Chloe, Chelsea, and Charmaine. From this distance, Noah and Lila look alike, almost like the twins that they are. But when Lila spies us, she glares, and I remember that that is where the similarities end.

"What are you doing here?" Lila snaps, coming forward.

If I thought that our newfound sisterhood was going to bond us, I was obviously mistaken.

"I wanted to be close to you." Noah tries to swallow her in a hug. "Just like in the womb."

Lila rolls her eyes, then, for a second, lets her gaze drift onto me. Is she thinking about Ms. Chancellor and the Society? Or maybe about how Dominic followed us through the streets this afternoon and how I ran away? I'll never know.

"Just stay away from me," she snaps at Noah, and I feel like I should say something, but all my witty banter has abandoned me, so instead I stand perfectly still for a long time, staring at the fire.

It's a mistake, and I know it. I can feel the flickering glow washing over me. But even if I turned away, I'd still see the way the light flits and moves across the trees, how the shadows dance in the sand. The whole party is bathed in the orange-red aura of the flames. Then the wind shifts. I smell smoke . . . and that's when I start shaking.

Noah and Megan have moved up ahead, talking to someone I don't know. Rosie is no longer by my side. I am alone in the middle of the party, surrounded by the music and the flames.

"Grace, no!" my mother screams.

I close my eyes and shake my head and try to keep the panic at bay, but it's here — it's always here — closing in on me. I spin, looking away from the fire, trying to find air to breathe that doesn't taste like smoke.

I push away from the flames and only realize how far I've walked when I feel the sand beneath my feet turn to rock and grass. The smoke is fainter here. The flickering light is muted, and I can feel my heart stop pounding and my head stop spinning.

I put on my shoes and pull a flashlight from my pocket. No one looks at me like I'm a freak because I have one. I just look . . . prepared.

There are noises in the trees. I hear a few shouts, some laughing. Couples who have peeled away from the pack for a few moments of privacy, overanxious boys eager to jump out of the woods and scare some unsuspecting female who has been told tales of monsters and ghosts.

No one dares to jump out at me.

I let the beam of my flashlight dance across the trees and bushes, the outcroppings of rock and the boulders that, upon closer inspection, look more like giant fists, fighting free of the ground. I step closer, let my light and my gaze sweep deeper into the overgrowth. Vines have almost overtaken the island. They climb and crawl, and I swear I can almost feel them wrapping around my ankle. I kick and claw, spinning.

And that is when I see it.

Someone has carved something into the trunk of one of the ancient trees. I step closer, shine my light directly on the words, and make myself say them aloud.

"Caroline and Dominic forever."

And just like that my blood turns cold.

Moms aren't supposed to have pasts. Not old crushes or first loves. But the words have been there for ages, I can tell, and it's far too easy to imagine another night in another year — another party filled with other kids. I can't help but see my mother here. Alive and young and in love. Long before my father. Long before me.

Long before everything went wrong.

Suddenly, I think I'm going to be sick. I want to cry, but I don't cry anymore. My grief comes out of me in other ways. I can feel it in my pounding heart, my running feet.

My promise to Noah is the furthest thing from my mind. Besides, I'm not wandering off. I'm fleeing, retreating, going deeper inland, exploring this new place that is actually incredibly old. I only know that I can't go back to the music and the fire and the laughing. I don't belong there. I'm far more at home in the dark.

When I reach something of a clearing, I let myself stop. I can feel the moonlight upon my face. The music is fainter and the smell of smoke is all but gone. Wonder takes the place of panic. I don't know how far I've run. I don't care. I'm too mesmerized by the sight before me.

A temple. A fort. Something is built into the side of a hill. I'm not sure what it is, but something draws me toward the massive pillars. Some still stand, and some have tumbled, spilling and breaking onto the ground, returning to the earth that bore them. Creeping vines cover almost every surface as if trying to pull the old walls down.

In the darkness, I have no idea how large it is. My light is too small, almost insignificant as it sweeps across something that must have once been an entrance. But now there are crumbling rocks and sagging arches. It's not safe — even I know that. But when my light catches the Society's symbol, I step closer. It's like a magnet drawing me into the dark.

"I thought that was you."

The voice startles me, and I spin, remembering suddenly that I'm not alone on this island. It's a voice I recognize but don't quite know, and it takes a second to find the figure standing in the trees, one hand held up to shelter his eyes against the glare.

"Lower the flashlight, will ya?"

Spence.

Spence has come to the party. Which means my brother is on this island.

"What are you doing here?" I ask when he steps closer.

"We heard there was a party," Spence says, but he's no longer looking at me. I watch him take in the trees and vines, the dim outline of crumbling towers and ancient ruins.

"So in other words, Jamie followed me."

"Yes." Spence flashes me a smile.

"And he sent you to keep an eye on me."

"No." Spence looks sheepish, charming. He gives me the kind of grin that probably goes over big with the girls around West Point. "I volunteered," he says, but I'm not flattered, and I don't say a single word.

"Wow. What is this place?" he asks after a while.

"Just some ruins," I say, protective. If I'm not supposed to be here, then neither is he. And I've never been good at sharing.

I should tell him to go. I should tell him I want to be alone, because I do. But Spence doesn't know the truth about my mother. He has probably never heard of the Scarred Man. This is the closest I can get to being alone while in the company of another human being, so I don't ask him to leave. I just think about how, when my mom was my age, she was coming to parties on this island. She was joining the Society.

She was falling in love.

For a moment, I think about Alexei. He must be back in Russia by now. Home and safely out of my blast radius. It should make me happy that I can no longer hurt him. But it doesn't.

I feel Spence coming closer. Soon his arm is brushing against mine, and I see him looking up at the symbol hidden among the ruins.

"That's cool," he says. "What is it? It looks kind of familiar."

I shake my head. "I don't know."

It's not a lie. I still have no idea what the Society is about or how it can be explained. I've been a member less than twenty-four hours, and I barely know more than I did as a kid, chasing after my mother down the streets of the great walled city. So I just tell him what everybody already knows.

"A lot of people have ruled in Adria. The Romans and the Turks and the Byzantines. That's probably the symbol of whoever built this place."

Despite the darkness, Spence jumps onto one of the fallen stones of the crumbling fortress. He looks like some kind of ancient marauder, claiming the island for a far-off king.

"So, Jamie told me you moved here at the start of the summer."

The change of subject surprises me.

"Yeah."

"He didn't tell me you were so pretty."

When he jumps off the rock and lands in front of me he is close. Too close. I step back, but there's a stone behind my foot and I stumble.

I reach back instinctively, bracing for the crash that never comes. Instead, Spence's arms are wrapped around me, holding me a foot off the ground.

For a second, I am suspended in the air, caught between two realities. I could be Grace, the messed-up little sister. The murderer. The crazy girl.

Or I could be the girl this stranger seems to see.

I think about Ms. Chancellor and Jamie and my grandpa, and how they all want me to be normal. I'm supposed to get over it, move on. Pretend. I think about Noah and Megan, the people on the beach. This is what being a teenager is supposed to be, isn't it? The Big Moments.

And in this moment all I really want is to be the kind of girl whose biggest worry is whether or not this boy is about to kiss her.

Then there is no more thinking. He is leaning closer and closer. I close my eyes and feel his lips brush mine. I try to stop thinking, worrying, being afraid. But my worries don't go away. If anything, they multiply. I'm consumed by a new kind of panic.

Who is Spence and why is he here and how am I supposed to face my brother after his friend's hands have been in my hair and his lips on mine and . . .

I'm stronger than I look, I know. And Spence stumbles back when I shove him.

"Sorry. I shouldn't have done that." Spence doesn't sound sorry, though.

"I should get back to the party," I say, and start to walk away.

"Wait. Hold up." In a flash, he cuts me off. "We're just talking."

"No. That was called kissing."

"Grace, I —"

"Why?" Whatever Spence was expecting me to say, it wasn't this. "Why did you do that?"

"Why did I kiss you?" He raises an eyebrow and sounds like he wants to laugh.

"Is it Take Pity on Your Friend's Kid Sister Day or something?"

"No." Spence runs a hand through his too-short hair. "The fact that you are Blake's kid sister is the one reason I shouldn't be kissing you."

"Then why'd you do it?"

"I don't know. I'm sorry. You're cute and nice and funny and I thought . . ."

He thought I was normal.

"What's wrong?" he asks.

I should answer, but I'm too tired of this place, this boy, this night. I want my bed and my mother's room. I want to go back to the demons I already know how to handle, so I spin and start across the clearing, back toward the trees and the beach and the party.

"Grace, wait up," he says. "I'm sorry. I didn't mean —"

Didn't mean to kiss me? Didn't mean to hurt my feelings? To incur Jamie's wrath?

I will never know how Spence meant to finish that sentence, though, because in that moment there is a movement in the shadows near the trees. For a second, I think it is my unreliable mind playing tricks on me, another ghost from my past returning to haunt the present.

Even when the figure yells, "Leave her alone," I don't let myself believe he's really here.

It's not until Spence turns, too, and looks at the shadow, that I allow myself to say, "Alexei?"

CHAPTER EIGHT

He's not supposed to be here, but even in my shock I don't say that. He's supposed to be in Russia, called home with his father for reasons no one ever explained. He's supposed to be far, far away from me.

Alexei is supposed to be safe.

It's what I want for him. But the emotion that floods my veins is enough to say that what I want for *me* is something completely different.

"Hey, Gracie."

There is tension in the look on Alexei's face, in the sound of his voice, pulsing like the beating of the waves or the pounding of the music I can barely hear.

"Who's your friend?" he asks, unblinking, his gaze firmly glued to Spence.

"Oh, this is John Spencer. Spence is a friend of Jamie's — they just got here from West Point. Spence, this is Alexei. He's —"

"The Russian," Spence says, and for the first time I realize that it's like I've wandered between a lion and a tiger.

"Alexei is Jamie's oldest friend," I say, as much for my benefit as for Spence's. It's a fact I've let myself forget. But my brother, I have to remember, is back now.

"What are you doing here with her?" Alexei asks the other boy.

"Jamie asked me to come find Gracie, make sure she was okay out here. She wandered off."

"She does that," Alexei says flatly.

But Spence isn't swayed. "Thanks for your concern, comrade, but the lady and I can take care of ourselves."

"Lady?" Alexei yells. "She is sixteen. She is a child."

"Um . . . no," I say, even though, technically, I know he's right. But my childhood ended years ago. I will never consider myself a *child* again. "I was perfectly content before either one of you got here."

"Stay out of this, Gracie," the two of them say in unison, their accents blending almost in harmony, so I throw my hands in the air.

"I give up." I whirl, heading for the trees and the beach and the sea. I'll swim home if I have to.

But Alexei's not going to let me go so easily. He falls into step beside me.

"Come on, Gracie," he orders, his accent heavier than I remember it. "I'm taking you home."

I can't take it. I face him down.

"Maybe I don't want to go home! Maybe I don't want *you* to take me anywhere!"

"Gracie, I —"

"What are you doing here, Alexei?"

Spence is behind us, lurking and listening, but I don't care.

"I heard Lila was throwing a party. I knew you would likely be here."

"I mean why are you *here*? In Adria. I thought your dad got transferred."

Alexei shrugs. "We are back."

"I can see that."

"My father . . ." Alexei starts, then trails off, risking a glance at Spence before lowering his voice. "My father is to be the new ambassador. There are to be . . . changes."

"Oh."

For a moment, I think Alexei wants to say something else — do something else. But instead he takes my hand, gentler now.

"I should get you home. Or at least back to your brother."

"I can do that." It's Spence's voice that slices through the moment. "She's not your responsibility."

"Don't tell me what she is," Alexei says, spinning on him. "I know Gracie better than you ever will."

"Well, you've never kissed me," I mutter, half under my breath.

Instantly, I know what a mistake I've made. Because I watch the realization wash over Alexei's features.

"But evidently you didn't see that part," I say as Alexei turns to ice.

"He kissed you?"

"Let's go find Jamie!" I say too cheerfully, bolting for the beach.

"Grace!" Spence yells, chasing after me, but I'm moving fast over the uneven ground. I've spent too much time in the tunnels underneath Valancia. My eyes are used to the dark. I'm like a creature of the night, and they can't match me.

When I reach the edge of the tree line I pause and search for Noah or Rosie or even my brother. I need a distraction.

But the pause is all it takes for Alexei to reach me.

"He kissed you?"

"I'm fine!" I shout, but it's too late. Spence has caught up with us, and Alexei isn't looking for an explanation. He turns and pulls back his arm in one smooth motion, dropping Spence to the ground with a single blow. Some might call it a sucker punch. I know Spence never saw it coming. He lies on the ground for a moment, sprawled and stunned.

He's older and he goes to West Point, but Alexei is a little taller and enraged.

Spence doesn't care, though. He lunges at Alexei's legs, toppling them both out of the cover of the trees and onto the beach. They land, tangled together, rolling and fighting as sand billows up around them, rising like a fog.

They are darkened silhouettes, black shadows outlined in fire as they tumble and twist and brawl closer and closer to the party.

74

Soon, other people see them. The crowd turns. And a mur-mur sweeps across the beach, a low, simmering echo. *"Alexei."*

But no one knows the boy who knocks him to the ground and pounds against him with a terrible backhanded hit.

I want to run to them — to stop it. But before I can move, Alexei reverses their positions and kicks, striking Spence in the ribs with a vicious blow that makes him double over for a moment before charging, unwilling to be knocked down. Not again. Not without company. They roll together, a tangle of limbs and aggression and blood.

When they get too close to the fire, a cry goes up.

That's when I see Jamie. He's nearer the water, barefoot in the sand with his jeans rolled up, surrounded by Lila and a mob of pretty girls that I don't know.

When Noah appears beside me he is entirely too calm, con-sidering two boys are trying to kill each other by the fire.

"So . . . Alexei's back," I say.

"I can see that. I'd go say hi, but he seems busy."

Jamie is in motion now, leaping over one of the burning logs that has fallen, smoking and smoldering, from the fire and onto the sand.

"Stop it!" he yells. For a moment, he sounds like our mother, scolding us for bickering and fighting and taking the risk of break-ing her favorite lamp.

But his friends don't hear him. It's like there's no sound on the beach but the sickly slap of skin against skin, the crunch of bones and sparking, burning wood.

75

Even the music has stopped playing.

When Spence throws Alexei to the ground, he rolls and comes up almost in one motion. Sand sticks to his sweat-covered skin. And the cry he lets out, the string of Russian curses . . . He sounds like a stranger.

Alexei lunges for Spence, feral and brutal. All strength and wounded pride and fury.

There's only one boy on the beach who is fast enough to reach them, strong enough to leap into the breach when Alexei charges again.

I watch Alexei spin as Jamie catches him around the waist, using his own momentum to change directions.

How many times have I watched the two of them play at battle, tussle and wrestle and fight like brothers? Jamie, older, always a little bigger. Alexei, always a little more wild.

But now it's not like that. It's like Alexei has been tackled by a stranger.

"Let me go!" Alexei shouts, pushing against the offending hands. He might not even recognize my brother.

And Jamie, being Jamie, laughs.

"It's good to see you, too, buddy. I heard you were in Moscow."

"I'm back," Alexei growls, then lunges for Spence, who is breathing hard and bleeding from a cut on his eyebrow. His shirt is torn.

"Control your dog, Blake," Spence shouts before spitting blood into the fire.

Alexei lunges again, breaking free. *They're going to kill each other*, I think. Before I realize it, I'm moving forward. My arms are around Alexei's waist. I can feel the sand that clings to him, the rise and fall of his chest. It's like trying to hold back an animal, but Alexei won't hurt me.

Alexei will never hurt me.

"Stop it!" I yell, forcing him back toward Jamie. I'm the weakest of us all, I know. But I have a power here, even if I can't name it. "Both of you." I stare down Spence. "You're causing a scene."

I glance toward the crowd that has gathered around us. Half of Embassy Row is represented here. Most of the partygoers have their phones out, capturing the whole thing on video. It doesn't matter that the island is too far from shore for anyone to have a signal. Word of this will spread eventually. It will spread far and wide and at the speed of light. It will live online forever.

But Alexei doesn't see, doesn't realize, doesn't think. He's pointing at Spence, shouting, "Touch her again, and I will kill you. Do you hear me? I'll kill you!"

"Hey!" I pull his arm down and make him look me in the eye. "Stop, Alexei. It's over."

And then it's like he sees me for the first time. I can actually watch the rage begin to fade. When Jamie grabs Alexei and pulls him toward the beach, a little farther away from prying eyes, I follow.

"What is going on?" Jamie's tone of voice would make most people cower. But Alexei only glares.

"I saw him follow Grace to the ruins."

Jamie spins on me. "You went to the ruins?"

Alexei isn't easily distracted. "And when I found them, he was all over her."

I see the words land. It's like a shadow crosses my brother's face. In the distance, someone turns the music back on. People begin to buddy up, return to previously scheduled programming in groups of twos and threes. But the three of us are near the water. And a lot of people are still watching.

They see when Jamie spins and takes three long strides in Spence's direction.

"That is my kid sister."

Spence tries to laugh. "It was harmless."

"She's sixteen," Jamie says.

"She seems pretty mature to me."

Jamie doesn't say a word of warning. He just hits him.

Spence's head jerks but he stays on his feet. Slowly, he looks back at my brother and brings a finger to his bloody lip. He doesn't fire back, though. Maybe it's an army thing, or a West Point thing. Or maybe just a guy thing — but I'm certain that Spence thinks he had that coming.

When Jamie steps closer, he lowers his voice. It's not the crowd he's trying to hide his words from, I know. It's me.

"You don't know my sister," he tells his friend, but his gaze echoes with the things he doesn't say.

She is not mature.

She is not responsible.

She is not to be trusted in the dark with strange, mysterious new boys.
She is not to be trusted. At all.

I only wish I could tell my brother that he's wrong. But Jamie is never wrong. And nobody knows that more than me.

"Touch my sister again and *he* won't get a chance. I will kill you myself." Then Jamie turns and glares at Alexei. "That goes for you, too."

I want to remind Jamie that Alexei is still his best friend, that Alexei was the perfect proxy. But Jamie is here because I've been in trouble. Because somehow, in his eyes, Alexei has already failed.

"This isn't over," Alexei says. Maybe to Jamie. Maybe to Spence. Maybe even to me. But I don't get a chance to answer, because Jamie is spinning.

"We're leaving."

My brother's tone is clear, and I have no desire to argue — I have no desire to stay. So I follow him to the little boat he and Spence must have brought from the mainland.

Spence smirks at Alexei, a flash of teeth in the moonlight. But when he starts to follow, Jamie blocks his way.

"Find your own way home."

Spence doesn't argue, and that may be the smartest thing he's done all night.

Then I'm in the boat, alone with my brother. Which, from the way he's looking at me, feels a lot like being entirely alone.

CHAPTER NINE

Valancia is asleep when we finally reach the shore. Jamie docks the boat and offers me his hand, but I jump onto the dock without him. I'm not as helpless — as broken — as he thinks I am.

I'm worse.

And I can never, ever let him know it.

In the distance, the island is lost to the darkness of the sea. But the moon still shines, its white light rippling across the water, guiding us toward the city gates. They stand open, and I walk with my brother toward the big archway in the city's outer wall — its first and best line of defense. For a thousand years it has kept intruders away, but Jamie and I carry our problems with us.

An old playground lies down the beach. A rusty swing blows in the wind, and the merry-go-round stands silent, but I can hear a woman's laugh and see my mother running through the sand, singing to the children who have long since grown up.

Hush, little princes, wait and see . . .

No one's gonna know that you are me!

She laughs and chases a memory. Then, just as quickly, she is gone.

I'm not sure how long I stand there, lost in thought, but when I come back to reality, Jamie's shoulder is touching mine.

"It's weird," my brother says, following my gaze. "Being here without her."

"You don't get used to it," I tell him. He nods, then turns and starts walking toward the wall.

"Are you going to tell me what happened out there?"

"No."

"You've got to talk to me, Gracie."

"Really?" I ask. "Where is that written? Is that Adrian law or something?"

"No. It's sibling law."

"I don't need a babysitter."

"Really? Because it looks to me like someone has to save you from yourself. What happened out there?"

"What happened is that Spence kissed me. And Alexei didn't like it." I stop just inside the city gates and spin on him. "And judging by the punch you threw, neither did you."

"You shouldn't have wandered off alone."

"News flash, Jamie: I am alone!" Technically, it's not true. I have family here. Friends. It would crush Noah and Megan and

81

Rosie if they heard me say such a thing. And yet it might also be the most truthful thing I've said in years. "I am always alone."

I hate the way my voice cracks, but I can't stop it, so I don't even try.

"That's not true, Gracie."

"Oh, Jamie." I shake my head. And in this moment, I pity him. I really do. "It is exactly the truth." I start up Embassy Row, my feet carrying me faster now. He practically has to jog to keep up.

"You weren't supposed to grow up, you know. I was supposed to have another ten or twenty years before I had to start punching guys who kissed you." Jamie is trying to tease me now, to make me smile. "And you weren't supposed to . . ."

"Remember," I say flatly as I stop and spin. "I wasn't supposed to remember. I was supposed to just keep thinking I was crazy. But I am crazy, aren't I?" I want to laugh with the irony, but then the shadows move. For a split second, I glance behind Jamie, at the presence on the dark side of the street.

I am crazy, but the Scarred Man is real, I want to tell my brother.

And he's standing right behind you.

For three years, Dominic lived in the shadows of my mind. I could point to him now, exhibit A that I am only partially insane. But I just smile and turn away from both of the overprotective alpha males who seem to watch my every move. Let Jamie believe what he wants to believe. It's what I did for three years, after all.

•　　•　　•

When I appear in the kitchen the next morning, Jamie is already there. His T-shirt is drenched in sweat, and I don't have to be told that he's already run five miles on the beach. Maybe six. Or seven. Or ten. It doesn't matter that his body is in a different time zone. He would have risen before the sun and pushed himself to his limit. It was all I could do to make myself brush my teeth before I stumbled downstairs.

Jamie studies me over the rim of his cup of coffee and smirks, so sure in his skin, so confident of his place in this world. "Are we going to talk about it?" he asks, and I roll my eyes. He doesn't sound like Dad or Grandpa, not even Ms. Chancellor. He doesn't even sound like himself.

"Did you talk to *Spence* about it? I'm dying to hear what he said. Did he tell you it was my fault? That I made it up?"

Jamie is silent, and it feels like an admission. I start to wonder if maybe Spence did say those things. If maybe Jamie believed him.

But then Jamie puts his cup on the counter and leans back. "If you must know, I didn't ask him about it."

"Why? Does that go against some sort of West Point code or something?"

"No. I would have asked, but he didn't come home last night."

I think about Spence, in a foreign country and left on some island, and wonder if Jamie is worried about his friend or if he's too mad at him to care. Spence is a grown-up, after all. A West Point man. He can take care of himself, and Jamie knows it.

He should have known better than to hit on the likes of me.

"Jamie, I —"

"There you are!" Ms. Chancellor's voice has the singsong quality that it gets when she's up to something. She practically floats into the room. "Good morning," she says. "Did you sleep well?"

"Yes, ma'am," Jamie replies. "It felt good to be home."

This isn't our home, but Jamie is good at this — this impressing-the-grown-ups thing. It is maybe what he does best. And that, of course, is saying something.

When Ms. Chancellor smiles at him it's like he's the sun and she's basking in his glow. Then her smile fades.

"Alexei is here," she says, and I can feel an undercurrent of tension in the words, as if she knows what happened on the beach. Then I realize that of course she knows. Ms. Chancellor knows everything. "He says he has been trying to call you all morning, James."

Jamie busies himself, looking through a big basket of fruit.

"I can't find my phone. I must have lost it." For a second, I actually wonder if my brother, the saint, might actually be lying.

"Well, Alexei is here now. Waiting outside."

"I don't want to see him," Jamie says, and Ms. Chancellor smiles and slowly shifts her gaze onto me.

"Well that works out nicely, then, since he is here to talk to Grace."

I wait for Jamie to be insulted, to get upset because, for once, he's the one being left behind. But Jamie isn't hurt, I realize. He's just angry.

I turn to look at Ms. Chancellor, who raises her eyebrows. "I don't understand boys," I say.

She pats me on the back. "It gets worse once they turn into men, dear. Now come along. Alexei is waiting for you outside."

When I step outside the residence's doors, I see Alexei standing on the other side of the fence. He's staring straight at me, not blinking, not smiling. He doesn't even say hello. I nod at the marine who opens the little gate and lets me out onto Adrian soil. Wordlessly, Alexei falls into step beside me.

His right eye is swollen and I know I'm in his blind spot, so I stare a little harder than I ordinarily would. His knuckles are bruised and red, like he tried — and failed — to wash the blood off. There is a cut at his hairline, a burn on his arm. I start to reach out and touch it, as if I have the power to soothe, but I don't. So I pull my hand back and cross my arms.

"Don't tell me," I say when the silence is too much. "I should see the other guy."

"I have no desire for you to see the other guy."

I still can't believe how much stronger Alexei's accent is. Maybe that's what happens when you return to your homeland and spend a few days speaking exclusively in your native tongue. Or maybe that is just something that happens when Alexei is angry or sad or deep in thought. I don't know, I realize. And then it hits me: There is so much about Alexei I may never know.

"Then you will be happy to hear that the other guy didn't come home after the party. At least that's what Jamie said at breakfast."

Alexei pauses for a moment, blinks, and looks back. It's like he is expecting — or maybe just hoping — to see we aren't alone.

"Jamie's still mad," I say, answering the unasked question.

"I had assumed as much."

We walk in silence toward the city gates. There are cars and bicycles passing, a few pedestrians and tourists snapping pictures from atop the big red buses that seem to circle Embassy Row on a perpetual loop. I wonder if, to Alexei, it feels like he's come home. Or maybe it feels like he's just left.

"You came back."

It's not a question.

"I did." He tries to slip his hand into his pocket, then winces like maybe he forgot about his bruised and bloody knuckles. "Moscow is concerned about . . . our situation. The ambassador is retiring. My father will assume the position."

What situation? I want to know. I'm sick of people dancing around the facts, treating me like a child. I'm sick of all of it.

But that's not what I say.

Instead I blurt, "What were you doing last night?"

"That man was touching you." Alexei's voice is almost like a roar.

Something about it makes me want to laugh.

"He's not a *man*. He's Jamie's age."

86

But when Alexei turns and glares at me I don't feel like laughing anymore.

"Jamie is a man now. *I* am almost a man."

"What were you doing, Alexei?" I can't help but notice he never answered my question.

"I thought you needed help."

"I don't need any help," I say, because it's instinct now. Automatic. It was my reply when I was twelve years old and following the boys over the wall. And it is my answer now. It will be the answer until I die.

In fact, it is probably the answer that will kill me.

"Yes." Alexei looks at me too closely; he sees too much. "You do."

And I can't help but stare at his swollen eye and bruised jaw. He looks like the god of war, damaged and scarred, but still standing. I'm not thinking as I reach up and gently run a finger across his battered face. Then I pull back, like I've felt a shock, and Alexei drops his gaze to the ground.

"I will make apologies to your friend if that is what you wish."

"He is not *my* friend."

Alexei nods. "To Jamie's friend. To your grandfather. I have lived here long enough to know that there are repercussions for my actions. I knew better than to behave as I did. I am sorry, but . . ."

"But what, Alexei?" I throw my hands out, confused. "If you knew better then why did you do it?"

The wind blows behind me, pushing my hair around my face. I must look wild, crazy. Free. I would give anything to feel free.

"Are you mad that I fought with Jamie's friend, Gracie? Are you mad that I interrupted the two of you? Or are you just mad that I left?"

"You don't get it, Alexei. I'm mad because you came back." I move away, just a step. Just enough to breathe. It's hard to read the look that fills Alexei's eyes. He has always been a little stoic, a little cool. He has a natural poker face, my father used to say. And now, with his black eye and bloody knuckles, it is hard to see past what happened last night. It's almost impossible to reach the boy behind the bruises.

Wordlessly, we keep walking, through the gates and toward the beach that looks and feels so different in the light of day.

"Grace, I —"

I don't know what he's about to say, because then the wind picks up, carrying the clear salty air and the sounds of shouting.

"Over here!" someone yells in Adrian.

There are more cries and shouts, screams that are the same in every possible language. Grief and terror have a tongue of their own.

I don't know what I'm going to see as I turn and look down the beach. There are men in the surf, swimming out against the tide. An older couple holds two children, pulling them away from the water and the cries.

Then someone yells for an ambulance and I see the thing that is floating in the water. It looks like a log or a tangle of seaweed that the tide keeps pushing toward the shore. But the men are swimming toward it. The tension builds and grows. And when they've hauled it to the beach, more cries go up as the crowd descends.

And then the yelling stops.

The silence is so much worse. There is nothing but the sound of the waves and the seagulls and the whispers of the people who gather on the shore.

Whispers that I can't un-hear.

Body.

Police.

And then the sentence that changes everything.

This says his name is Blakely.

It feels like maybe someone else is screaming. I hear the bloodcurdling yell that causes people to turn. Panic is contagious; I learned that long ago. And the people in the crowd don't know what to make of me, the wide-eyed girl who is screaming and clawing, fighting her way toward the body.

"Jamie!" I'm yelling. "Jamie, Jamie, Jamie, wake up. Wake —"

"Grace, wait."

Strong arms are around me, pulling me back. Still, I fight against the bond. My arms are squeezed tightly to my sides as I try to claw and flail and kick.

"Jamie!" I yell again, but my voice is muffled as Alexei turns me, presses my cheek against his chest.

"I have to go help Jamie!"

"Shh. It's okay." Alexei takes my face in his hands and forces me to look into his eyes.

"No, I —"

"Grace, it's okay! Jamie's at the embassy, remember. Jamie's at the embassy. Jamie is okay."

Finally, I exhale.

"Jamie's at the embassy. Jamie is okay." I say it like a mantra, the words bringing calm.

But my blood still pounds inside me. The crowd has parted now, no one wanting to stand in the way of the crazy girl. They look at me like I'm something else to fear. The bystanders slowly fade away, a blurry, distant reminder that lingers on the outside of my vision as I stare at the boy in the surf. His West Point–issued jacket. His too-short hair and broad shoulders.

"That's Spence," I say, pulling away from Alexei, who surges to grab me again. "I've got to get him. I have to help him."

"You can't help him," Alexei says, taking my face tightly in his hands. He's not going to let me turn my head. He's going to make me keep staring into his blue eyes — eyes that are bruised and swollen, yes. But eyes that are alive. I have seen too much death already in my short life, and I have no doubt Alexei knows it.

"I have to help him," I say, numb.

But Alexei shakes his head.

"He's Jamie's friend," I say, as if that changes things.

Alexei pulls me against him.

"He's dead, Gracie. He's dead."

CHAPTER TEN

The embassy looks the same when we reach it — there's no black wreath upon the door; the flag isn't flying at half-mast. No, the US embassy isn't mourning. Yet. I have to remember that Spence's body is still lying on the beach, waiting to be identified. Tests will need to be run, calls will need to be made. It might be hours until someone tells my grandfather that a cadet from West Point has washed up on Adria's shores. Until someone tells Jamie.

Someone is going to have to tell Jamie.

"Grace." Alexei's hand is on my arm, and that's when I realize I've started to tremble. "It is okay."

"No." I'm shaking my head. "I thought it was him. I thought . . ."

"Jamie is safe."

"I know. It's just . . ."

The marine holds open the gate, waiting for me to make up my mind about whether or not I'm coming in, and I can't help myself . . . I hesitate. I'm not used to being the bearer of bad news. Usually, *I am* the bad news. A part of me wants to keep walking, past the gates to Russia and China, all the way to Iran and the hills that climb high above the city. I look at the embassy that stands before me, currently at rest. Like a pebble thrown into a very still pond, I know the ripples are coming. A part of me fears they will make waves.

Spence is dead. Spence is dead. Spence is dead.

I know the words are true, and yet they have no meaning.

It's not even ten a.m. yet. Twelve hours ago he was alive. Alive and standing on a beach. Talking. Fighting. Kissing.

He was the first boy I ever kissed. And in the deepest, darkest part of me I have to wonder if that's what killed him.

It's not as ludicrous as it sounds. After all, if Spence hadn't kissed me then Alexei wouldn't have hit him. If Alexei hadn't hit him then they never would have fought on the beach. If they'd never fought on the beach then Jamie would never have left Spence on the island. And if Spence hadn't been on that island then his body would have never washed ashore this morning.

I know it's not rational. I know it's not true. But knowing something and believing something are two totally different things, and right now I believe with all my soul that Spence is dead and I'm somehow to blame.

Spence is dead.

When I feel a hand on my arm I remember that Alexei's still beside me. I'd give anything for him to be a thousand miles away.

"I'll call you later," I say as I step through the narrow gate and start to close it behind me.

"I'm not leaving you," Alexei says, catching the metal latch before I can pull it closed. He sounds a little shocked I'd even think it.

"He won't take the news well."

Alexei steps closer, staring me down. "And that's why I'm not leaving you."

I could argue. I could fight. But it feels too good having him beside me, to know that, at least in this, I'm not alone. I step toward the doors and feel Alexei's hand take mine. Wordlessly, he follows.

The lights are off in the foyer. I stand for a moment on the black and white tiles, watching. Listening. Light streams through the narrow windows on either side of the door, slicing through the shadows. I look up the stairs, listening for the sound of Ms. Chancellor's high heels, ringing phones, and worried whispers, but the US embassy is business as usual. For now.

Should I find Ms. Chancellor or my grandfather first? Ms. Chancellor, I decide. She'll know what to do, who to call, what —

"What's he doing here?"

Jamie is standing on the stairs, looking down on us. His hair is still wet from the shower, but he doesn't look refreshed. He's looking at Alexei in a way I never thought I'd see. They were inseparable every summer of my childhood. They came home with scraped knees and knowing grins and secrets — so many secrets. But now I know something Jamie doesn't know, and it doesn't feel the way I always thought it would, being on the inside. I'd give anything not to know.

"There's something we need to talk about." Alexei glances at me, and, if possible, Jamie grows more distant.

"I'm not giving you my blessing," he snaps.

"What?" I ask, then shake my head. "Never mind. Come on down, Jamie. We need to talk to you."

"If you've come to say you're sorry about last night, you can save your breath," he says, passing us and glaring at Alexei. "You don't owe me an apology. You owe one to Spence, and he's not here. But as soon as he gets back —"

"Spence is dead."

I didn't mean to say it. Not so quickly. Not like that. But the words have been on a perpetual loop inside my mind and now they're out, tumbling free. I know I should have broken the news gently, eased Jamie off the cliff. But eventually, he had to fall. And I have never been one to fall when I can jump.

"What are you talking about, Gracie?"

He thinks I'm lying.

Or maybe he's just wishing, pretending he didn't hear or trust my opinion on this — or anything, really. Never before has anyone wanted me to be so wrong. I can see it in his eyes.

"Spence's body just washed ashore. I'm so sorry. He died."

"I don't know what you think you're saying, but —"

"Jamie. It's true," Alexei says, and I know that this confuses my brother.

"No." Jamie shakes his head. "Spence is nineteen. He's not dead."

"He is." I grab hold of my brother's shirt. It's an old one from before West Point and it's a little too tight across the chest. Buttons pull and gap. With the tiniest tug, he might break free. "We were on the beach and . . ."

I can hear the breaking of the waves, the screams.

This says his name is Blakely.

"Blakely," I whisper as my vision narrows, filling with spots. It's like the world is running out of air.

"It's okay." Alexei's hands are on my shoulders, gripping tight. "Breathe, Gracie. Breathe."

"Why is she saying that?" I hear Jamie ask. He sounds so confused. Stunned. This is a bad dream. It has to be.

"Your friend must have been wearing your jacket. For a moment, she believed it was you."

I hear my brother cuss. And then he takes Alexei's place beside me.

I can hear him, see him, feel him. And yet I can't stop hearing the voice on the beach.

This says his name is Blakely.

"Gracie —"

"I'm okay." I force the words out. This is no time for me to fall apart. "I'm fine."

"Gracie, why would you say that Spence is dead?"

"*Because he is*. We were on the beach and . . . Jamie, his body washed ashore."

"I don't believe it." Jamie steps back. "He's a US citizen. They would have told Grandpa. You have to be wrong."

"They haven't identified him yet. We just came from the beach. We were just there."

"No. No. You're *wrong*."

"I'm so sorry," I say.

"Did you see his face?" my brother shouts.

"He was wearing your jacket. That's why they thought his name was . . . It was him."

"It *wasn't*." Jamie's acting like denial can make something true. But it can't. And no one knows that better than me. "It can't be —"

"James." At the sound of Grandpa's voice, my brother's face goes white. Slowly, he turns, and just that quickly Jamie knows. Grandpa doesn't have to say that someone called the embassy — that it's official. That it's true. And there is nothing anyone can say to change it.

CHAPTER ELEVEN

It takes a long time to fall asleep, and when I do, I dream of bodies.

I dream of ghosts.

Some are floating on the waves and others lie in clouds of smoke, but all are just out of my reach. I'm far too late to save them. And yet I try, over and over, tossing and turning until my legs are tangled in my sheets and I'm covered in sweat.

I blame it on the chaos that's filled the embassy for hours, on the meds that I'm not taking. It's natural, I tell myself, to be haunted. But as I lie somewhere in that place between sleep and wake, it takes a while to realize that I'm not making up the voices.

"Ah, she looks so sweet."

"Should we wake her?"

"Don't touch her! I touched her once. It was a mistake."

Slowly, the whispers penetrate the haze that surrounds me and pull me gently from the dream.

When I open my eyes, Rosie's face is inches from mine. "Good morning!" Her voice is too chipper and entirely too loud. I don't know what time it is, but the room is bright, and decidedly not empty.

"Good. You're up," Megan says, plopping down on the foot of my bed.

"Now I am."

Slowly, I push upright, trying to hide my worry. Was I talking in my sleep? Did they hear me? What dream was it this time? I have to wonder as I look at my friends, hoping they didn't hear enough to figure out any of my secrets.

"What are you two doing here?"

"Three!" a voice calls through the window.

I throw off my covers and go over to look out at Noah. He's trying to ease his way onto one of the limbs of the tree outside, but he's bigger than Megan and Rosie, and the limb is bending under his weight. He has a death grip on the tree trunk and all the color has drained from his face.

"Rosie, how do you make this look so easy?" he asks.

Rosie shrugs. "I'm little, but I'm strong."

"Noah," I say slowly, "why don't you try coming in through the door?"

Noah shakes his head. He keeps his gaze on the ground. "Can't."

"Noah, you're gonna get yourself killed breaking into the US embassy. And I'm pretty sure, diplomatically speaking, that's frowned upon. Now climb down and come to the door like a sane person."

I have no right to question anybody's sanity, but my friends don't know enough to say so.

"That's the thing, Grace . . ." Rosie looks up at me. "We had to climb over from Germany because the main gates are kind of *busy*."

I'm just starting to say something when the limb cracks. Noah winces, and I turn and yell, "Are you coming in or aren't you?"

"I'm good out here. You guys just . . . talk loudly."

"Talk about what?" I'm still half asleep, and I really need to go to the bathroom. I want to eat something and go back to bed and wake up when I can convince myself that the last twenty-four hours were a dream. But they weren't. I can tell by the looks on my friends' faces. "What are you guys doing here?"

Megan and Rosie share a glance, and then Megan steps slowly forward.

"Grace, we have a problem." That's when I notice she's holding her phone.

There's a video paused on the screen, and Megan presses PLAY. At first, the screen is too small for me to make out the moving image. For a second, I don't know what I'm watching.

"What is it?" I ask.

Megan turns up the volume and instantly the audio fills my silent room. Only then do I recognize the flickering light of the bonfire, hear the sickening sounds of the hits.

And when Alexei shouts, "Touch her again, and I will kill you," the words are as clear as a bell.

"There were four different versions from four different angles uploaded the morning after the party," Megan says. "You can hear him say it on every one."

"That's online?" I ask, panic rising. "Who put it up? We've got to get it taken down. Now."

But Megan is shaking her head. "You don't understand, Grace. It's on the *Internet*. It's *everywhere*."

I remember that night on the beach, the panic I felt as I saw people were recording the fight, and I realize that a part of me always knew this was going to happen. But no part of me ever guessed that Spence would be dead when it did.

"There are millions of videos online. I mean, nobody's gonna see it, right? Megan, tell me nobody will see it!"

"Grace . . ." Megan starts.

But Rosie has already picked up the remote control and is turning on the little TV I never watch. One of the perks of embassy life is that we get pretty much every station. All the ones in Adria. A lot of the news outlets covering Europe and Asia and the Middle East. And, especially, the US.

I'm not sure which channel the TV is on, but as soon as the picture becomes clear, I recognize the fire, the hits, and the words of the boy next door.

"I will kill you."

I grab the remote control and click to the next station. And the next. And the next. On every one, the footage is the same — a constant loop of violence mixed in with the droning of "experts," none of whom actually know Alexei. But that doesn't stop them from talking. Words like *diplomatic immunity* and *Adria* and *murder* fill my room like a fog. Like smoke.

And on the bottom of every screen scrolls the same clear message: *Murdered West Point Cadet Brutally Attacked and Threatened by Russian Ambassador's Son.*

We live in a twenty-four-hour news cycle, and as I slept, the world started to care about a stupid fight at a stupid party. About two stupid boys who just had to lash out at each other.

Because of me.

"Where are you going?" Rosie says when I bolt from my room. I can feel her behind me, keeping pace at my heels, but I don't slow down.

"Grace, where are you going?" Megan calls.

"To fix it."

"You can't fix it!" Megan says, but I'm not listening.

"Where's my grandpa?" I ask her, barreling down the stairs of the residence, racing toward the offices. "Have you seen him? We have to issue a statement, or . . ."

It's not until I reach the landing that I hear the noise — the yells. It's different from the shouting on the beach. These aren't cries of fear or terror. No, it's lower somehow. A steady, rumbling hum on the other side of the big round window that looks out onto the street.

And then I see them. The entire street is blocked off, and where there are usually buses and pedestrians, at least a hundred people stand. They carry signs and American flags and chant, demanding justice. Russia's gates are tightly closed against the mob, but their cries fill the street.

Rosie cuts her eyes at me. "It's too late to fix it."

My friends don't follow me to my grandfather's office, and I can't blame them. Embassy kids are supposed to be good at blending into the wallpaper and making ourselves scarce. We're not supposed to charge into the center of international drama. But I'm pretty sure we're not supposed to cause any international drama either. That's why I find myself pushing down the hall, rushing toward the big double doors that are almost always closed, especially to me.

But when I notice they're open just a crack, I stop. When I hear voices, I can't help myself. I listen.

"We will have to speak with her." I don't recognize the woman's voice, so I risk creeping a little closer and allow myself to peek through the slim crack in the open door.

"Now, I just don't think that's gonna be possible." Grandpa's tone is hard, but the Tennessee is heavy in his voice. Whatever he wants, he's trying to get it with his own special cocktail of charm and determination.

"You may posture and complain all you like, Mr. Ambassador. But Adrian officials must be allowed to interview the girl."

"Absolutely not," my grandpa says, and I don't have to wonder what girl they might be speaking of.

The girl who is too fragile.

The girl who is too weak.

The girl who is too broken.

"Why don't you question the boy?" From Grandpa, it isn't a question. It's a challenge. And my first thought is my brother. Grandpa sees no reason to hide Jamie.

But then the woman says, "The boy is here on a black passport. Of course we haven't questioned him."

Now I know they're speaking about Alexei.

I'm not surprised to hear the Russians are playing the diplomatic immunity card, but I wish they weren't. After all, Alexei doesn't have anything to hide. Alexei isn't me.

I hear the clicking of high heels, watch a white-haired woman walk across my grandfather's office, admiring the art on the walls as if she has all day to answer the US ambassador's questions.

"I have come as a favor, Mr. Ambassador."

"Are we really going to be so formal, Madame Prime Minister? You used to call me Bill. Or William when you were angry."

"And you used to be a better flirt," the woman says. "I didn't have to come to you myself, you know."

"I do know." Grandpa nods. "And I thank you."

"I could step outside right now and tell the world that the US is refusing to cooperate with this investigation. Would you prefer I do that?"

"Threats, Alexandra? And here I thought we were having so much fun."

"I am here because we want a resolution."

103

"As do we," Grandpa says.

"We cannot have this spiraling into something more of a spectacle than it already is."

"You call the death of a West Point candidate a spectacle?"

"With all due respect, Mr. Ambassador, there are approximately two hundred people and two dozen television cameras outside at this very moment who are proving my point for me."

"A United States citizen is dead and —"

"Alexei didn't do it!"

When I push open the doors and step inside I see them look around as if wondering whether or not their discussion might have conjured me. Well, now I'm in their midst, and I can tell that neither of them is entirely sure what to do about it.

"Gracie," Grandpa snaps. "Go to your room. I'll speak to you later."

"Oh. I'm sorry, Grandpa. Is this a bad time?"

I grin and turn to study the woman in my grandfather's office. I look from her white hair worn in a sleek, chic bob all the way down to the tips of her designer heels. She's so polished she reminds me of . . . Grandpa. But the Adrian Lady version. She is diplomacy personified.

Something in my look must tell Grandpa that he'd have to summon the marines to drag me from this room, so he finally gestures in my direction.

"Madame Prime Minister, would you do me the courtesy of allowing me to introduce my granddaughter, Grace? Grace, you have the privilege of meeting Adria's acting prime minister, Ms. Alexandra Petrovic."

The last time I was this close to an Adrian prime minister I was at the wrong end of a gun. But I guess a week can change things. A week can change everything.

"Hello, Grace," the woman says.

"Isn't it your first week on the job?" I ask her.

"It is," she says with a laugh. "It seems I'm going to have to — what is it you Americans say? — hit the ground running."

The smile she gives me never quite reaches her eyes. This isn't a chat, a friendly visit. I have to wonder what she's heard about me. Does she know I'm the reason the man who had the job before her is in a coma right now and probably isn't going to make it?

Well, I think, remembering, *I'm* part *of the reason.*

There's a small door that separates my grandfather's office from Ms. Chancellor's. It doesn't look like a door, though — the red wallpaper and white wainscoting simply swing forward on a nearly invisible hinge. As a kid, I thought it was the coolest thing I'd ever seen. My very first secret passage.

The very first of many, I have to think as the door swings open and Ms. Chancellor steps inside.

"Oh, good. Here you are," Grandpa says, gesturing her closer. "Madame Prime Minister, you know my chief of staff, Eleanor Chancellor?"

Ms. Chancellor steps forward and takes the prime minister's

outstretched hand. "Madame Prime Minister, so nice to see you again. Please forgive me. If I'd known you were coming I would have met you downstairs myself."

But the prime minister pushes Ms. Chancellor's worries away. "That's quite all right. It was an unexpected stop. I'd prefer to keep this visit . . . informal."

That prime ministers don't just pop by to visit foreign ambassadors is something nobody in the room says but everyone in the room knows.

"To what do we owe the pleasure?" Ms. Chancellor asks, and I can feel the air start to turn. Grandpa can flirt and cajole, thicken his accent and lay on the charm. But that's not going to work on the new prime minister of Adria, and Ms. Chancellor knows it. Probably because she knows it wouldn't work on her either.

I look from Adria's new prime minister to the woman who shot the old one, and for a second my heart begins to pound and my mouth goes dry. I forget about Spence and Alexei and the protesting crowds outside, and I think about what would happen if the truth about that night ever came to light, if the Society and their cover-up failed.

If that happened, there would be no end to the shouting.

I'm looking at Ms. Chancellor, trying to keep the panic from my eyes, when Ms. Petrovic says, "We would very much like to ask Grace some questions."

"Absolutely not," my grandfather interrupts. "Grace, you —"

I don't let him finish. I just tell her, "I don't have anything to hide."

I have everything to hide.

"We have found ourselves in a bad situation at a very bad time."

Ms. Chancellor raises an eyebrow. "When exactly is a *good* time, Madame Prime Minister?"

"I simply meant that —"

"I know what you meant," Ms. Chancellor says. "The Festival of the Fortnight begins tonight and the streets will be overrun with tourists. The death of an American citizen is bad for business."

"Tourism is Adria's largest industry. I won't apologize for that fact. I can't have Americans making speeches on television and calling for Russian heads on spikes. We haven't done that in Adria for two hundred years, I'm happy to say."

"Yes. Well, the last time it didn't end so well, did it?" Grandpa challenges, finally getting into the fight.

The prime minister studies him, a glint in her eye. "No. It did not. And I believe we shall all spend the next two weeks remembering."

"Irony is an amazing thing, is it not?" Ms. Chancellor says.

The women stare each other down with cool indifference that has to be anything but. Does she know the truth about Ms. Chancellor and her predecessor? Does Grandpa? How deep and how far does this conspiracy go?

But the adults around me are so calm. I half expect my grandfather to smile and say *By the way, Alexandra, did you know Eleanor is the one who shot your predecessor and then had her secret society librarian friends orchestrate a massive international cover-up? Would you like some tea?*

It's Ms. Chancellor's voice that finally breaks through my foggy brain. "Grace went to the party at about nine. She was home by ten-thirty. She and her brother would have passed at least two dozen surveillance cameras between here and the city gates, and you are welcome to check ours if you would like."

"Mr. Spencer stayed at the party?" the woman asks me.

"Yes."

"And the fight?"

"You've seen the video."

"Yes. I have." Her smile is so cold that I can't help but remember that the last man who held her job wanted me dead. I start to wonder if that's one of the responsibilities that comes with the position.

"There. Was that so hard?" the prime minister says. "However, I do also need to ask you to control your people, Mr. Ambassador. These things do have a tendency to turn ugly."

"They are not my people. And they are not out of control."

The woman laughs. "There is a mob outside, sir, who would disagree with you." She pierces my grandfather with a glare and reaches for the door. "Valancian police will monitor the crowds and keep the peace on our side of the fence. I strongly urge you to do what you can from your side." She shifts her gaze onto me. "Grace, it has been so nice to meet you. Now, I'm afraid I should be going."

"Of course," Grandpa tells her. "It's a busy day. I appreciate you taking the time."

When she reaches the door she stops and looks back. "We'll reach a solution, William. And the US will be happy with it."

As soon as the prime minister is gone, I look at Grandpa. I'm pretty sure he's already noticed that it wasn't a question.

CHAPTER TWELVE

After I leave my grandpa's office I lie on my bed for hours, wondering what's worse, the chanting of the mob outside or the pounding that fills my head. Over and over and over. I know that it can't kill me, and yet I think it might. Maybe a part of me wishes that it would. Anything to make the pounding stop.

I have to make the pounding stop.

Before I realize it, I'm bolting from my room and down the stairs at the back of the building. They're only used by staff, so no one sees me as I push out into the courtyard, chasing the *pound*, *pound*, *pound* that beats like a telltale heart, reminding me over and over that something is terribly wrong. After all, it's not the first time I've found Jamie shooting hoops behind the embassy. It's just the first time I've ever found him here alone.

"Jamie!" I yell, but it's like he doesn't even hear me.

"Jamie!" I shout again, but my brother keeps dribbling the basketball, bouncing it hard against the pavement. He doesn't even look in my direction.

At the back of the embassy, the noise from the mob is softer, but I can still hear the chanting — the steady roar that rages, demanding justice be done. But no one asks for the truth.

When I walk closer, Jamie stops dribbling long enough to take aim at the basket. The ball swooshes through — nothing but net — and my brother grabs it, starts dribbling again. *Pound, pound, pound.* It makes me want to scream.

"Hey!" I shout. When Jamie shoots again, I grab the ball as soon as it drops through the net and hold it just out of my brother's reach.

"Give me the ball, Gracie." It's like he's just now noticed that I'm here.

"How are you?"

"How do you think I am?"

He's right. He doesn't have to answer my question. I can see the truth in his dark eyes and the set of his jaw. There's an anger in my brother that I have never seen before. He's pulsing with it. And a part of me wonders if that was really the pounding that has filled my head all day.

"Spence's parents called Grandpa today to make arrangements for claiming his body. I'm going to have to shake his father's hand and salute his mother and . . . Can you imagine that? They have to bury their son."

Three years ago Jamie and Dad brought our mom's remains

here. To Adria. Now the Spencers have to make the opposite journey with their child. I can't imagine anything worse. And by the look on his face, neither can Jamie.

"I can't tell them that their son died a hero. I can't hand them a folded flag and say it was all in service to his country. No. He died because he trusted me enough to follow me to that island."

There's a chink in Jamie's armor now. He is vulnerable and flawed and it's the most terrifying thing that I have ever seen. I need Jamie to be perfect. I need it so badly — so I don't have to be.

"Jamie, it's not your fault."

"Spence was alive when I left him, Gracie. When *I left him*." Jamie looks away and shakes his head. For the first time, I realize how much he looks like Dad. "I left a man behind. Do you know what that looks like? What that *feels* like? I'm going to have to go back to West Point and tell my teachers — tell my *classmates* — what happened here. Someone is dead because of me. Do you have any idea what that —"

I *do* know what that feels like — better than anyone. And Jamie just remembered. "It wasn't your fault," I tell him, but Jamie just shakes his head.

"He's never been here before. He doesn't . . . he *didn't* know his way around." Jamie grimaces as he remembers his friend is in the past tense now. "He didn't speak the language."

"Every person on that island goes to an English-speaking school, Jamie. And you know it."

"He's dead, Grace!" Not *Gracie*. "And when I left he wasn't."

Three years ago, on a dark night in a smoky building, I pulled a trigger and someone we loved died. What Jamie did — or didn't do — is different. But guilt isn't smart. It isn't logical. It doesn't only live in the places it belongs.

So I, better than anyone, should know just what to say to make my brother feel better. But it's a trick question. The truth is, there's nothing anyone can say.

"Jamie, talk to me. Or, fine. Don't talk to me. Talk to Alexei!"

At this, my brother only glares.

We're behind the embassy, right by the wall. Alexei is just on the other side of the fence, but Jamie is acting like they're strangers.

"Have you talked to him?" I ask.

"Of course I haven't talked to him," Jamie says, and I can't help myself. I take his basketball and throw it with all my might, high over the fence, into Russia's backyard.

"Hey!" my brother snaps.

"Alexei's probably home." I shrug. "Go ask him for your ball back."

"Brat," he tells me, and starts toward the doors.

"What can I say? I'm mentally unstable."

"Don't joke." Jamie is spinning on me.

Instinctively, I step back. "You used to have a sense of humor."

"Not about that. Never about that," he says. "Besides, someone murdered my friend, Grace. Forgive me if I don't crack up."

"Who said anything about murder? We don't know what happened."

"Oh," he says, turning slowly to look at the Russian embassy, "I think we know a little bit of what happened."

I follow his gaze, but I can't believe them — the words he isn't saying.

"No, Jamie. You can't possibly think that Alexei . . ."

"He never left the island. Did you know that?" Jamie turns again, this time as if he can see through Adria's great outer wall, as if he can look all the way out to the island, back into the past. "Spence. He was killed out there."

"You don't know that."

"Our grandfather is the United States ambassador to Adria, Gracie. He gets briefed on these things."

And Grandpa briefs Jamie. Nobody ever briefs me.

I try to follow where Jamie's going with this. "So Spence never left the island. Okay. Maybe he got drunk and wandered off and fell. Hit his head. Drowned."

"He didn't drown, Gracie. His neck was broken."

"So he fell and broke his neck!"

I am so used to Jamie being the calm one, the smart one. I'm not used to him being the cold one. But that's exactly what he is as he looks back at the Russian fence.

"He'd been in a fight."

"You can't think Alexei did this. You can't really, honestly think that."

"Alexei's been doing a lot of things I never thought he'd do."

"Like what?" I demand.

"Like you guys got close."

114

"You're the one who asked him to look out for me."

"Did he take advantage of you?"

"Did he . . . Ew. No!"

"Don't lie to me, Gracie. I see the way he looks at you. How you two are together."

"Spence is dead and that's *awful*. It is so, so awful, and I'd give anything to go back and change that night. I know you would, too. But we can't. Spence is gone. But if you don't stop this you're going to lose Alexei, too. And that would be tragic. Because that is something that you can still stop."

"Maybe some men deserve to be left behind."

I know this isn't just some army thing, some West Point thing. Spence was alive and now he's not, and Jamie isn't mad at Alexei. He's mad at himself. Alexei is just the closest target.

Alexei is my brother's Scarred Man.

"Spence was an adult, Jamie. He could take care of himself. He wasn't your responsibility."

"Like you're not my responsibility?"

"No," I tell him. "Don't you remember? You gave that job to Alexei."

"Well, then I guess I've made a lot of bad decisions this summer."

Jamie is my family. My blood. If I ever need a kidney, he is totally my first call. But we have never been so alike until this moment. He is changed. Broken.

It's the one thing I had hoped we would never have in common.

115

"Ms. Chancellor?" I say. She's in front of one of the big round windows upstairs, looking out onto the street, when I find her. Dusk is falling, but she holds a coffee cup with both hands, slowly sipping. It's the middle of summer on the Mediterranean, but it's like she's standing beside a pane of frosty glass, watching it snow. I can feel the cold descending.

The crowd is smaller now, here at the end of the day, but there are still protestors chanting, clogging the street and blocking off Embassy Row. Are these people angry with us or the Russians next door? Sometimes it's hard to say. Some people, after all, don't care who they yell at as long as they have a reason to keep shouting.

"It's not going to go away quickly, is it?" I ask, staring at the crowd.

Ms. Chancellor takes a sip. "No, dear. I don't believe it will."

"That's why the prime minister was here, wasn't it? Because of the crowds?"

"Because of what they represent, yes."

That's when I realize Ms. Chancellor isn't looking at the street — not at the protestors or the massive television trucks that stand right behind the barricades. No. Her gaze is locked on the building next door. There's an almost identical window on the Russian side of the fence. I half expect to see Alexei standing there, staring back.

On the street below, people are pushing through the crowds, going somewhere. There is a charge in the air, and even inside I can feel it. The sun begins to dip below the horizon and the shadows come to Embassy Row.

"You know Alexei didn't do it," I tell her, but I'm still surprised to hear her say, "Of course."

"Do you know who did?" I ask.

I don't know what I'm expecting her to say, but I'm disappointed when she shakes her head. "No, dear. I do not."

I think about the secret rooms and tunnels and the memory of Ms. Chancellor in a nearly abandoned street, holding a smoking gun.

"Ms. Chancellor, about the prime minister . . ."

"Alexandra Petrovic is *acting* prime minister, dear."

"I wasn't asking about her."

Eleanor Chancellor isn't a cold woman. But the look she gives me might turn the Mediterranean to ice. But I can't stop — not now.

"About what happened . . . did I ever say thank you?"

For being there. For believing in me. For saving my life.

"Really, Grace." The smile she gives me is almost blinding. "I'm sure I don't know what you mean."

But she does know. Of course she does. But the truth is one more thing that I know she'll never say.

"Now go on," Ms. Chancellor tells me with a playful push toward the stairs.

"Go where?" I ask.

"Out. The Festival of the Fortnight begins tonight, you know." She looks at me over the top of her glasses. "Oh, Grace, don't tell me you've forgotten. It's a very important part of Adrian history. And a very big party." There is an uncharacteristic twinkle in her eye. I think for a moment that she might be teasing. Then I think better of it. Eleanor Chancellor does not tease.

"I'm not in a partying mood," I tell her.

"I'm not asking, Grace. You need to get out of this building and enjoy yourself for a little while." She points toward the stairs. "Now go. Your guests are waiting."

Is she speaking as my grandfather's chief of staff or as my surrogate mother? Or maybe this is part of the Society. Maybe I'm not supposed to know.

Then I wonder, *What guests?*

CHAPTER THIRTEEN

When I reach the entryway, Megan and Noah are already there. She is leaning against his shoulder as they both look at her phone. His cheek touches the top of her head. Their embrace is so comfortable, so easy, that I almost feel guilty for having seen it.

"Hey," Noah says when he sees me. He doesn't pull immediately away from Megan, though — as if they've been caught. They aren't doing anything wrong, I guess. Technically, there's no shame in being happy.

"Awesome. You're here," Megan says, and Noah reaches for the door. "I told you not to underestimate Ms. Chancellor," she tells him before stepping outside.

"Come on," Noah almost yells over the chants of the protestors. "Let's go."

I haven't seen him this excited in ages. Not since the night we met, when he took me to Lila's party on the cliffs. It was only a few weeks ago, but it seems like a lifetime. It was *Before*.

Before my brother came and his friend died. Before the streets were filled with protests and cries. Before I knew the truth about my mother and what I did.

Before I figured out that I am the villain of my own story.

I want to pull away from Noah, go back inside. But his grip on my hand is too strong as he loops an arm around Megan's shoulders and leads us out beyond the gates.

Dusk is settling over Valancia, and the crowd is smaller. But barricades still line the sidewalk, keeping the protestors in the street. Adrian police officers rush toward us, ushering us farther from the embassy, away from the chanting mob.

We walk through the bright lights that shine upon the reporters who stand in the street with US and Russia over their shoulders, the embassies spotlighted in the glare. It's the middle of the day in the States, I have to remind myself. And cable news isn't going to let this story die. Not yet. We live in a twenty-four-hour news cycle and this story has only begun.

When we reach the edge of the crowd I know I'm safe, but I have to look back — like Lot's wife. I'm almost afraid I'll turn to salt. But I don't see the city burning. No. I see a boy with black hair and blue eyes standing before a second-story window of the building next door.

Alexei raises his hand in something that isn't quite a wave but isn't a salute. It's more like he's pushing me away, telling me to save myself.

So I look straight ahead. I swear I won't look back again.

When we reach the Israeli embassy we turn and start up the street that rises steadily to the palace and the center of town. The farther we get from Russia, the more the city seems to change. The angry cries grow fainter, but the streets are anything but empty, and the closer we get to the palace, the rowdier the crowd becomes. We are surrounded by laughter and talking, big raucous groups of tourists and older couples who walk together, hand in hand. It's like all of Adria is heading toward the palace.

Then I think about Alexei — about Jamie.

Well, *almost* all of Adria.

"So what is all of this, exactly?" I ask.

Noah turns, walking backward for a moment, shocked indignation on his face. "You spent every summer of your childhood here and you don't know what tonight is?"

It's like I've just told him that I think all puppies are evil.

"You never came to the Festival of the Fortnight?" He gapes.

"No," I say.

"Never?" Noah asks, not letting it drop. "Little Grace never crawled out of her window and ran away to see the bonfire?" he teases. "Or *set* the bonfire . . . or tossed petrol upon the bonfire . . ."

"No," I say, sounding almost defensive of Past Me. "Mom would have killed me."

121

There's a huge group of people coming up behind us, singing songs I've never heard. Noah and Megan and I step aside to let them pass, but one of them knocks into me anyway. He mumbles something, slurring his words, and his breath smells like liquor.

As the drunk moves along, I look at Noah. "Mom said it wasn't exactly 'kid friendly.'"

Noah nods. "I can see her point."

When we reach the streets that surround the palace, the crowds grow thicker, heavier. Somehow hungrier. We are tossed and pushed and shoved. Noah holds both of our hands, keeping us lashed together, until we finally find a place beside one of the barricades, right in front of the palace. I turn and look up at the tall iron fences, the almost impenetrable facade.

"You *do* know about the War of the Fortnight, don't you, Grace?" Megan asks me.

I look at the palace and try to recall the night last month when I accompanied my grandfather to an official state function. I remember walking through the ornate ballroom, studying the walls that were covered like patchwork with priceless paintings of kings and queens. That night, the prime minister told me the story of one of those kings. But at the time that same prime minister was also trying to kill me, so, in hindsight, I'm not exactly eager to take his word for it.

"Remind me," I say, and Megan and Noah share a look.

Noah rubs his hands together, trying his best to be dramatic.

"Okay," he says. "Picture it! Adria. Almost two hundred years ago. A terrible drought has crippled the land. Rivers are dry. Crops have failed. The people are hungry — literally starving for revenge. And since they can't take it out on God, they go after the next best thing . . ."

Reverently, Noah turns, and we all look at the palace. I can feel his countenance change. He isn't teasing; no one's laughing anymore.

"One night, the palace guards left their posts and threw open the gates, and an angry mob pulled the king and his family from their beds," I say, almost to myself.

Noah and Megan stand beside me. Together, we ease a little closer to the fence.

"The king," Megan says. "The queen. Two princes, and a baby girl who wasn't even a month old yet. Five of them. They pulled them from their beds, and they killed them." She points to a line of windows in the center of the palace. "That's where they hung their bodies."

For a second, I think about Alexei and the crowds that have taken over Embassy Row. What would it take for that mob to pull him from his bed? How easy would it be? But then I remember that there are some questions to which you never want to know the answer.

"And that, Gracie" — Noah leans against the barricade and eyes the palace — "was the start of the War of the Fortnight. Fourteen days that changed Adria forever."

Fourteen days, I think. Noah seems amazed that change can happen so quickly, but I know better. It doesn't even take that long. The whole world can change far faster. In the time it takes a thirteen-year-old girl to point and fire a gun.

Some people in the crowd carry torches, and the air is filled with smoke. Gaslight shines from sconces that adorn the palace's fence. The light that surrounds us is the color of fire.

In the distance, I hear a child laugh. A mother yells. And I close my eyes, try to block out the din of chaos that fills the air. I want to run, to leave. I don't know why, but I know I need to get away from these people before it is too late.

Frantically, I push away from the fence and am just starting to turn, to leave, when the trumpets sound. The sound is so foreign and ancient and regal that I stop. Then I remember where I am, standing outside an ancient palace, looking through the fence at history.

The crowd stands still. It's like even the fire in the torches stops moving. Everything is absolutely quiet as the palace doors open.

That is when I notice the rich red carpet that runs from the doors to the gates. A few weeks ago, that was where I ran, clutching a ball gown in my hands, away from the Scarred Man and my mother's memory. But tonight the people who exit through those doors are walking slowly toward the hordes that gather on the other side of the fence.

The king is in the center, the queen to his right. On his left stands the crown prince of Adria. And beside him his wife, Princess Ann.

The royal family keeps walking until they reach the fence, and then the most amazing thing happens. Slowly, the gates open wide until there is nothing between the crowds and the four royals who stand, almost at attention, as if daring history to repeat itself.

Two hundred years ago, someone threw open those gates and the people of Adria rushed *in*. But now the gates stand open and the royal family looks *out*.

I expect cheers from the crowd, applause of some kind. But the people outside the palace stay silent, as if imagining that centuries have not passed. As if they have traded places with their ancestors and are pondering this chance to do things differently.

But I know better. I know you never really get a second chance.

The king leads his family toward four black wreaths that sit on stands before them. They each pick up a wreath and carry it through the gates. Slowly, the royal family members raise their wreaths and place them in front of the palace, directly beneath the place where the king's ancestors once hung for all to see.

Again, I expect applause, but there is no sound except the buzzing of the gaslight, the solemn breathing of the crowd.

It's like all of Adria is waiting, watching as the king picks up a nearby torch and brings it to the wreath he'd carried. I can't believe it as he lowers the flame to the wreath and lights it. In a flash, the fire spreads, and soon all four wreaths are ablaze.

I realize then there is a small path through the crowd. Barricades hold the people back, and soon I know why when the fire shoots away from the wreaths, chasing the darkness toward the wide grassy promenade where just last week the closing of the G-20 summit was held.

But now the grassy area is filled with the silent crowd that stands, watching, as the fire hurtles toward them from the palace, then leaps onto a massive tangle of timber and broken furniture, tree limbs and debris. In a second, it ignites. The fire shoots and spreads, spiraling up into the night.

Only then does the crowd applaud, the sound almost a roar as they stand in the orange-red glow of the spark that the king himself sent into their midst.

It's supposed to symbolize something, I'm certain. But I'm not quite sure what. Maybe it's a sign of peace. Maybe it's a warning.

Like a rainbow, is this supposed to be a sign that the people will never destroy their king again? But I know better than anyone just how quickly the world we know can turn to flames.

"It will burn for fourteen days," Megan says, but I only half hear her.

The king and queen and their son are turning slowly, solemnly away from the crowd and starting the walk back toward the palace.

Only the trim, beautiful woman remains.

For just a second, Princess Ann stands silently, looking right at me.

CHAPTER FOURTEEN

I don't know how I lose Megan and Noah but they're gone.

All I know for certain is that the air is filled with smoke and the sky is the color of fire, and my mother's best friend was just looking at me as if maybe she might see what I see, know what I know.

"*Grace!*" I hear a woman yell, but I don't turn. I don't want to see my mother's shadow in the crowd.

"*Grace, honey, no!*"

Then Princess Ann turns and starts back toward the palace, away from the commoners. Away from me. And I start pushing away from the gates and whatever little safety I'd clung to on the edges of the crowd. I have to find Noah and Megan. I have to go home. I have to keep moving, pushing against the current of people that keeps pushing back, too hard.

It's growing late and the crowd is too close. I hear a popping sound, like gunshots. I imagine the glass breaking in the window of my mother's shop, the burst of fresh fire as soon as the oxygen rushes inside.

"Grace!"

And now I don't care about Noah and Megan. They're together. They'll be safe. They are probably holding hands and kissing somewhere. I would just be in the way, I tell myself. But the truth is I just need to be anywhere but here.

"Grace!" I hear my name again, but it's too much. I close my eyes tightly against the memory. Like the flames of the bonfire, I expect it to explode inside of me, to leave me shaking with terror and guilt and grief.

If I can just make it to the tunnels, I might be able to climb inside and slip away, escape into darkness and silence. I might be able to have my attack in peace.

So I push against the crowd that seems to be growing thicker, wilder, by the second. People chant and cheer. Even as I get farther and farther from the bonfire, the pressure of the people around me doesn't lessen. It just grows darker.

"Grace!" I hear my name again, my mother's voice.

I stop.

I want to scream.

But then there is a hand on my arm, turning me.

"Grace, are you okay?"

And it's not my mother. I look up into the same blue eyes that just a short time ago watched me from a Russian window. And, suddenly, I am completely unconcerned about myself.

"What are you doing here?"

Alexei shrugs. "I was getting ready to ask you the same question." He looks around. "Where are Noah and Megan?"

I shake my head. "I'm not sure. We must have gotten separated and I . . . I was going home."

"Yes," Alexei says. "We must get you home."

"And you," I say. "You shouldn't have come, Alexei."

It's a mistake. I know it as soon as I say his name.

There are too many people. The Festival of the Fortnight isn't just an Adrian tradition. It's famous. Visitors come from all over the world. Like people collecting beads at Mardi Gras or running with the bulls in Pamplona; the city fills with tourists. In the past ten minutes I've heard five different languages.

And just this morning another crowd gathered on another street. The setting and the cause are different, but all mobs are the same.

I don't recognize the man who turns toward us, but I know him. I know the way he stumbles and the cadence of his words as they slur. "Hey, I know you."

He is drunk on smoke and fire and the darkness of the streets, the heady mixture of whatever primitive drug seems to come with night and torchlight.

Valancian police are on patrol, but the crowd is too big. It always is. It's why our mother locked us in the embassy, forbade us to leave. This place, this night — these people.

Are dangerous.

I see it in Alexei's eyes as he reaches for my hand.

I speak to him in Adrian. "Let's get out of here."

Alexei nods and we start to push our way down the hill and back toward Embassy Row. But before we've even taken a step, the big man blocks our way. His friends see and circle us. Two of them carry torches. They are staring at Alexei and me as if we are their next meal.

"Well, what do we have here?" the leader asks. He's not much older than Jamie. Maybe they're American college guys. Maybe they are backpacking through Europe. Tourists.

But these guys aren't content with the fire and the crowds and the music that is coming from somewhere deep within the city.

I know in my gut that they were outside the embassy today. I know that they have been looking for a fight for maybe their entire lives. A sick feeling fills me as I realize that they've found one.

"You're him," the leader says. It isn't a question.

I speak in Adrian again, pull harder on Alexei's hand, but it's no use.

"It's the Russian!" one of the men with the torches yells. The world is full of Russians. He doesn't bother to specify which one.

Someone shoves Alexei, and he stumbles back, crashing into me.

"Grace, I'm so —"

But as soon as Alexei speaks, the mob descends. Hearing him — his accent — is proof enough. Besides, they don't care about justice. They aren't here to take Alexei to the cops, turn him over for questioning.

In the crowd, I hear words like *murderer* and *communist* and *diplomatic immunity*. It is the last phrase that really does it.

The fist that hits Alexei knocks him nearly off his feet. He doesn't see it coming. I don't know which one of the men swung first, but now the floodgates have opened. I can feel myself getting pushed, almost knocked to the ground. I lash out, kicking a man in the knee as he lunges at Alexei. But two other men are already upon him. I feel a sharp, searing pain in my side. I think about the torches and the bonfire and the smoke. There is so much smoke.

"Grace, run!" Alexei manages to yell as he knocks one of the men away, but no sooner does that man fall than two others take his place.

"Let him go!" I shout, then jump onto someone's back and elbow the ringleader in the nose.

He curses and blood begins to stream down his face. And then there is a loud bang and, for me, the world begins to spin. Perhaps it is the motion of the man trying to throw me from his back, but the pain that slices through me is real, even as the sights and sounds that fill my mind descend to shadow.

The sound of the shot.

The smell of the smoke.

And the fire that grows and grows, filling the space and climbing up the stairs.

Most of all, I see blood. There is so much blood.

"Grace, no!" my mother yells.

And I know that I have to break free of these thoughts that fill my mind. I have to help Alexei. I have to be stronger, smarter, tougher.

I see the Scarred Man rising, walking through the smoke. I hear him yell my name.

But this is different. The Scarred Man has never spoken to me before, not in the flashbacks or the nightmares. I feel his hands on my arms.

"Grace, are you okay?" Dominic yells. And just that quickly, fresh air fills my lungs. Terror is replaced with a different kind of panic.

"Alexei," I say. The mob is growing. "Help Alexei!"

Dominic presses me up against a wall, as out of the way as I can be, then starts toward the center of the mob. But before he can even reach Alexei, I hear a voice crying out, cutting through the madness.

"Let him go!"

Jamie has always been tough. He was raised by our father, a born soldier. But what I see isn't his West Point training; it's not the result of years of wrestling with our dad on the living room floor.

No. What I am seeing is sheer rage as Jamie battles ahead of Dominic, plowing through the crowd. He tosses grown men aside as if they were rag dolls. He knocks bullies to the ground like the toy soldiers he and Alexei used to play with on the embassy stairs. He is turning them all to dust because they touched his friend.

Jamie starts yelling, warning the college kids to back off, but it's Dominic who pulls Alexei from the mob's clutches. He drags him toward me while, behind him, Jamie keeps fighting like a man possessed by demons no one can ever exorcise or name.

I want to stop him. To hold him. To let him pummel *me* until I feel as bad on the outside as I do within. But Dominic is thrusting Alexei toward me.

He limps, and one eye has already swollen shut. Blood is soaking through the front of his white T-shirt.

"I'm okay, Gracie," he chokes out, and the smile that follows makes me want to fall to the ground and cry.

"Get him home," Dominic orders, pushing Alexei forward. He gives me a knowing look. "You know the way."

I don't wait for Jamie. He's with Dominic. He'll be fine. I just place Alexei's arm around my shoulder and drag him into an empty alley. It's the very place I saw the Scarred Man disappear weeks ago. Alexei leans against me, heavy and warm, but I don't stop to explain as I reach down and trigger the opening of the tunnel. I just hope that Alexei can make it down the ladder as I push him toward it, the two of us descending into the dark.

CHAPTER FIFTEEN

There are hundreds of miles of tunnels and catacombs beneath the city. The Romans built them, or so I'm told. They are thousands of years old and twist and turn, climb and fall. People died here, are buried here. But I am not afraid. As soon as the tunnel entrance closes overhead, there is nothing but darkness and the dank, musty smell of a damp enclosed space.

It smells a little bit like home.

That's why I let myself rest against the old stone walls. My shoulders rise and fall as I try to breathe deeply. It hurts — but if there is one thing I'm good at it's not letting myself think about the pain.

I reach for the flashlight in my pocket, and when I turn it on, Alexei flinches. It's like the bright light actually hurts. I shift the beam away from him, but there is still enough light for me to see the details that I didn't have time to fully notice on the dark, crowded street.

Scrapes and blood cover his knuckles. There is a split in his lip. Old bruises blend with new. The cut on his forehead has come open again, and his black hair is coated with red blood that still trickles slowly down his right temple.

"Don't," he says. I think it's because I'm reaching for him. I'm bringing my sleeve to his cut, wiping his blood away.

"No, Gracie. Don't look at me like that. I'm fine."

"You are not fine!" I run my fingers through his hair, pushing the strands away from his forehead. "They're monsters."

"Come on." He takes my hand. "We should get home," he says, but doesn't move.

He stands too close. He looks at me too long. I think, for a second, that maybe *he* is going to kiss me.

I think maybe I am going to let him.

Thousands of people fill the streets above us. We are just feet away from an angry mob. But we are also alone in the glow of my flashlight's narrow beam.

"Gracie." Alexei exhales my name. He pushes my hair away from my face with one hand and holds on to me with the other, slipping his arm around my waist and pulling me close. It hurts but I can't say so, not when he breathes deeply and says, "What are we going to do?"

Not *I*.

Not *my government*.

Not *the embassy*.

We.

What are we going to do?

Alexei and I are a *we* now, I realize. At least right here, right now. In this moment. And with the way he rests his forehead against mine and closes his eyes, I feel like maybe this feeling — this togetherness — is going to follow us when we finally decide to go back into the light.

Alexei doesn't speak again. He just holds me to his chest while he takes long, deep breaths. I feel my body moving with his chest.

Spence kissed me.

But this is more.

More intimate. More gentle. More emotion pounds through my veins than anything any boy has ever made me feel. For a second, we both just breathe, him out and me in. Me out and him in. It is like we are sharing breath, the very air that will keep us both alive. And in this moment, I stop thinking about my mother.

"It will pass, Alexei," I say, remembering Ms. Chancellor's words.

"Will it?" he asks. But it's not really a question, I can tell. He pushes me away but takes my hand. He's still holding it when I aim the flashlight down the long tunnel, to the place where it curves out of sight. It's what the old explorers must have felt like, seeing the earth disappear over the edge of the horizon.

I know where we're going.

And yet I can't help but fear that beyond this point there might be dragons.

・ ・ ・

"Where have you been?"

Sure, Jamie's hair is mussed and his shirt is ripped. Bruises and scrapes seem to cover every part of him. And yet it's almost like he's bulletproof. I knew he'd be okay, but as soon as I see him, I exhale and slump against the door, breathe a sigh of relief. I didn't even realize how worried I was until I croak out, "You're back."

"Of course I'm back," he tells me. "I'm worried about *you*."

I just saw him take on a half dozen grown men, and yet I almost knock him off his feet when I say, "Thank you."

He can't decide whether to be mad at me or just happy that I'm here in the embassy, safe and sound.

"Where were you?" he asks instead.

"I helped Alexei home. We had to take a . . . back way. We couldn't let anyone else see us."

"What were you thinking, Gracie? *Were* you thinking? Going out there? Tonight? With *him*? Are you trying to get yourself killed?" He jerks back. It's like the most awful thought in the world has just occurred to him, a thought he can't *un*think. "Are you?" he asks again. It's not hyperbole, an exaggeration.

Jamie thinks I have a death wish.

He reaches for me, but I wince and pull away. My brother fought off a mob tonight, and yet this is what hurts him, I can tell. He didn't save Spence. And this is one more reminder that he is three years too late to save me. Jamie's armor isn't quite so shining

137

anymore. Which is probably a good thing. If I were to look in it, I know I wouldn't like what I'd see.

"I wasn't there to get hurt," I assure him. "I'm fine. Alexei is fine. Thanks to you."

This should bring them back together, mend whatever rift Spence's death has caused, but Jamie hardens.

"I wasn't there for him. I was there for you."

"And *I* am fine," I say again.

"You were literally being chased through the streets by an angry mob carrying torches!" Jamie yells, then shakes his head. His anger fades, and all that is left is a deep-seated fear as he whispers, "Mom hated this night."

Compared to the shouts of the protestors and the noise of the crowd, the embassy is too quiet, too empty. So I say the words that, someday, Jamie is going to have to hear.

"He didn't do it. Alexei isn't a murderer."

"You don't know what he is."

"I know he's your best friend."

Jamie looks like maybe he wants to tell me something. But in the end he just shakes his head again and steps away. I know he wants to climb up to his old room, maybe take a shower, and crawl into bed. Or maybe he intends to stand guard all night, a sentinel against whatever ghosts might try to slip beneath my door.

"When are you going back?" I ask, suddenly not wanting him to leave.

He takes a couple of steps. His hand rests on the railing.

"Jamie," I call out, "when are you going back to West Point?"

He doesn't look at me. He just says, "I think maybe I should stay."

I wonder what that would be like, having him always here to fight my battles. I would hate it. And I would love it. But that's not how this story is supposed to go.

"You can't stay, Jamie."

"Yeah." He spins on me. "Well, right now I can't *leave*."

"I'm okay," I tell him, easing forward. "Don't give up West Point because of me. Because I am okay."

"Are you? Are you really, Gracie? Because my room is next door to yours, you know. When you wake up screaming in the middle of the night, I'm the one who hears you."

I don't talk about the nightmares. Not with Noah or Megan or Rosie. Not even with my psychiatrist, Dr. Rainier. It's not that I can't remember them once I wake up. It's that they are always there, like a movie playing in the background of my mind. Sometimes, though . . . sometimes I can't turn the volume down.

"They aren't that bad," I tell my brother. And the amazing thing is that it's mostly true.

He reaches out for me again, but I wince involuntarily and Jamie stops. I am the wild thing he doesn't want to frighten.

"I don't blame you, Gracie. You know that, don't you? I don't blame you for what happened to Mom." Jamie stalks toward me slowly. One heavy step and then another. They punctuate his words. "I. Don't. Blame. You."

His forgiveness is supposed to release me. I know I'm supposed

139

to slump to the floor and cry. I should be able to get better now, but Jamie doesn't know that my tears dried up ages ago.

So I just look at him.

"Then you're the only one."

He doesn't follow me up the stairs. He doesn't say another word. And I'm glad of it because I don't know if I could take it, not his words and not his touch. I don't want him to see me sway, unsteady on my feet as I walk down the hall.

I don't want him to notice how hard it is for me to open my bedroom door or how I collapse against it once it's closed.

But, most of all, I don't want my brother to see the dark stains that have spread across my black tank top. When I pull off my cardigan, I wince. When I try to stretch my arms over my head and peel off my shirt, I scream. But the water is already running in the shower, pounding against the tile and filling the bathroom with steam. I am alone as I look at the too-thin girl who is reflected in the mirror. Her hair is tangled and her eyes are sad, and her right side is covered in blood.

I try to touch the slice that pierces my skin, but the pain is too much. I can't pass out. Not now. I can't ask for help.

But, most of all, Jamie can't see this — know this. He already feels too guilty about Spence, and it's not like anybody needs another reason to worry about me, so I won't give them one. I'd rather die first.

I look at the bloodstained girl who is disappearing into the steam.

I'd rather die.

CHAPTER
SIXTEEN

I sleep later than I should. It's for the best, though. Easier to avoid Jamie that way. And Ms. Chancellor. But not Grandpa. I never have to worry about Grandpa.

Or so I think.

I'm halfway down the stairs when I hear voices in the foyer. There are a half dozen men and women being ushered into the formal living room on the other side of the black-and-white-checkered floor. It's the room where Grandpa hosts his standing poker game, but no one in the foyer has come to play, I can tell.

They wear their best suits and their most serious expressions as Grandpa shakes their hands and welcomes them inside. But it's the final man in the line who makes my breath catch.

Alexei's father is taller than his son, broader. More stoic, which I never really thought was possible. For a moment, he and

Grandpa stare at each other. Then, slowly, Grandpa extends his hand, and Alexei's father takes it. It looks like something knights might have done five hundred years ago, right before they battled to the death.

There are no cameras in the foyer, no press. I have no idea how they got the Russians into the embassy without causing the mob outside to go wild. Maybe they crawled over the fence? *Wouldn't be the first time*, I think. It's a shame I wasn't there to offer pointers.

"Grace?" Ms. Chancellor stands at the bottom of the stairs, looking up at me. "Is everything okay, dear?" Her gaze is as sharp as a knife, and that makes my side hurt. I'm pretty sure I wince. "Grace, are you ill? You seem pale."

"No. I'm just . . . I didn't sleep well."

"Yes, well —" Ms. Chancellor glances to the doors that are closing behind her. "I'm not surprised."

"What are they doing here?"

"That's not for you to worry about, dear. Are you *sure* you're feeling well?"

I want to yell that Alexei's not a killer. I want to storm into the room and tell everyone how he pulled me from the mob last night — that Alexei is a good guy. He saved me.

"We have to help him," I tell Ms. Chancellor. "You know as well as I do that Alexei didn't do this, so we have to do something."

The people in that room with my grandfather are nothing compared to the women in the Society with Ms. Chancellor.

142

"If they can make a gunshot disappear they can fix this," I tell her, but Ms. Chancellor gives me a slight shake of her head.

For the benefit of anyone who might be listening, she says, "I'm not sure what you mean."

I know I'm supposed to shut up now, like our trip to the Society's headquarters three days ago never happened — like I didn't see what I saw or hear what I heard. I guess I'm supposed to act like it was just another illusion of my messed-up mind. But I know what happens when you start treating the truth like fiction, and fiction like the truth. I know how the lines blur, and I can't let it happen again.

So I don't shut up.

"What does the Society know?" I ask quietly, taking a step closer. "What aren't you telling me? You've got to help him. You have to go in there and —"

"Eleanor?" My grandpa is standing at the door, calling to her. "We're ready."

Ready to do what? I want to yell, but do not say. It's just another thing that no one will ever tell me.

So when Ms. Chancellor looks back at me and says, "Grace, whatever is wrong, dear, I hope you know that I'm here. That I'll listen." I just nod. I don't even bother to lie anymore.

As I walk through the front doors, the sound of the protestors booms in my ears. They're back, of course. If anything, they're louder. They probably heard about the brawl last night. No doubt things are going to get worse before they get better.

Things can always get worse.

There are two marines on duty today, and neither of them says a word. I'm pretty sure they don't notice the way my right arm hangs oddly, too gently at my side. If anyone questions why I work the gate with my left hand they don't ask.

Protestors press against the barricades, and the sidewalk has disappeared into a narrow strip. People jostle and push, and every step is like a hot poker trying to stick between my ribs. When I touch my T-shirt, my fingers come away tinged with red.

I need help, of course. Even I know that much. The smart thing to do would be to turn around and go bang on the closed door until Ms. Chancellor opens it, to go to Jamie. Even Noah and Megan would help. But I know what will happen if I go to the hospital.

US Ambassador's Granddaughter Stabbed in Brawl with Russian Suspect.

I might as well go ahead and start World War III right now.

So I tell myself, *I'll be okay. I'm fine. Really. He'll be there*, I practically chant.

He's always there.

Then I see him, on the other side of the street, just far enough from the crowd to keep the whole thing in perspective. He sees me. In fact, he sees everything. And for the first time, I let myself double over. My steps falter.

I practically fall into the Scarred Man's arms.

"I need your help."

I sway. My vision blurs. I must have lost more blood than I realize because the Scarred Man's grip is too tight. I'm fragile and vulnerable and all of the things I hate. He practically carries me down the street.

"Come on."

The light in Dominic's kitchen is too bright. He makes me sit on a stool in the middle of the fluorescent glare, and I can't help but feel like I'm in an old-fashioned movie and he's a cop or a spy trying to sweat the truth out of me. But, of course, Dominic barely says a word. So I use the light to study *him*.

There is not a scratch on him, save the obvious. It's like there never was a fight, as if there was no mob. Last night? The guys on the street? They were *boys*, drunk and rowdy. Standing before me is an actual *man*. They never stood a chance.

"I'm sorry." I don't say for what. For getting into trouble, for bringing my problems to his door. For killing the love of his life. There's so much to choose from that I don't even try to be specific.

"Where are you hurt?" Concern seeps into his voice, but also annoyance.

I pull up my shirt. My dad is an Army Ranger and I spent half of my childhood in some kind of brace or cast. I know how to clean and bind a wound. But now blood is oozing through my makeshift bandages. The cut must be deeper than I thought. I must look as hideous as I feel.

"From last night?" Dominic rips the bandage away and I wince. He cocks an eyebrow, as if I'm being a baby.

When the Scarred Man drops to his knees and leans toward me, I tell him, "I got cut."

"You did not get cut, Grace Olivia. You got *stabbed*."

It's the first time he has ever used my full name. My mother used to do that. It's no doubt where he heard it, and that makes me sway again.

I blame it on the blood.

"You're not going to tell me I should go to the hospital?" I ask, even though I already know the answer. It's why I'm here. But still I hold my breath as the Scarred Man looks at me.

"You have seen enough of hospitals, I would expect."

I don't bother to agree. It would be redundant, and I'm coming to learn that Dominic is the kind of person who doesn't waste anything. Not a movement; not a moment; not a breath.

I sit on my stool while he rummages through a cabinet filled with old bottles. He pulls on a pair of gloves and takes out a toolbox stuffed with the kinds of tools that have nothing to do with home improvement. I see scalpels and tweezers and bandages. There are pills in a half dozen colors and clear vials of thick liquids that carry no labels.

"Raise your shirt again," he says, matter-of-fact. I do so, showing him the gash in my right side.

"It isn't too deep." He sticks a gloved finger into the wound, probing it, and I cry out in agony. "My apologies," he says, but I don't think he means it. The wound burns as he cleans it, but I stay silent. When he reaches for a needle and thread, I brace myself for what's coming.

"Do you want something for the pain?"

"No," I say.

Finally, he smiles as if maybe I'm starting to gain some of his respect.

The Scarred Man works in silence. There's no lecture, no fatherly concern, as he sews me back together.

"Shouldn't you be at work?" I ask, but silence is the answer. "I met the acting prime minister. Are you a part of her security team now?"

"The last man under my protection is currently in a coma."

"It was a heart attack," I say, the words a reflex now.

Dominic cuts his gaze up at me as if maybe I've forgotten he was there — that he of all people knows better. I wonder for a moment if Ms. Chancellor and her Society even tried to rewrite *him*. I wonder if they'd still be breathing if they had.

"Well, as far as everyone knows, it was a heart attack," I try.

Dominic goes back to work. "Nevertheless, Grace Olivia, my services are not precisely in demand at the moment."

"Oh," I say, then add one more item to the list of things that are my fault. "But I guess you have lots of free time, then. You know, to take in the sights . . . Enjoy the festival . . . *Follow me.*"

Dominic keeps working, his stitches smooth and even. He's better at this than Dad, but I can never tell him that.

"You were there last night," I say dumbly.

"I was."

"Why do I get the feeling you weren't just in the neighborhood?"

I ask, but he doesn't look up. "Why were you there? Why are you always there?"

"I was following you."

"Why?"

I should know better than to make demands of a man sticking a needle in and out of my skin, but I've never been known for my stellar decision-making. "If there's something you want to ask me, just ask it. If there's something you want to say, just —"

"Your friend . . ."

"His name is Alexei. And if you knew him —"

Finally, Dominic stops. Stares at me. "Oh, I know him." He knots the thread and clips the end, then rubs some sweet-smelling cream over the place where I'll no doubt have a scar. "You would do well to avoid him in the future."

"He didn't kill that cadet."

"And yet someone is going to a great deal of trouble to make it look as if he did."

"Why are you following me?" I don't yell. It's almost like a whisper.

Dominic stands. He pulls off his gloves. Slowly, he begins to wrap a bandage around my ribs, around and around and around, binding me tightly, holding me together.

"I could not save her."

I see it in his eyes then: He's going to save *me*.

For the first time in a long time, it doesn't feel like my guts are going to spill right out.

"There." He pushes away. "How does that feel?"

148

I look at him. "Hurts."

He nods as if he understands completely, then he turns and pulls a small glass bottle from one of the shelves. It's little, with an old-fashioned stopper. It looks almost delicate, like something a fine lady might dab on her wrists. The liquid inside is thick and clear.

"Take this," he says. "Mix a little with water. No more than a few drops, though. You're small. Too much will knock you out."

"Okay," I say, standing and slipping the vial into my pocket. He offers me a bottle of water.

"Here. Now go."

"But —"

"Go home, Grace Olivia. Today, you rest."

"Okay," I say again. There is no doubt I've been dismissed, so I start toward the door. I'm almost gone when Dominic calls to me.

"And, Grace . . ." I turn back. "Your friend . . . he should be careful."

"He didn't do it," I say again.

Dominic just looks at me as if I should know better. "That is precisely *why* he should be careful."

"Why? What are you talking about?" Worry stirs within me. "What do you know?"

But Dominic doesn't care that I am desperate. It's almost like he doesn't notice that I'm scared. I watch him fade and drift away. I can see some old worry settle into the lines around his eyes. And I know he's not talking about Alexei, not about Spence.

He is thinking of my mother when he tells me, "Bad people do not like loose ends."

A darkness descends. My blood turns cold. It's like it's someone else who is asking, "What does that mean?"

Dominic looks into my eyes. His voice is low, a warning. "It means your friend should be careful."

CHAPTER SEVENTEEN

The Scarred Man bound my wounds, but I'm still sore. And yet it is another ache that claws inside of me. Dominic's words echo in my mind, and even though I know I told him I'd go straight home, I can't take the chanting crowds or the closed doors. I can't take much of anything anymore.

Bad people don't like loose ends.

A prime minister with a bullet wound was a loose end, and that went away. The question I don't want to ask is simple.

What about a dead cadet?

"Gracie!"

For a second, I'm sure I must be hearing things, but the word comes again.

"Gracie, wait."

I tell myself that I'm wrong, that Alexei can't be outside of

Russia's walls and chasing after me. But he is. I see him running up the hill, and a new kind of panic takes control.

"What are you doing out here? Are you crazy? You shouldn't leave the embassy. Wait — how did you leave the embassy?"

We're at the top of the hill, near the base of the cliffs and almost to Iran. I can see the mob and the blocked street below. I can actually hear the chanting, but Alexei only shrugs.

"You aren't the only one who can climb the wall, you know."

It's hard to imagine Alexei climbing onto the ancient wall that circles the city, running along the top like a fugitive. Like me.

But Alexei is stepping closer, pulling me over to the cliffs, near the Iranian fence. It's so calm here, almost like the night before didn't happen. But even in the shadow of the fence I can see the black that rims Alexei's eyes, the bruises on his jaw and the cuts that mar his skin.

"You shouldn't be here," I say again.

Alexei shakes his head. "I had to come."

"No. It's not safe. We have to get you back before —"

"I came to say good-bye."

It's maybe the only thing he could have said that might stop me. My mind reels with all the things that he might mean. But there is one obvious answer: Alexei is returning to Moscow. Alexei is leaving. Again. And a part of me hopes he will stay away forever. Another part hopes he'll take me with him.

"Oh. I see. Okay. I guess this time you'll have to stay in Moscow for good." I tell myself that it's okay. Prudent. Totally for the best.

I'm in no way prepared for when Alexei says, "I will not go to Moscow."

"What do you mean?"

"I mean that, in fact, the opposite is happening. I am renouncing my diplomatic status. I'm going to turn myself in."

When I was twelve I followed Alexei and Jamie up the big wall that circles the city. I wanted to chase them and catch them and be just like them for a little while. And when I couldn't listen to Jamie scold me for my foolishness any longer, I did something truly stupid: I jumped.

That is what this feels like.

Not the mind-blowing pain of a shattered leg, but the whoosh of air that leaves my lungs, the jarring crush of the earth rushing up to greet me. For a moment, I forget where I am. It's like I'll never breathe again.

"No," I say, as if I can forbid it, stop it. "You can't."

Was this what the meeting at the embassy was about this morning? Was this the deal my grandfather brokered while I was out having the Scarred Man bind my wound? I want to run down the hill and yell at the mob that I'd be dead if it weren't for Alexei. But I can't say a thing.

Alexei puts his hands in his pockets and shrugs. "My father is holding a press conference denouncing my immunity even as we speak. They are readying an official vehicle to take me to the central police station in about an hour. It is not an arrest. I will answer their questions, that's all. I have nothing to hide."

It's what I wanted at first, for the Russians to stop shielding themselves behind immunity. For the world to see that Alexei has nothing to hide. But in my mind, I hear the Scarred Man's words — the Scarred Man's warning. Terror fills me and I can't let Alexei see it.

"This is insane!"

"No. It's not. It is for the best. I can turn myself in, and there can be a full investigation, without all the politics."

"This is Adria! There will always be politics!"

"Grace, my father is worried what all of this unrest will lead to. It can't be good for diplomatic relations and —"

"Do you think I care about diplomatic relations?" I shout. "Well, I don't, Alexei. And you shouldn't either. Think about it." I grab his shirt. I refuse to let him go. "None of the politicians care about what happened to Spence. Not what *really* happened. They just want to make this problem go away. Make *you* go away."

I can feel Alexei's heart pounding against his chest as I grip his shirt, holding him to me and this place and this time. I force him to look into my eyes. I have to make him see.

I finally understand what Dominic was really saying: Sometimes good people stand in the way of bad things. Sometimes good people get hurt. But maybe if I'm smart enough, strong enough, clever enough, this time I can find a way to stop it.

"You have to go back to Russia. Now! You have to get out of here."

But Alexei is stepping back, shaking his head. "I will not run away."

"You can't go to jail, Alexei."

A brief glint fills his eyes. "Are you worried about me?" he tries to tease, but this isn't funny. None of it is funny.

So I yell, "Yes!"

Alexei is taken aback.

"They're saying someone killed Spence, Alexei. They think someone *murdered* Spence, and now you are conveniently willing to take the blame for it. Someone *wants* you to take the blame for it."

Alexei shakes his head. "You don't know that."

It probably seems too improbable for Alexei to believe, this cover-up. My crazy theory. He doesn't know what I know — he hasn't seen what I've seen.

I look at the Iranian embassy. It is still dilapidated. Still forbidden. It seems like a lifetime ago that my friends and I huddled in its basement, speculating on the Scarred Man's every move. I miss that feeling — the certainty that came with knowing who the boogeyman was and what needed to be done to stop him.

But right now the villains are nameless and faceless, omnipresent and filling every shadow. Maybe I'm becoming paranoid in my old age. Or maybe paranoia is the only thing that will allow me to see seventeen.

"I know it, Alexei. And if you'll stop and think about it you'll know it, too."

"Grace —"

"We don't know who killed him," I say. "Or why. But do you really think this was a mugging or some random act of violence?

155

You saw his body on the beach that day. Did that look like a boy who'd been in an accident?"

He puts his hands over mine. They are warm, pressing against my skin.

"I'll be okay, Gracie."

I used to hate it when he called me that. I used to say he didn't have the right — that it was reserved for Jamie and Jamie alone. But my nickname sounds different when Alexei says it. Maybe it's his accent, or maybe it is something else. Something . . . more.

Again, I think about Dominic's words, the unspoken danger that pulsed beneath the moment. My mother got hurt. Someone wanted her dead. And I killed her.

I vow here and now that I will never again let someone get hurt if I can help it.

Never again.

"I'll be okay, Gracie," Alexei reassures me, but I turn my back on him, look up at the Iranian embassy, the rotten fence and overgrown weeds. Another country. Another world.

"My father said that as soon as the political aspect can be set aside we will be able to pursue justice instead of vengeance. He says —"

"He wants the mob to go away, Alexei. And he's willing to sacrifice his own son to make it happen."

Alexei pulls away. He can't face me when he says, "It's not like that."

"It is exactly like that."

For a second, the silence stretches between us. It's almost quiet here, on the north end of Embassy Row. The protestors are still chanting in the distance, but the wind has shifted now. It blows their cries toward the sea.

"Please do not be angry with me."

"You think I'm angry?" I snap, then soften. I have to make him see. "Alexei, I'm terrified."

"I'm sorry," he says.

For leaving me?

For scaring me?

For hurting me?

I can't tell and he doesn't say. So I hold out the bottle of water Dominic gave me.

"I'm not thirsty anymore," I tell him. "Do you want this?"

It's just a bottle of water, but in the diplomatic world it's never just that. It is an olive branch. A peace offering.

Alexei takes it with a smile.

"Thank you," he says, taking a sip.

"Don't let it go to waste, you know. It might be your last taste of freedom."

Alexei's eyes look like he wants to keep smiling as he drinks faster, deeper. But then, even though he's standing still, he stumbles.

His hand goes limp. The bottle tumbles to the street and starts to roll down the long, sloping hill. But I don't care about that. I put my arms around his waist and hold him tightly.

"Grace, I don't feel . . ."

I know exactly how he feels, but I don't say so. I just grip his waist tighter with my left hand while, with my right, I slip the nearly empty vial of medicine into my pocket.

Alexei's gait is uneven as I lead him past the Iranian fence. His legs wobble. But thankfully we are out of view of the street by the time he passes out completely and falls, sprawling into the weeds.

I look down at the sleeping boy who, for once, looks helpless. Innocent.

"It's for your own good," I assure him.

Alexei doesn't say a thing.

I'm almost to Brazil before Noah and Megan see me. He looks worried something bad has happened. He has no idea.

"I got your text. What's going —"

"Come with me," I say, and sprint toward the city gates.

I can hear Noah and Megan behind me, but I don't stop or look back.

"Grace, slow down!" Noah yells, but I am running down the beach like there is no looking back. And there isn't. Not for me. Not anymore. I will not stop to consider what I've done, that it might be a mistake. I did what I had to do. And if I can't make Noah and Megan see that . . .

I have to make Noah and Megan see that.

My side no longer hurts. It's the adrenaline, I know. I have to keep moving, keep fighting. I have to keep us safe and make them see.

When we reach the cliffs that mark the north end of the beach, it's like we've reached a dead end. Almost.

Then they see it.

"No." Noah pulls back and shakes his head. He has no intention of following me through the small, arching doorway that was once a hidden passage through the great wall of Adria. Forty years ago, it was the gateway that allowed the Iranian embassy private access to the beach. It's rusty and overgrown now, but it still works, I know, and I push through it, desperately needing my friends to follow.

"Grace, I thought we talked about this!" Noah calls after me. "I thought we said that maybe Iran wasn't the best place for us to . . . you know . . . *hang out*." He glances nervously around, but this stretch of beach is deserted. There is no one here to see. "Especially those of us who are, you know, half Israeli."

"And American," Megan adds. "Americans should really keep out as well."

"Guys." I look at them and then do something truly desperate. I say, "Please."

"Grace, wait," Megan calls to me, but I'm already through the gate and running across the stretch of sand that lies between the wall and a wooden fence that has been beaten down by more than two decades of salty air and neglect.

"Grace!" Megan's voice isn't fading, and I know she's right behind me, running through the weeds that are so thick and high that when I see him, I have to freeze, slamming to a stop.

I feel Megan collide with me, then Noah. For a second, no

one speaks. We just stand quietly, staring at the boy asleep on the ground.

His hands are bound with shoestrings, his feet with his own belt. He lies on his side, lifeless and still.

"Alexei!" Megan rushes to his side and shakes him. Her hands push back his hair, looking for some kind of wound.

But Noah doesn't panic. He just looks at me.

"He's okay, Megan," I say. "He's just sleeping."

"In the weeds in the backyard of the Iranian embassy?" Noah sounds like he wants to shout but is afraid to.

"He's drugged," I say.

"How did he . . ." Megan starts, then realizes she already knows the answer. "No. No. No, Grace. Tell me you didn't drug the son of the Russian ambassador and restrain him on Iranian soil. Please tell me you didn't do that."

"I had to!" I tell her.

"Oh, she had to," Noah says, cutting his eyes at Megan and then at me. "Tell us, Grace, exactly why you *had to* drug Alexei."

"He was going to give up his diplomatic immunity. He was going to turn himself in."

I stand, waiting, watching. And that is when I see the look that passes between Megan and Noah like a secret.

"What?" I ask, but they stay silent. "What is it?"

Noah eases toward me. "Alexei's dad just finished the press conference. It's done. They're expecting Alexei to come in for questioning" — Noah glances down at his watch — "now. Right now, in fact."

Megan shifts her gaze onto me. "If Alexei doesn't show up . . ."

"He can't show up," I tell them.

"He has to!" Megan says. "Without diplomatic immunity, *not* showing up will mean violating all kinds of Adrian laws. He has to turn himself in. It's too late."

"No," I say. I'm not shouting. My voice is even and low. "He didn't do it, and he is not going to turn himself in. Now come on." I reach down and grab Alexei's arm. "Help me get him inside. I would have done it myself, but he's heavier than he looks."

I pull and tug, but Alexei barely moves across the overgrown grass. Neither Noah nor Megan moves to help me.

"We have to get him inside," I say again. "We have to hide him. If we hide him then he'll be okay. We can —"

Noah's hand is on my arm. Calm radiates through his skin and into mine. It's enough to make me want to cry, so I pull harder.

"Grace," he says.

"Help me get him inside!"

"Grace," he says again. "What's wrong?"

But a better question is: What's right?

My mother is dead and so is Spence. They're both *dead*, and it's too late to save them.

But it's not too late to save Alexei.

"Alexei is innocent," I say, my voice so soft it's almost a whisper.

"So?" Noah prompts, and I look into his big brown eyes that have always felt as comforting as chocolate. I want to make him see. But I don't want to make him change.

"So sometimes innocent people get hurt."

Megan and Noah see them then, the ghosts that follow me. They hear the things that I can't say.

"Grace," Megan says, easing closer, "Alexei can't stay here."

"Of course he can't. But he's harder to move than I thought he would be."

"No." Noah's voice is so soft it's like he's speaking to a child. "I think what Megan was trying to say is that Alexei has to turn himself in."

"No. He's got to go back to Moscow. He'll be okay there. I think. At least, I hope so. They probably can't get to him in Moscow."

Neither Megan nor Noah asks who "they" are. They don't mention my cracking voice or my shaking hands.

"I know I sound like a crazy person," I tell them. "I know it. But you have to believe me. If he stays —"

"Gracie." The voice is too far away. I only realize who is speaking when Megan drops to her knees and helps Alexei sit upright.

"What happened?" he asks.

Noah gives me a skeptical look before telling Alexei, "You took a little nap, my friend."

While Noah works on the belt that binds Alexei's feet, Megan pulls a pocketknife from somewhere and cuts through the shoestrings around his wrists.

"Alexei, don't yell," I tell him. "Just listen. You have to listen to me. Please. You have to go back to Moscow."

"No!" It hurts for him to shout, I can tell, but he does it anyway. And when he stands, he's a little unsteady, but that doesn't stop him. "No. I will not run. I will do the honorable thing for my country and for yours. I must do this!" Then something seems to dawn on Alexei. "What time is it?" he asks.

Noah gives a somber nod. "It's time."

Alexei mumbles something in Russian then starts through the lawn, around the corner of the embassy and toward the street. I'm no longer worried that someone might see us at the top of the hill. I'm too afraid of what lies at the bottom.

"Alexei, don't do this," I plead.

"I must do this," he says.

"No, you don't have to. Okay. So you don't want to go back to Moscow. Fine. Then stay here. Lay low until we can figure out who really killed Spence. Just —"

We're on the street when Alexei turns. "It is a matter of honor, Grace."

"Honor is overrated."

"I will cooperate with their investigation, and the truth will come out."

"No!" I grab his arm and stop him, lunge forward and block his way. "It won't if they don't *want* the truth to come out."

"Who are 'they,' Gracie? Tell me." Alexei's voice is soft, worried. But not about the situation. About me. He thinks the world is too big and vast, too full of checks and balances for the truth to stay hidden forever. He still thinks the good guys always win.

"I . . . I don't know. But don't go, Alexei. I don't know why, but I know it is a huge mistake. Please, don't go."

Reporters are in position, overlooking the mob and the Russian embassy. The press conference must have sent the cable news networks into a feeding frenzy. I can almost hear the talking heads now, speculating on exactly when the Russian ambassador's son will appear and make the trip to police headquarters, when the next chapter of the story will begin. They keep their cameras trained on Russia's gates.

"I'm late." Alexei glances down the street as a long black car with Russian flags flying near the headlights pulls through the crowd and into the Russian courtyard. "I should be on my way to the police station by now."

He looks at Megan and Noah.

"It'll be okay," Noah says. When he glances at me, I know he's not talking about the police. "We'll take care of her."

"Yeah." Megan stands on her tiptoes and kisses Alexei on the cheek.

Then he turns to me. I'm sure that I'm not crying. There has to be some other excuse for the way my eyes go blurry and my throat begins to burn. And yet when Alexei's fingers come to my cheeks, I notice that they smooth away moisture, but that can't be right. I'm supposed to be all out of tears.

"I am okay, Gracie," he tells me, my face still cradled in between his hands. "Do you hear me? I'm okay. I'm going to be okay. No one is trying to hurt me."

I want to believe him. I swear, I really do. It's not like I enjoy this terror that consumes me, this never-ending pulse of fear that pounds in my veins and echoes in my mind so hard that even when I cover my ears I hear it.

I don't want to be right.

But I'm too terrified of what might happen if Alexei is wrong.

Down below, the car sits idling in the Russian courtyard, and the crowd waits with bated breath. They are watching the front doors of the embassy, not the far end of the street. They haven't seen us. Yet.

Alexei looks toward them, certain of where he must go and what he must do.

"We're going to figure out who did it," I tell him. "We're going to find Spence's killer. Before it's too late."

"What do you think's going to happen to me, Gracie?" Alexei says it with a grin. It's almost like a dare.

But that must be too much irony for the universe to handle, because, just then, the big black car explodes, fire and black smoke filling the sky.

CHAPTER EIGHTEEN

The room was probably beautiful once. But now when I pull off the white sheets that cover the furniture, a cloud of dust billows up. Moldy drapes cover the windows, but Megan pulls them aside just a crack and peers out onto Embassy Row. From the second story of Iran we can see the street. The chaos. That's why we aren't in the basement. No, we're here, watching the black smoke rise into the sky, listening to the constant chorus of sirens, shrill and piercing, playing like an old-fashioned phonograph turning in another room.

The protestors have been replaced by spectators who push against barricades. Police cars and fire engines and every news crew in Adria fill the streets. The story has changed, and for a moment, the crowd waits, reverent and still.

But soon . . . soon they're going to start looking for Alexei.

The world is right outside that dirty window, but we stay in this dusty, decaying shell of an embassy, none of us certain what comes next.

"We can't stay here." Noah can't stop pacing. He's right, of course, but I don't say so. We know the Scarred Man used to meet the prime minister here — maybe other people come here, too. It's a risk that we can't take, and Noah knows it.

"Do you think we'd be better off out *there*?" Megan points to the street.

"We can use the tunnels," Noah says.

"And come out where?" Megan asks. "Where are we supposed to go? Where is *Alexei* supposed to go?"

"I don't know," Noah snaps. "But I know we can't stay *here*."

"You're right," I say. For a moment, I consider the Society and its massive underground headquarters. Ms. Chancellor said that she didn't think Alexei was guilty, but she didn't offer to prove that he's innocent either. I could ask her to hide him. I could ask the Society to help. But they've already become embroiled in one international conspiracy on my behalf. And if I'm being honest with myself, it scares me.

If I'm being really honest, a part of me can't help but fear they might be in the midst of another.

"Grace?" Noah is at my elbow. "Grace, what do you think?"

"You're both right. We're probably stuck here until the sun goes down. We'll find someplace safe for tonight, but eventually we've got to get Alexei out of the country. Noah, can you get your mom's van?"

"Yes, but I won't."

"You have to!"

"We can't just smuggle a hot Russian across the border," Noah snaps, then realizes what he's said. "I mean, a *fugitive* Russian. Not a *hot* Russian. Not that Alexei isn't extremely attractive. You are, it's just that . . ."

"We get it." Megan places a hand on his arm and stops him, saving Noah from himself.

Through it all, Alexei is silent. He hasn't spoken since the street. Maybe it's the trauma. He almost died. I know how that feels, and the sensation takes a while to get used to.

Megan and Noah are watching him, too. He doesn't rock, doesn't shake. It's more like he's still seeing it, a nightmare on a loop inside his mind.

He's so quiet that when he finally whispers, "I knew him," I'm not sure if Alexei even realizes that he has spoken aloud.

Then he looks at me.

"The man in the car. His name was Mikhail. He was my father's personal driver. I know him. I mean . . . I knew him. He taught me to ride a bicycle."

"I'm so sorry, Alexei," Megan says, patting his hand. "We're all so, so sorry."

Spence is dead. And now Mikhail. *People are dying!* I want to scream as I look out the window at the chaos that still fills Embassy Row. I'm three years and thousands of miles away from my mother, but it feels like I will never outrun the smoke.

"Grace!" I hear a voice echoing up from the basement. "Grace, are you in —"

"Second floor!" I call, but Rosie is already racing up the stairs. She has a large bag in her hands and the look on her face is sheer terror.

"Grace, I got your text. Where is he? Is he . . ." But then Rosie sees Alexei, sitting on Iran's old couch, all color drained from his face but very much alive. She hurls herself across the room and into his arms. Alexei rests his cheek on the top of Rosie's head as she comes down to rest, cradled in his lap.

"I was so worried," she croaks out.

"I am okay, Rosemarie. All is well."

All is not well, but now might not be the time to say so.

"Did you get it?" I ask Rosie, who hands me the bag.

"Of course. It's a madhouse out there. The embassies are all closed off and the street is blocked and there are television cameras everywhere. But it was easy," Rosie says, then shrugs. "No one paid any attention to me."

I open the bag and look down at some men's clothes and bottles of water, a few protein bars. And, finally, four shiny cell phones. I pull one out and eye it.

"The embassy keeps those for staff and visiting dignitaries," Rosie says. "No one has used them in months. They won't be missed."

Perfect. If Alexei is going to go on the run, he'll need to be on his own. Or at least it needs to *look* that way. No one has a reason to be watching Germany.

169

"Rosie, I love you," I say.

Rosie shrugs. "Most people do."

She snuggles closer to Alexei, and he squeezes her tight.

"Don't worry," I tell him. "We're going to keep you safe until we can find a way to get you out of Adria."

"I'm not leaving the country." His voice is strong now, sure.

"You're not safe here," I tell him.

"I will not run away like a coward."

"If you stay here, whoever blew up the car is going to find you. And they are going to kill you. And maybe not just you. Don't tell me you still want to turn yourself in?"

This, at least, hits home. I can almost see the gears in Alexei's head start spinning.

"I must return to the embassy. I'll be safe there, and in the meantime —"

"Alexei! Stop!"

Finally, it's Megan who is screaming and not me. I'm so relieved to be the quiet, sensible one, if only for a moment.

"It was a *Russian* car, housed and maintained in a *Russian* garage. And it exploded." Megan eyes him as if waiting to see him catch on. "Someone got to it from *inside* the Russian embassy. Which means . . ."

"You can't go home," Noah finishes, then places a hand on Alexei's shoulder.

The honorable part of Alexei is struggling with the idea, but the sensible part of him knows better. What if Mikhail isn't the only person who gets hurt?

"I know a place," Rosie says at the exact moment Megan blurts, "We'll hide him!"

"Where?" Noah asks Megan.

"I know a place," Rosie says again.

"Is there another embassy that would take him?" I ask. "I know the US won't do it, but what about —"

A piercing whistle fills the room. Slowly, we all turn to look at Rosie.

"As I was saying," she starts slowly, "I happen to know a place. It's just that" — she looks skeptically at Alexei — "it may be a little . . . rough."

For the first time since black smoke and fire filled the street, Alexei grins. "I can handle rough."

"Don't worry. You aren't in this alone," I say, but my words are hollow. I mean them. I swear, I really do. But I have been the one in danger — the one at the center of a secret. And no matter how many people surround you, that is still the loneliest place on earth.

"Do you have everything you need?" I ask for what has to be the twentieth time. At least. And for the twentieth time, Alexei looks at me.

"I will be fine, Gracie. Thank you."

I look around at the hodgepodge of things that lie scattered on the dirt floor.

Rosie's "place" is high in the hills that rim the north edge of the city. I don't know how she found it or how long she's known about it, but I am sure that no one is going to stumble across Alexei here anytime soon. The entrance is narrow, barely wide enough to slip through. And the stone ceiling overhead has cracks that show the stars, enough air circulation that it is safe to build a fire.

It's as good a place as any to hide, but I'm not a hider. I'm a runner and a fighter. It goes against my every instinct to sit on the ground in this cold, dark place, waiting for things to get better, but that is exactly what Alexei has to do.

"Noah's dad likes to go camping," I say, desperate to fill the silence. "He managed to smuggle out a stove and a sleeping bag, and we have some water and protein bars in that bag. You're supposed to be able to make coffee with one of those contraptions, but the instructions are in Portuguese, so —"

"Grace." Alexei's hands are on my arms. His skin is warm against mine. I was starting to worry I might never feel warm again.

"We're going to take turns bringing you food and stuff, so don't worry. Someone will be here tomorrow with —"

"Grace, I'm fine." Alexei's voice is steady, but my hands shake.

"If there is anything in particular you'd like, just let me know. You've got Rosie's phone and all of our numbers, but we probably shouldn't use them except for emergencies because —"

"Grace," Alexei says again, pulling me closer. I am trying to be strong, for him and for me. But the trying is too much sometimes — too hard — and I feel myself fall against him.

I'm not fighting anymore.

"When I saw that car explode . . ."

Alexei smooths my hair. He rests his cheek against the top of my head and holds me tighter.

"I know," he says.

"I smelled smoke," I somehow mutter. "I hate the smell of smoke. My mom . . . There was a fire. And ever since then . . ."

I'm shaking now, even as Alexei holds me tighter. The wound in my side hurts and I wince but I don't want to pull away.

"It's okay," he says even though he's the one who almost died, even though I should be comforting *him*.

"I'm sorry," I say, because it's what I always say. To Jamie and my grandpa and the world. I'm always sorry. Because the world broke a long time ago, and it was my fault. This is my fault, too. I just know it. And I have no idea how to fix it. "I'm sorry, Alexei."

But, somehow, he laughs.

"I have never been drugged before. It was a new experience for me. And considering it saved my life . . ."

"Not for that." I pull away and wipe my nose on my sleeve. "For my country. For how quick we were to hate you. I'm so sorry we're so out for vengeance."

Alexei is silent for too long. Even in his arms, I can feel his stare. "Are *you* not out for vengeance, Gracie?"

I push away from him and put my hand on my side, hurting. "Not from you."

I don't talk about the Scarred Man or the Society, the prime minister or whatever villain is still out there, unknown and unnamed.

Vengeance is like gravity for me. Always present, pulling me in a direction that I can no longer feel. It is simply the fact of my life, of who I am. Someday, though, I'm going to break free. And when that happens, I may very well just float away.

Alexei leans down and turns on one of Noah's father's lanterns. Its yellow glow fills the cave. Shadows dance across the walls. Overhead, a small sliver of rapidly darkening sky is the only thing that reminds me that there is a world out there, beyond the safety of this stone cocoon.

"It's getting late," he says. "You should go home. It would not do for your grandfather and Jamie to worry."

"What about you?"

"What about me?"

"I mean, should someone tell your dad that you're okay?" The dad who wanted to throw Alexei to the wolves just this morning.

"Everyone at the embassy will know I wasn't in the car. They will feel nothing but relief."

He's right, of course, but still I do not move.

"They're going to think . . ." But I trail off. The truth is I have no idea what anyone is going to think.

"Grace?"

"Yes?" I sway closer.

"I'm going to be okay," he tells me, and I try to believe it.

"Of course you will," I say.

"And, Grace . . ." Alexei brushes a piece of hair out of my face, tucks it behind my ear. "You'll be okay, too."

But as I slip through the narrow opening in the cave and out into the coming night, I can't help but believe that Alexei is no longer perfect — that, for once, Alexei is most certainly wrong.

CHAPTER NINETEEN

A man and woman are waiting in the upstairs sitting room when Ms. Chancellor summons me the next morning. Most of the time, we call it the family room, but these people are not family.

"Grace, these police officers would like to ask you some questions," Ms. Chancellor says as soon as I walk in the room.

Prime Minister Petrovic already asked me some questions, I think but don't say. Things have changed, after all. Outside, the street still smells like smoke, and even though the crowds have grown, they're oddly silent. Reverent. But sides are forming. I can tell.

Embassy Row is filled with fire trucks and police cars that stand with swirling lights, and every news channel in the world is broadcasting live, all of them busy speculating on what happened.

None of them know the truth.

Some people think Russia blew up its own car to curry sympathy or let Alexei get away. Others believe it was an act of retaliation by the US — an answering strike that might lead to an all-out war. Some blame terrorists or extremists who want to see the US and Russia come to blows. And some are conspiracy theorists who rant and ramble and just sound crazy.

I'm one of the latter.

I don't bother saying hello. I just eye the two cops and ask, "Do you know who blew up the car?" What I don't add is that I'm almost afraid of the answer.

This isn't about a dead cadet anymore.

This isn't even about an international embarrassment or situation.

There is no longer any question of whether or not Spence's death was an accident.

Someone killed him. And now someone has tried to kill Alexei — someone *did* kill the Russian driver — and, finally, the authorities have noticed. Finally, the authorities might care.

"So?" I ask again. "Do you know who planted the bomb?"

The look that passes between the two strangers is equal parts guilt and confusion.

"We actually have several questions for you, Grace." The man in the suit speaks to me in English. "Would you prefer we discuss this in Adrian? I was told you are fluent."

"I am." I try to nod and smile.

"But perhaps this is a good opportunity for me to practice my English," he says with a slight British accent. "I attended Eton."

"And now you're a cop?"

"A detective, yes." He glances at one of the uncomfortable chairs in the formal living room.

"Won't you sit down?" Ms. Chancellor asks.

Her voice is so even, so kind and cool. She doesn't look like a woman who, just a week ago, shot and seriously wounded the prime minister of Adria. No, she looks like a woman who really wants to get back to her filing.

But Ms. Chancellor isn't going to leave me. The police probably aren't supposed to question a minor without a parent or guardian present. I guess on Embassy Row it's a parent, guardian, or the guardian's chief of staff.

There's a female officer, too. She must speak English, but so far she hasn't said a thing. She just sits there, scowling. There's not a doubt in my mind that she will remember every word.

Cautiously, I sit down next to Ms. Chancellor. My side aches, but I'm glad the back of my chair is so straight, the seat so hard. I have a feeling it would be a great mistake to get too comfortable around these people.

"I am very sorry about what happened to your friend," the man tells me.

"Thanks. But they said on the news that he wasn't in the car, so he's probably okay." I think about Alexei, all alone in that cave in the hills. "I hope he's okay."

"No." The officer shakes his head, smiles. "I was talking about John Spencer."

178

And then it hits me: They aren't here about the bomb. Or not directly. This isn't about the attack on the boy next door.

"John Spencer wasn't my friend," I say too quickly. "I mean, he was my brother's friend. I barely knew him. You should talk to Jamie."

"We'd love to. Where is he?" the man asks.

I don't want to tell him I don't know, that Jamie's room is right next door to mine, but in so many ways it's like he's still on the other side of the world.

"Maybe we'll just talk to you first, okay?" the man says, and leans back. He keeps smiling at me, though, a look that is supposed to put me at ease. He doesn't know that I have been questioned by police officers before. Lots of times. I don't need him to tell me to relax.

"So, Grace," Officer Smiley says after a moment. "Where is Alexei Volkov?"

"I thought you were here to find out who killed John Spencer?"

"That investigation is ongoing. We're here because of the manhunt."

Manhunt.

From the moment I gave Alexei that drugged bottle of water I knew this was coming. I knew I was making him a fugitive, an outlaw. Suddenly, the Mediterranean coast feels more like the Wild West, and Alexei is supposed to be some villain on the run. It's absurd.

"Manhunt?" My voice is shaking again, but this time for an

entirely different reason. "Manhunt!" Fury consumes me. I'm aflame with righteous indignation. "Two people are dead. One more person should be dead except sheer dumb luck meant he wasn't in the car at the time."

"Now, Grace . . ." Smiley starts, but I don't care what he has to say. I know they aren't here because they're worried someone tried to kill Alexei — worried that next time they'll succeed. They aren't even worried about who killed Spence. No, they're here because Alexei is in the wind and Adria is embarrassed. And the crowds . . . the crowds aren't going to go away.

"Do you know who tried to kill Alexei?" I ask. "Who killed his driver? Do you even care?"

"Grace." Ms. Chancellor places her hand on my sleeve, pulls me back.

"The car had a mechanical malfunction." Officer Smiley's face is so straight, his expression so earnest, that it's almost like he believes this ridiculous theory.

"Oh," I say. "Is that what they're calling bombs these days?"

"Grace," Ms. Chancellor warns, but I shake her off.

"It was on a timer, wasn't it? The bomb?" I wait, but of course they don't answer. That doesn't stop me from seeing the truth in their eyes. "He wasn't supposed to be late. Alexei is never late. If I" — *hadn't drugged him* — "had to guess, I'd say whoever set the bomb knew that."

"The Russian delegation is handling this situation internally. It was an official embassy car on official Russian territory. We haven't examined the wreckage, haven't removed any bodies.

We know only what they tell us. And they tell us *mechanical malfunction*."

I can tell by the way he says it that Officer Smiley doesn't think there was a driver, a body. Now at least I know the Adrian police are buying into one conspiracy theory. They just have the wrong one.

"Someone killed Spence. And then someone tried to kill Alexei right before Alexei was able to talk. You can't possibly think that's a coincidence."

"So you're saying that you think there is some vast international conspiracy at play here? Some cover-up?"

It's all I can do not to turn and stare at Ms. Chancellor. "It wouldn't be the first time."

Smiley leans a little closer, places his elbows on his knees, like we're confidants. Like we're friends. "Now, come, Grace. We know you have an active imagination."

Times like this I want to yell, I want to scream. I want to tell the world that I was wrong about the Scarred Man, but I was right, too. I was just a different kind of —

"Crazy."

The officers stare at me, not blinking. I go on. "That's what you meant to say, isn't it? That I was institutionalized? That I have a history of psychotic breaks? It's okay if it is. I really am —"

"Gracie?"

I turn at the sound of Jamie's voice. He's standing in the doorway, hurt and confused. He looks like maybe I've betrayed him. I'm talking about his little sister, after all. It would be easier if I'd just act like everyone else. Pretend.

"What's going on here?" my brother asks Ms. Chancellor as both cops rise to their feet.

"James Blakely?" the woman asks.

"What do you want with my sister?"

Smiley extends a hand, but Jamie lets it hang, empty in the air.

"Well," the officer says, pulling back. "Good to meet you. We were hoping to have a moment of your time as well. We have a few questions about —"

"Gracie, come on. We're leaving." Jamie jerks his head toward the door.

"Mr. Blakely, please come in. Have a seat." That Officer Smiley doesn't have the right to offer anyone a seat in the US embassy is something that no one mentions.

Jamie stays at the door, his own form of rebellion.

"What's going on here?" he asks.

"These officers had some questions for Grace," Ms. Chancellor tells him.

"Please, join us, Mr. Blakely. We have some questions for you, too."

Jamie doesn't budge until Ms. Chancellor says, "James. Please."

Grudgingly, Jamie comes around and takes a seat beside me. It feels like I have a guard, a protector. It's something I haven't felt in ages, but I don't let myself think about how much I've missed it.

"Do you have any idea *why* Mr. Volkov wasn't in the car yesterday?" Smiley asks me.

"No. But I know John Spencer is dead and the boy who was getting ready to start talking about that night is *supposed* to be dead. So please tell me you people don't still think this is just about some kids trying to blow off steam at some party."

He doesn't speak, so I cross my arms, defiant. "Fine. You don't have to tell me the truth. But please don't treat me like I'm stupid."

"Let's talk about that night. Tell us about the party," Smiley says.

"It was nothing special. My friends went. So I went. It was just your typical, run-of-the-mill high school party."

Smiley slides his gaze onto my brother. "But you and Mr. Spencer are no longer in school, are you, Mr. Blakely? So why did you go?"

"We felt like it," Jamie says, and Smiley turns back to me.

"And you talked to Mr. Spencer there?"

I nod. "Sure."

"What did you talk about?"

"Nothing really," I say, honestly not evading the question. It just seems so irrelevant. So far in the past.

I will not tell this man that Spence kissed me. I will not tell him how that made me feel or what happened next.

"Where did you talk to him?"

"At the party." I'm so exasperated I do everything shy of roll my eyes.

"I mean where, exactly, at the party? What parts of the island did he make it to?"

"Oh." I think a bit. "The beach, of course." Everyone nods. After all, they've already seen the video. "And we might have wandered just a little bit."

"Wandered where?" the cop says.

"Inland. There's kind of a clearing. We saw some old ruins and looked at them for a little while."

"Have you heard enough?" Ms. Chancellor asks, shifting, reminding everyone that she is still my grandfather's pit bull. A pit bull in high heels.

"Almost. Mr. Spencer and Mr. Volkov got into a fight that night, did they not?" This time he looks at me.

"Boys are idiots," I say.

"Why don't you tell us about the fight?" Officer Smiley leans back and crosses his legs, like we're just chatting, like at any moment Ms. Chancellor is going to ring for tea.

"I thought you were here because of the *manhunt*," I tell him, but Smiley just raises an eyebrow. It's almost like a dare. "It was a fight, okay? A bunch of hitting and grunting and showing off in front of girls in bikini tops. It was exactly what that fight always is. I know you've seen the video."

"Yes. We have. But perhaps you can tell us what Mr. Spencer and Mr. Volkov were fighting over?"

The officer eyes me. We're playing a game, I realize. Him asking questions to which we both already know the answer. But I don't like games, so I don't say another word.

"You don't have to talk to them, Gracie," Jamie says.

Smiley ignores him. "Were they fighting over *you*, Ms. Blakely?"

Beside me, I feel Jamie tense, but I have to laugh at the thought of it. It's so absurd.

"They were fighting because that is what alpha males do when they are thrown together in close proximity. Herd dominance. Survival of the fittest. Alexei had been gone. Spence was new. So they were the designated fight of the night. Go to any high school party in the world, and chances are you'll find one."

"But one of the fighters doesn't always end up dead."

Smiley has a point, but I don't say so.

"Did you give Mr. Spencer a ride off the island?"

It's the woman, Officer Scowl, who asks this. I'm taken aback for a moment. I'd half forgotten she was here.

"No," Jamie says. "My sister and I left early. We didn't see Spence again."

Until the next morning.

Until he was already dead.

"Did you see Mr. Volkov?" Scowl asks.

"Not until the next day," Jamie says. "He came to tell me . . . He and Grace were there when the body washed ashore."

"Have you seen him since then?" Smiley asks. Jamie shakes his head, so Smiley turns to me. "And when did *you* last see him?"

"Yesterday morning," I say. "Not long before someone *tried to kill him*."

"Do you know where he might have gone?" Smiley asks.

"No."

"Do you know anyone he might go to for help?"

"Sure. Anyone who *doesn't want him to be killed*."

185

I'm being ridiculous, the grown-ups think. A kid. An innocent. A crazy girl with fantasies about conspiracies and wrongly
accused boys with pale blue eyes and soft black hair. I am what
happens when people just refuse to listen to reason, I can see it in
Officer Smiley's eyes. And I really can't blame him. Sometimes
the lies are so much less work to believe.

"Mr. Spencer died on the island, Ms. Blakely." Smiley isn't
calling me Grace anymore, I notice. "Now that we've spoken to
the two of you, we have officially interviewed every person who
was there that night, except for Mr. Volkov, of course. It's been
a diplomatic nightmare, but we have done it. And what we've
learned is that Mr. Spencer didn't get a ride off the island with
anyone. No one saw him on any boat. The current is strong that
time of night — too strong for even a young, fit man to swim
that distance. So listen to me carefully. Your friend John Spencer
died on that island. And on that island there was only one person
who might have wanted to hurt him."

When the pair of officers stand, Officer Smiley closes his
notebook and gives me a grin.

"Don't worry. We have officers posted at the airport and all
the private airstrips. All trains in and out of the country are being
searched, and his picture is posted at every port. If he's still here,
Alexei Volkov isn't getting out of Adria." Then the man cuts his
eyes around at the embassy — the fortress — I live inside. "And
I highly doubt he can hurt you here."

"You think Alexei would hurt me?" I actually laugh. "That
would be like being afraid of my own brother."

186

Smiley cocks an eyebrow and glances from me to Jamie, then back again. "But Alexei Volkov is not your brother, is he?" the man asks, and I sit for a moment, thinking hard about the answer.

They're almost to the door — I'm almost free of them — when the woman stops and pulls something from her pocket.

"One more thing. We were wondering if any of you recognize this?" She's holding a plastic bag, but it's what's *inside* that draws my attention. A piece of leather is looped through what looks like some kind of medallion. It's the size of a quarter but the color of a penny. For a minute I think it must be some kind of European coin. But then I stand and move closer, and it's easy to recognize the symbol that I have been seeing around Valancia for weeks, leading me down beneath the city and into the Society's web.

It takes everything within me not to turn to Ms. Chancellor, not to gape. But it's Jamie who breaks the silence. "That's Spence's."

"What an unusual piece," Ms. Chancellor says, her voice so calm and casual.

"Yes," the officer says. "We found this in Mr. Spencer's pocket."

"In his pocket?" Jamie asks. "Not around his neck?"

"You sound surprised." Smiley studies my brother.

"Spence always wore that. Always. He said his grandmother gave it to him — told him to come to Adria someday and it would lead him to . . ."

"Go on," Smiley says.

When my brother exhales, it's like the world's smallest, saddest laugh. "Treasure."

There's a twinkle in Officer Smiley's eye. "Did he find it?"

No one says the obvious: that John Spencer found something far, far worse.

I can feel my brother's gaze on me long after Ms. Chancellor escorts the cops from the room.

"He's okay, Gracie," Jamie says. "He's probably back in Moscow by now — was probably halfway there by the time the car exploded."

"He was going to renounce his diplomatic immunity."

"That's what the Russians said, but it's not true."

"Of course it's true!"

"Grandpa says the Russians did it themselves. Probably to buy time or change the headlines. Or both. The windows were tinted and no one saw a driver get into the car. It could have been driven by remote. Easy. The army can fly a drone from the other side of the world. Trust me."

I can't tell if Jamie believes it or if he only wants to. Which version of the truth might scare him more — that someone killed one of his friends and tried to kill another? Or that our grandfather has been right for all these years, and we never should have made friends with the boy next door?

"Either way," Jamie says, "by the time that car blew up, Alexei was long gone."

"No. He wasn't."

Something in my face must tell him that I'm serious. That I'm right.

"How do you know that?"

"Because I really did see him. Earlier yesterday. He came to tell me what his father had agreed to do. He was going to go to the police station. He was going to be in that car."

I can actually see this wash over Jamie. One of his friends is dead, and one should be. But Jamie's anger is a lifeboat. He's not letting go just yet.

"He was lying."

"No, Jamie." My voice is soft, gentle. "He wasn't."

"You heard the cops. No one else on that island had reason to hurt him."

"Maybe they didn't talk to everyone on the island. Maybe there's more here than meets the eye. Maybe . . . This is Adria, Jamie. There's always more under the surface."

I love my brother. And I've missed him. And I need him. I should stop and tell him all of that, but the officer's words are still ringing in my ears. The sight of Spence's pendant is still burned into my brain. Questions are swirling inside of me, about to come screaming out, and if I don't ask them soon I may explode, so I start for the door.

"Gracie, do you . . ."

"Like you said" — I turn and give him a knowing look — *"he's okay."*

Then I practically run down the hall and to the center staircase.

I'm going to search the embassy, the tunnels, the entire continent for Ms. Chancellor if I have to. I don't care how loud I have to scream or how far I have to run, I'm going to get answers this time if it kills me.

Then I stop. I let myself wonder if that's what killed Spence.

"Grace."

She's standing at the bottom of the stairs as if she's been waiting for me. Of course she has, I realize. She knew I was going to give chase, cause trouble. Ms. Chancellor is no fool.

I'm almost to the bottom of the stairs when she looks me straight in the eye and says the only two words that might make me hold my tongue.

"Not here."

When she walks through the embassy's doors, I follow.

CHAPTER TWENTY

Spence had seen the symbol before. Of course he had. I should have realized it that night at the ruins. I should have recognized his lies when I heard them. They sounded so much like my own.

He was looking for something.

The only question now is whether or not he found it.

As soon as we step out the embassy's doors, I smell smoke and feel tension. Two marines are stationed at the gate. Next door, Russia has a half dozen armed men guarding their high walls. Maybe more. Adrian police patrol the barricades that hold back the crowds, but I can feel a thousand eyes upon me; I can almost hear the people wondering who I am and why I'm allowed inside the fences. But Ms. Chancellor doesn't falter, doesn't care. She's walking quickly in her high heels, past the end of the barricades, pushing through the crowds.

When we reach Israel we turn and start up the steep incline toward the city center. I expect her to turn into the narrow alley that leads to one of the entrances to the tunnels, but Ms. Chancellor keeps walking, higher and higher, faster and faster.

Her heels don't get stuck in the cobblestones. Her breath doesn't come even a little bit hard. She's practically floating up the hill, and I follow right behind, but I refuse to ask any questions that I don't think Ms. Chancellor will answer, so I don't say anything at all.

When we reach the palace, Ms. Chancellor walks up to the gates. I half expect them to swing open, to welcome both of us inside. But the gate stays closed, and Ms. Chancellor stays silent.

Until, finally, the silence is too much.

"Tell me," I say.

Ms. Chancellor draws her hands together. It's almost like a prayer.

"You're probably wondering why we're here and not down in the tunnels, aren't you, Grace?" I nod. "The truth is, the answer to your questions are here. The stories Spence heard from his grandmother, they all started here. Because of this."

Her voice is distant, like she's remembering a dream, but I don't understand.

"Because of what?"

"The festival," she tells me. "No. That's not true. The war. The rebellion."

Slowly, Ms. Chancellor turns and stares through the wrought-iron bars of the fence. Guards in ornate uniforms with bright gold buttons stand, unblinking, at the gates. The sun shines and a light wind blows. Tourists snap pictures all around us. But in the center of the square the bonfire still burns. A hint of smoke taints the air. I think I'm going to be sick.

"You know the story, Grace. Everyone knows the story. There was a drought and a coup and a massacre. For eight hundred years the Society had been here, watching history, guiding fate. But two hundred years ago we didn't see the rebellion coming. And we should have. Truly. We should have known. Trouble such as that does not happen overnight, doesn't come out of the blue. The drought was severe and the people were restless, and we should have understood that a mob was forming."

I think about the crowds that are filling Embassy Row, blocked by barricades and still pushing toward the scene. Two hundred years have passed, but I can't help but see the truth.

A mob is always forming.

Ms. Chancellor places her hands in her pockets. She doesn't face me as she says, "But by the time word left the palace it was too late. Some of our sisters reached these gates only to find them open and the royal family . . ."

Ms. Chancellor raises her hand to point, as if looking back in time.

"They were already hanging the bodies, Grace. From those windows. There. In the center of the palace, see? The king and queen and the children, too. They were in their nightclothes, or so the story says. Snow-white muslin practically glows in moonlight except . . . except when it is stained with blood."

Ms. Chancellor's hand was steady as she shot the prime minister, but her voice trembles as she tells this story. It happened centuries ago and yet it feels like her mistake, her failure, her burden, I can tell.

"We were too late to save the family, and the palace was in chaos. But the Society knew the building well, so as quickly and carefully as possible we went inside and gathered all the artifacts and relics that we could. Looters were everywhere, and more were filing in by the minute, so we collected the things that mattered most. That night the Society did what we always do — we guarded Adria's history."

She turns back to the windows where, two hundred years ago, the royal bodies hung. "I only wish we had done a better job of guarding Adria itself."

Ms. Chancellor shakes her head, as if trying to wake up from a dream.

"Three of our elders took responsibility for guarding the things we salvaged. Some say they were taken from the country for safekeeping. Some say they were tucked away in the hills or in the tunnels or catacombs beneath the city. Personally, I like to think they were hidden in plain sight. But whatever the case, the people who knew the location were killed during the War of the Fortnight, and the truth died with them."

"So the treasure . . . it's real?"

"Quite real. But also quite lost. And almost forgotten."

"You think Spence was looking for it, don't you?"

"I think he probably heard stories about it from his grandmother, yes. For a thousand years Adria has been whispering about us, as if we are angels. As if we are ghosts. I have no doubt his grandmother delighted in telling her grandchildren the story. But, Grace, that story had nothing to do with his death. It's just that. A story."

"How can you say that?"

"Because two hundred years have passed, and now it is an old wives' tale. A legend. Like most legends, it was a little bit true once upon a time. But that time was centuries ago, and, besides, the Society has never cared about gold or rubies — those things were left to the looters and the murderers and the people who came through the gates. The Society values *information*, not material wealth. This so-called treasure is not for you, Grace. It's gone. And you should forget about it. You should just move on."

How many times have I heard those words? A hundred? A million? I was supposed to forget about my mother's murder and the Scarred Man and the fire. For three years, I was told to leave well enough alone. To *move on*. I should learn from that, I know. But Alexei is in a cave in the hills, and this time I'm not fighting my own dragon. Ms. Chancellor, however, doesn't care.

"You are not the first young girl to hear the word *treasure* and have her head fill with ideas. But listen to me, and listen to me carefully, Grace. Don't think about that. Don't let it consume you, too!"

Ms. Chancellor seems to realize that she's yelling because she almost recoils with the words. Then she turns away from the palace and the bonfire and the tourists. She starts back toward Embassy Row as if nothing has happened at all. We walk together in silence, hearts beating, feet pounding.

"Why?" After a few minutes, it's all I can think to say. "If it wasn't because of the treasure, then why was Spence killed? Why go to such extreme lengths to cover it up? What aren't you telling me?"

She stops. For a second, I'm not quite sure she's heard me, so still does she stand upon this hill. From here you can see the embassies and the wall and the deep blue waters of the sea. But that's not where Ms. Chancellor is looking.

The crowd blocks the street below us, filling Embassy Row. When someone throws a bottle it crashes to the cobblestones in front of Russia, shattering, splintering, and I know this isn't a crowd. It's not even a mob. It's a powder keg, and Alexei is a spark.

"Look at it, Grace. Look at what's happening."

I think about the words she said just a few days before — how history always repeats itself. And how it's almost always written by men. The truth about what happened two hundred years ago lives in an ancient room beneath this city. And the woman in front of me is one of the few people who know it.

"Mobs are powerful things," she says, as if that answers my question. And I guess, in a way, it does.

"You think *this* is what they wanted? You think this is why Spence was killed?"

Ms. Chancellor shakes her head. For the first time since I've known her, she seems genuinely unsure. "Honestly, Grace. I have no idea."

"You have to help him," I say.

"No, Grace, we do not."

"Then why did you tell me all of this? The Society stood aside and let a mob make a mistake two hundred years ago. Is your point that you're going to let it happen again?"

"It's my point that Alexei should leave the country," Ms. Chancellor says.

"You mean run."

"I mean he should get far away from Adria. He's gone now. And he should stay gone. At least for the time being. *If you see him*" — she eyes me knowingly — "you should tell him that."

"So you agree? Someone is trying to kill him? Someone is going to kill him?"

"I know I don't want you to get hurt."

It's been almost two weeks since Ms. Chancellor shot a man to save me. *She shot a man*, I have to remind myself. Then I want to laugh with the irony, because, in that respect, Ms. Chancellor is far more dangerous than Alexei will ever be.

When I watch her walk away, I remember that I owe her my life. But do I owe her my obedience? My blind devotion?

My trust?

I might not trust Eleanor Chancellor, I finally admit.

And I don't like it.

"They're not going to help, are they?"

197

When I spin, I see Lila standing with her arms crossed, defiant.

I guess my face shows my answer because Lila rolls her eyes. "I knew it," she says then mutters a word that is some kind of Portuguese insult. It's like she's daring fate to talk back.

"Well, at least he's someplace safe," she says, then raises an eyebrow. "I mean, you do have him hidden somewhere safe, don't you?" Lila doesn't really wait for an answer. Lila isn't the type to wait for anything. "You and my brother and Megan. Maybe that little German freak."

"Insult Rosie one more time and you and I are going to have a problem," I say.

Lila raises her hands as if in truce. "Fine. Don't tell me where he is. Just promise me he's okay."

Lila seems worried. No. Lila seems *scared*. But then I can't help myself. I think about what the cops said, what I told Jamie. Spence was killed by someone on that island, but it wasn't Alexei, I know it in my soul.

Lila was on the island. For the first time, I let myself wonder: What did she see? What does she know?

Does she know about the prime minister and what the Society has already covered up this summer? Does she know that the Society is likely what got my mother killed? Does Lila know about the treasure that may or may not be hidden in the hills or beneath our feet? Somehow, I don't think I'll ever know.

"Alexei was the first friend I made in Adria," Lila says then slowly turns to me. "It was three years ago, and our father had just been posted here. Mother had already come. It was during the divorce, and Noah and I knew no one. We were citizens of two countries, but in so many ways we were without a home. Then Alexei became our friend."

"Ms. Chancellor says he should leave the country and I should stop sticking my nose where it doesn't belong. If I were smart, I'd probably do what they tell me for once, but —"

"You're new," Lila says. It's almost like an accusation.

"I've been coming to Valancia every summer since I was born, so I'm *not* new."

Lila doesn't seem mad. She just shrugs and goes on. "You're new to us. To me and Noah. You didn't know us. Before."

"Before what?"

"Before our parents got divorced? Before they relocated to Adria? Before our world turned upside down? Take your pick. You didn't know us before everything went to pieces and Noah learned how to please everyone." Lila pierces me with a glare. "I learned there's no use trying to please anyone."

"So?" I ask.

For the first time I can remember, Lila actually smiles at me.

"So if the Society isn't going to help and the police think he's guilty, and his own father was willing to throw him to the wolves . . . what are we going to do about it?"

"We?" I ask.

"Alexei was my friend long before you came back and started stirring up trouble. So, yes, what are *we* going to do?"

199

CHAPTER TWENTY-ONE

Are you sure this is a good idea?" Noah asks as he looks up and down the deserted stretch of beach. We're too far from the city gates for tourists or even the locals to bother us. The sun is high and there's no wind coming in off the sea. It's the hottest day of summer so far, and I'm starting to sweat, but even though we haven't seen a soul in ages, I can't blame it entirely on the heat.

"I mean, are you *absolutely certain*?" Noah asks again.

Is he asking if I'm sure I wasn't followed out of the tunnel that took me from inside the US to the alley behind a mosque deep in the heart of the city? Is he wondering if this is the best use of our time and limited resources? Or maybe Noah, like the rest of us, is just terrified that this is yet another in a long history of Grace's Very Bad Ideas.

I'm not certain, so I look at Megan.

"According to my sources," Megan says, which I'm pretty sure is code for *I hacked into the police mainframe, but please don't tell my mom*, "the police are finished on the island. They've combed every inch of it for clues, and no one is planning on going back."

Which is good because it means nobody is going to bother us.

Which is bad because it means that there's probably nothing out there to find.

But the police weren't there that night. They never met Spence. They don't know Alexei. And as long as there's a chance, no matter how slim, we have to take it.

"Besides," Megan adds with a shrug, "if the police do show up, well . . . we're not the first kids to go out to that island. I think the whole world pretty much knows that by now."

I look at the island in the distance, floating and shimmering like a mirage. Spence died there. Part of me never wants to set foot on those rocky shores again. Part of me knows I won't sleep until I do.

"Should I go get the boat?" Megan asks, but I shake my head.

"We have another ride coming," I say.

"Who?" Rosie sounds concerned.

But there's already a boat on the horizon coming this way, and coming fast. A silky black ponytail waves in the wind, and before the boat even slows down, Noah starts shaking his head. He's actually backing away.

"Grace, you can't be serious." Noah stares at his sister, slack-jawed and a little afraid.

"Lila is going to help us."

For a second, my friends stand silent.

Leave it to Rosie to say what everyone else is thinking. "Are you sure we can trust her? I mean, she was there. Maybe she killed Spence? I mean, could Lila kill someone? At least I think Lila could kill someone."

We all turn to Noah, who seems offended we would have to ask. "My sister? Oh, she could absolutely kill someone. But then she'd look you straight in the eye and tell you why she did it and how much better off the world is for her bravery. Lila might be a killer, in other words, but she's no liar."

"Plus, she was there that night, and she's spent a lot of time on the island." I think about the Society and Lila's mom and how she's been a part of this longer than I have. Some might say I'm keeping my enemies closer, but I just repeat, *"Lila is going to help us."*

Noah stumbles a little. "I'm sorry. I cannot get used to hearing my sister's name and the word *help* in the same sentence."

We all watch as Lila pulls the boat up to the pier and lets it coast into position. I know I should say something, to defend Lila or maybe just my own good sense. But it's no use because Lila's already staring up at Noah.

"I know that island better than any of you," she says. "So I'm coming."

"Perhaps," Noah counters. "But I know you better than any of them, so excuse me if I'm a little concerned about how much help you might actually be."

"Noah . . ." Lila begins, but what follows is a stream of Portuguese so fast I could never hope to follow.

Noah throws his hands in the air and shouts back in Hebrew.

Another Hebrew insult from Lila followed by Noah's favorite Portuguese swearword.

Lila huffs, offended. But she doesn't turn and stomp away.

The fight swirls, a cloud of language and flying hands, insults the same in every language.

Finally, Rosie looks at me. "You want me to handle this?" she asks.

"Be my guest," I say.

What comes next is a sound like nothing I have ever heard before. Part whistle. Part yodel. It pierces the air, a sound so fierce that Megan actually puts her hands over her ears. In the distance, dogs begin to bark. And, on the pier, Noah and his twin finally stand silent.

"Thank you, Rosie." I give her a smile then turn to the others. "Now, as I was saying, Lila is going to help us."

"But —" Noah starts, and Lila cuts him off.

"I'm not here for you," she snaps. A smug smile crosses her face. "I'm here for *him*."

When the door to the boat's small cabin swings open, it seems to happen in slow motion. Even though we're far from town and took every crazy and overly cautious detour to get here, I'm terrified when I see Alexei step out into the sun.

Dark stubble covers his jaw, and his hair is going in about a dozen different directions. But he's here. And, most important, he's safe.

"You made it," I say. I didn't realize how worried I was until I see him standing on the deck of the boat, squinting against the glare of the sun as it bounces off the water.

Lila smiles at me. "I told you no one would follow me. We didn't see a soul."

Noah smirks at his sister. "Oh. Okay. This makes sense. My murder wouldn't get her out of bed before ten."

Lila snaps back in Hebrew and soon the two of them start again. This time, I step between them.

"Enough! Noah, leave your sister alone," I say in my best Ms. Chancellor voice. "And, Lila, if you don't want to go to the island, feel free to use your time otherwise. I'm sure there is something your little party-going minions didn't tell the authorities, for example. If you don't want to go with us, then go question them. But I'm not going to listen to the two of you argue all day. Do you understand?" I ask. They both stay quiet. *"Do you?"*

"Yes," they answer in unison.

"Okay," I say, turning for the pier. "Let's go."

At this time of day it's easy for the blue water of the Mediterranean to disappear into the blue of the sky, and as we reach the island, I can't fight the feeling that I'm returning to someplace I've never been. It looks so different, here in the light of day. There is no bonfire, no music. Instead of a beach covered with partying teens, there are long scrapes in the sand where things have been dragged ashore. The grass and bushes at the back of the beach have been trampled. It's like walking into a ghost town, something once so full of life that now stands empty.

Spence died here.

And now I have to find out how.

"What now?" Rosie asks.

"Spread out, I guess," I say. "We need to find out where he was killed, if we can. Just . . . look. For something. Anything that doesn't belong. Anything that might prove . . . something. Anything that could indicate that there was someone out here that night besides Spence and Alexei."

"And you," Noah says. Something in his gaze unsettles me.

"And me," I say. "Meet back here in two hours?"

Everyone agrees, and slowly we start to spread out down the rocky beach. Lila and Megan start toward the forest. The island feels bigger than it did in the dark, farther from land. Our phones won't work here, and I know we're all alone, miles from shore — from civilization. There's nothing but the sound of the waves lapping on the beach, the wind in the trees. It's supposed to be paradise. But it feels like something else entirely as I climb a huge stone outcropping and —

"Ouch!"

Sharp pain shoots through me as I trip over a stone that protrudes from the hillside. "What the . . ."

"Uh . . . guys?" Noah calls. He's already climbed the rocky ridge and is looking down on the beach and the water and . . . me. "I think you need to see this!"

There's something in Noah's voice that frightens me, so I run up the embankment as quickly as I can. Noah clutches my hand and helps pull me the rest of the way. The others have taken the long way around, but soon I feel my friends gather at the edge of the ridge, all of us peering down at the same eerie sight.

I didn't trip on a boulder or an outcropping of rock, I realize. I tripped on a —

"Face!" Rosie says what everyone else is thinking. "That big rock is a face!"

"I think it's some kind of statue," Noah says, his voice flat, but there's no doubt that he's right.

I lean over the edge and peer down into the face that stares back at me from the ground. Years of age and erosion have dulled the features. The nose is smaller than it probably once was, but the lips are still closed, as if keeping a secret. And the eyes stare up at me like a giant who's been buried alive.

Like a god who was cut down in his prime.

"Neptune."

Part of me had just assumed that the tale Ms. Chancellor told me was some kind of myth. Or legend. Or fairy tale. But now I stare into eyes that are the size of washing machines, at a nose the size of a tiny car. In its prime, the statue must have been massive, and now it's easy to imagine a great stone idol rising into the sky, looking out over the blue waters of the sea.

"What do you think it is?" Noah asks.

"A statue used to guard the bay before the Crusaders came," Lila says. "I never thought I'd see it. I thought it was all gone. But it's . . . here." She gestures toward the parts of the statue that we can now identify strewn across the beach.

"Is that a foot?" Noah points to a huge stone. There are fingers, and long, massive pieces that are probably broken arms and legs. The hill has tried to reclaim it, but from this vantage point we can clearly see the statue's base.

"Why would someone tear it down?" Rosie asks.

Lila shrugs. "False idols and all that, I guess. But if you ask me, they didn't want someone else sneaking up and stealing Adria from them after they went to so much trouble to steal it from the Turks or the Mongols or whoever it was they stole it from in the first place."

Lila and I share a look. We could tell them about the knights and the angel that guided the *Grace* through the storm. We've both heard the same story, but it's one that I'm pretty sure we aren't supposed to tell.

"No wonder people say this place is haunted," Rosie says. Then, undeterred, she turns, ready to get back to business.

Slowly, we pair off. Megan and Lila start toward the rocky cliffs at the far side of the island. Rosie and Noah comb the beach.

"I guess that leaves us," Alexei tells me.

Together, we start toward the trees.

•　　•　　•

I know exactly where I'm going. My feet move on their own. The sun burns above us, but its light is fractured as it cuts through the trees, shifting, swirling. *I'm inside a kaleidoscope*, I have to think as I make my way toward the clearing.

I close my eyes and try to remember it as it was that night. There was music in the distance. Shadows played across the forest floor. But in the light of day, I see the details that were invisible then, especially as I stare up at the high structure that disappears inside a rocky hill.

"Wow," Alexei says. "It's . . . bigger than I thought."

The stones of the structure itself are staggered, so it looks almost like a pyramid built into the hillside, so utterly out of place among the trees and crawling vines, the thick bushes that almost swallow one side of it whole. From the air, you'd never even see it, and I know now how this place has remained almost a total secret for so long.

As I creep closer I see flowers and smell honeysuckle — see a piece of a hand coming out of the ground, as if Neptune is trying to wrench a sword free from the flowers and the vines. It feels like I'm stealing into some ancient burial ground and if we disturb anything the giant is going to wake.

But a part of me swore I'd never wake a sleeping giant ever again. That's why I'm careful as I head toward the place where Spence and I stood not long ago. The emblem is right where I remember it, so much clearer in the light of day.

"What is that?" Alexei is right behind me. I can feel his chest against my back as he leans closer to see.

"I don't know," I lie.

He's too close.

We're back at the place where it happened — the kiss, the argument. The fight. And it's like we're both only just realizing it.

"Grace." Alexei's breath is warm on the back of my neck.

When I turn, he's just right . . . there. I don't even have to reach out to touch him.

"I didn't mean it," I say.

"What?"

"The kiss. Kissing Spence. He was here and he seemed like he liked me and I thought maybe he did like me. He was just . . . new. He didn't know me. So I thought that maybe . . ."

"You thought that no one who *does* know you could possibly like you." Alexei is still too close. He sees too much.

"What I'm saying, Alexei, is I'm sorry I dragged you into this. I'm sorry."

"This isn't your fault."

Everything is my fault.

"If I hadn't kissed Spence — or let Spence kiss me — then you wouldn't have fought with him and there wouldn't be any stupid videos online and you wouldn't have to live in a cave for the rest of your life."

Then Alexei does the strangest thing.

He laughs.

"Oh, Gracie." He leans closer, takes my face in his hands and looks straight into my eyes. "I am fairly certain the cave is temporary."

I hit him in the chest. "You know what I mean!" I say, but Alexei just laughs harder.

He glances at the massive overgrown fortress behind us.

"Now. Are we going in there or aren't we?"

It takes a half hour to find the entrance. It's covered by brush and vines. But here, at last, there are signs of life. The vines are crushed, like they've recently been pushed aside. And maybe it's my imagination, but in the dirt I can almost swear that I see footprints.

"Spence?" Alexei asks.

"Maybe," I say. "I doubt the police would have looked here very hard. Spence was a pretty big guy. If he'd been killed here, it would have been hard for him to end up in the water."

I squeeze through the vines and step inside, dragging my leg after me. A moment later, Alexei follows. I can feel him at my back as my eyes adjust to the dark. It's still the hottest day of the year so far, but inside the narrow opening, the air is so much cooler, darker. Dust dances in the slim rays of light that slice through the darkness beyond the entrance. But it's too dim to see much, so I reach into my pocket for the flashlight I always carry. The light slashes across the space. I watch it sweep across the ancient walls. Moss grows between the cracks in the mortar. The stone floor beneath my feet is dirty and damp. And in it I see footprints, too big to be my own.

Alexei's gaze catches mine, and I can almost hear what he is thinking. Probably because I'm thinking it, too. And so we follow those footsteps into the shadows, no matter where they might lead.

CHAPTER TWENTY-TWO

It's not a tunnel. Not really. I know I'm not underground, at least not yet. It's more like a corridor made of stone. Only tiny slivers of light cut through the darkness. Moss and vines creep through the cracks. I see signs of wildlife, too. Probably some small animals have nested here, but there is no other living thing inside the passage now. No movement. No sound. Alexei and I are alone as we walk on and on.

We're inside the hill by now; we have to be. We've been walking for too long, and it's too dark — too quiet.

Then the passage ends, opening into some kind of chamber or room. All I know is that the air feels different here. When I try to sweep the beam of my flashlight across the walls, the beam stretches then fades, reaching out so far that it doesn't find an end.

"What is this place, Alexei?"

He says something in Russian, low and under his breath. Then he mutters, "I have no idea."

Carefully, we go on. When the beam flashes across a giant urn I inch forward. It's stone, but the interior is black. I rub my finger along the inside and realize it's coated with soot.

Alexei looks at me. "This is where they used to light their fires," he explains.

I walk forward, down a wide staircase onto the sunken floor. My light catches other urns. Some stone pedestals that look like places where ancient pillars might have crumbled. I point my light up and see mosaics covering the ceiling above us, catching the light, and I just know in my gut that it is inlaid with gold.

Alexei cranes his head upward, following the light. "Have you ever seen anything like it?"

I have, but I can't say so.

Alexei looks at me. I can feel his gaze through the darkness. Our hands brush.

"Grace!" Alexei points in the dim light, so I flash the beam across the dusty floor, past cracks in the stone and plants that grow, even in the darkness. "Grace, are those . . ." I follow Alexei's gaze, and then my light catches them.

"Footprints. Spence?" I ask.

"Who else?" Alexei shrugs.

Neither of us asks how a West Point cadet could have died here and ended up in the sea. Neither of us worries that in the dark there might be nothing we can find. We just ease forward, following in the footsteps of a dead man.

There are vines overhead. A bird squawks and I jump, suddenly grateful Alexei's beside me.

"Don't leave me in here, okay?" he asks, grinning and taking my hand. "This place is freaking me out." In Alexei's Russian accent, that sounds almost funny, and I can't help but smile.

"Don't worry, tough guy. I'll protect you."

We cross the massive room, following the footsteps until, as if by magic, they disappear. There's a wall ahead. A dead end. I turn quickly, sweeping the beam of my light across the floor, but I can't see where the feet might have retreated. Maybe they did, walking on the section of floor that isn't as dusty. Or maybe . . .

I step away from the wall and look at it from a new angle.

"Okay," Alexei says. "I suppose this is a dead end. I'm sorry, Gracie."

I can feel him turning, backing away, but I can't stop looking at the wall. I can't stop thinking *Spence was here.* I know it. I can feel it. He was too intrigued when I saw him outside, and, according to Jamie, he wore his grandmother's necklace every day of his life. He wasn't the type to turn back just because something looked to be off-limits.

He came here.

And then he ended up dead.

"Gracie," Alexei says. I can feel his hand on my arm. "We should go find the others. Perhaps they have had better luck."

"No." I shake my head. "Not yet."

I start in the upper-left-hand corner of the wall and slowly sweep my light across it, moving in a gridlike pattern. I cover every inch. Every brick. Every loose piece of mortar and —

The mortar is loose, here in the right-hand corner. I step forward, reach out to touch the stones the way I've seen Ms. Chancellor do, pressing and pulling.

"Gracie, please. It doesn't look stable. We should go."

I know Alexei is looking at me like I'm a crazy person. I can hear it in the way he says my name. But it's too late for looking crazy to bother me.

"Just a second. I think maybe . . ." The stones are turning, they're easing into position, and a moment later, the floor shakes a little. The wall moves, sliding aside, revealing an empty space of echoing darkness, but as soon as I shine my light upon the floor I see more footprints.

Alexei is mumbling something that I think must be the Russian equivalent of *Oh my freaking goodness*.

But I don't stop to think or reason, I just follow the footsteps to the other side of the wall, where there is nothing but blackness. The air feels different here — fresher. Even though the walls on either side of me are closer and the room feels smaller, when I shine my light forward it stretches out farther and farther and I know we're not even close to the end.

"Gracie, we shouldn't be here," Alexei says, but even his voice is filled with wonder.

I turn my light upward and see that even here the ceiling is covered with images, faded but clear. In the first, a king is surrounded by six knights, each of them bowing before him, offering their swords.

"Look at that one," Alexei says.

I cast my light over an image that looks vaguely familiar. It's the room we just left, I realize, but it's filled with piles of gold. Rubies, emeralds, and pearls overflow from chests, spilling out onto the floor.

Treasure.

Even though we're standing still, my heart has started to pound too hard. The light shakes as my hand trembles.

"They almost look real," Alexei says as the gems in the pictures catch the light, gold shining, diamonds glowing. A cold dread grips me.

"I think they *are* real," I say, and just that quickly . . . I know.

We aren't supposed to be here.

Spence wasn't supposed to be here.

The last person who came to this place looking for treasure died, and it doesn't matter that he ended up miles away from here — I know it isn't safe.

"Gracie, I think we'd better get out of —"

But before Alexei can finish, we hear it: a faint scraping, the sound of small rocks being ground into dirt as something heavy moves across an ancient floor.

We spin in time to see that the wall is moving again, closing, locking us in. Alexei races toward the entrance, but he and I have wandered farther inside than we realized, and even with his long strides, I know that it's too late.

A second later the wall closes, trapping us inside the black.

"No!" I yell, as if that can make the wall open again.

There must be a trigger, I think. I pray. But the wall is almost solid stone, and on this side the pieces of the puzzle aren't moving, aren't working. If there's a trigger to open the door I can't find it, and as my hands move over the stones, I feel my fingers scrape — my hands bleed. Panic blooms inside me.

"No," I say, almost to myself. "No. No. No."

Darkness surrounds us. I realize too late that I've dropped my flashlight, and it's started to roll away, faster and faster. The floor must slope downward, because the flashlight is picking up steam, and a new kind of panic fills me.

I jump to my feet and race across the floor, chasing after the rolling beam of light.

Then the beam flashes across . . . nothing.

I can sense as much as see the flashlight teeter, tipping, falling away, but I dive, sliding through the dust and the dirt, and grasp the end just as it falls over the edge of the cliff.

And then it hits me: *We're on the edge of a cliff.*

It's not a long room or a corridor; it's a dead end, and I can feel myself slipping, sliding. I claw against the air as if I can propel myself backward, but then Alexei's arms are around me, jerking me back into the safety of his chest.

"I got you." Alexei breathes against my temple. "You're safe. You're well."

216

We aren't well. We're trapped, and I know it.

Behind us, there's an ancient doorway that is closed. Locked. In front of us is a sharp drop to nowhere.

Only then do I feel the real blackness descending.

My breath comes too hard. Even though my flashlight is bright in the total darkness, I can feel my field of vision starting to close in. My heart is pounding too hard inside my chest. It's going to burst free and I'll never be able to stop the bleeding.

"Grace." Alexei's voice is too far away. "Gracie!"

Alexei has seen me have an attack before, so I don't even bother being embarrassed. What use would that be when I know I'm going to die here on this dirt floor in a place where no one besides Spence has been in decades? Maybe centuries.

Our friends are on the island. Our friends will eventually miss us, I know it in my head. But in my gut I know that they may never find this room. They may never open the door. This place that looks and feels so much like a tomb is going to serve as ours, I'm just certain.

And that's when I begin to rock. I try to slow my breathing. I try to tell myself that there's no reason to panic. Not yet. I have to think. I have to move. I have to fight.

The door behind us is closed, locked. In front of us there's a sharp cliff and a long way down — into what, I do not know. I may be the girl who jumped off the great wall of Adria, but even I have my limits.

"If we die," I say, not knowing where the thought comes from, "it'll kill Jamie."

"There's a way out, Gracie. There has to be. And we're going to find it." Alexei turns with my flashlight and starts scanning the space. In front of us, there's nothing but a sheer cliff and an expanse of black. The secret door and hidden chamber must lead into some kind of massive cavern, and we are standing on a ledge so high that we'll never find our way down, so Alexei turns back to the way we came. The light plays over the walls and the ceiling, the dusty, cold stone floor.

"Wait!" I yell, just as Alexei freezes. Something small and white lies in the dirt — something decidedly man-made and a few thousand years out of place.

"What is that?" Alexei asks.

"It's a phone." I crawl toward the wall and pick it up.

"Is it Spence's?"

"No," I say, examining the *ARMY* cell phone cover that I got my brother for Christmas. "It's Jamie's. He told me he lost it the night of the party."

Frantically, I try turning the phone on. It comes to life, almost fully charged, but of course there is no signal here, so far from the mainland and locked in this place so dark and deep.

"Has Jamie been here?" Alexei sounds amazed, and for a moment I'm confused. Then I remember.

"No. Spence was wearing Jamie's jacket. It must have fallen out of the pocket when he was down here. That's why Jamie couldn't find it even after . . . It wasn't on Spence's body."

For the first time, my panic wanes. Breath comes easier now, and I feel steady, certain.

218

We found Spence's body. We saw it wash up on the beach. So, one way or another, Spence made it out of this dark chamber. The only question is how.

"If Spence was here," I say, looking up at Alexei, "then he made it out."

I take back the flashlight and crawl on my knees, inching toward the sharp edge of the cliff. My light plays across the stone on the far side of the huge ravine, thinking there might be some other passage. Maybe there's a bridge.

And then I see it: a staircase. It's rickety and ancient — the stairs just a few inches wide — but they're there. And they stretch, spiraling, leading to whatever lies below.

Alexei and I move slowly, practically inching our way around and around and around. But with every step, the air gets fresher, clearer. It's boiling hot outside, but in here the air is almost chilly, and a low, rumbling hum grows louder the lower we go.

"Do you hear that?" I ask. Alexei glances back at me.

"Water?" he says, and I nod.

Eventually, we see the underground river that runs through the bottom of the massive cavern. The water is black and it feels like we're about to reach the River Styx, but we don't have the luxury of being afraid of what lies on the other side.

"If someone built the stairs, then they have to go somewhere. Right?" I look at Alexei, who flashes me his most boyishly charming smile.

"Of course."

This is Alexei trying to be so positive — so overwhelmingly charismatic — that I forget to be afraid. And it might be working. Maybe. Just a little bit.

The stairs end, and Alexei puts the flashlight in one hand and takes my hand with the other then steps down onto a floor of solid stone. The river isn't wide, but it's deep and moving quickly. There's a narrow path along its edge, and we walk until the river runs into what looks to be the side of a mountain. A kind of tunnel or cave surrounds it, and I can imagine this underground river cutting a path through the stone for centuries, leading away from this place — but to where, we do not know.

I look at Alexei, and, wordlessly, we follow.

"So," he says, moving carefully along the river's slick black banks, "how is Jamie?"

I guess we're going to make conversation. I guess we're going to pretend that this is just another outing — just another day.

"He's upset," I say. I'm not sure how else Jamie would want me to answer. Once upon a time, he and Alexei told each other everything. But now I'm not so sure.

I always thought Embassy Row's secrets were the result of diplomacy and politics, old alliances and the new world order, but now I'm walking through a tunnel in the middle of a mountain, following a river that leads away from some sort of ancient treasure chamber. Something tells me Adria was full of secrets long before the embassies were built along its wall.

"I think the hardest part is that he wants to blame himself," I say.

"So he blames me instead," Alexei fills in.

I want to tell him that he's wrong, but Alexei is a smart guy. Alexei already knows better.

"How are you?" he asks next.

I don't say a thing.

The cavern-like path seems to go on forever. Stalactites hang from the ceiling. Or are they stalagmites? I never could keep them straight. But now I'm surrounded by them, and I know this place is not man-made. And yet, it's easy to imagine the Romans or Byzantines or some other ancient civilization exploring this cavern — these caves — expanding, searching, looking for a place to hide.

My side hurts from so much walking and climbing, but the stitches hold and soon I'm shivering underground. We walk for what feels like hours. Eventually, the river runs away and the tunnel continues on. Sometimes it branches. Sometimes we find that it's caved in, and then we backtrack and start again.

I have the vague sense that the ground slopes down for a long time and then back up again. Then the tunnel subtly shifts.

"I think we're climbing," I say. "This one's probably caved in, too."

Alexei nods. "Maybe it is."

"I mean, it's probably nothing," I say, even though my heart is beating faster. Alexei grips my hand harder. "We're probably wasting our time. I mean, it can't possibly be —"

The tunnel turns — and Alexei and I freeze because, up ahead, there is a door. Not a trapdoor. Not a hidden, secret wall that spins or a tunnel that spirals. No. It's an actual door. And, well, technically, there are two. They're wide and made of a deep, dark wood. I reach out and touch them — they're smooth, but, most of all, they're real.

I want to cry, but I'm so thirsty that my eyes don't make tears. I want to scream, but I'm half afraid someone won't hear me.

And I'm half afraid somebody will.

"Do we dare?" I ask, but Alexei's hand is already on the handle. And slowly — carefully — he turns.

CHAPTER
TWENTY-THREE

As soon as Alexei opens the door, I know where we are. I don't recognize the room we enter or the corridor we try to creep down, but I *know*. From the moment Spence and I spied the symbol on the ruins, I knew that place was linked with this one. I just didn't realize the link would be quite so literal.

"Where are we?" Alexei asks.

"I'm not sure," I say, and tell myself it isn't even technically a lie.

Alexei's hand is tight in mine. I try not to think about how accustomed I've become to the weight of it, the feel of it. *It's not a talisman*, I tell myself. I'm certain I'd be fine without it, and yet the warm pressure soothes me in a way that I don't dare consider long.

The corridor has low stone ceilings that arch overhead. Gaslights burn in sconces, lighting the way, but I know I didn't see this corridor with Ms. Chancellor.

We pass old oil paintings — the kind like they have in the palace — and cabinets that are tightly locked. There are more corridors, other rooms. Alexei and I go on, following the flickering gaslight, hoping it will light the way, but the place is built like a maze, and for a second I wonder if Alexei and I have been trapped in some terrible loop — like we may never find our way out.

"We have to find one of the tunnels," I whisper to Alexei. "We have to get you out of here."

"Out of *where*?" he asks, spinning me to face him.

"I think we're back on the mainland. I bet this leads to one of the tunnels. From here, we can get you to Iran then back up into the hills."

I try to pull away, but Alexei holds me steady. "What aren't you telling me?"

"Alexei, I can't —"

"Wait." Alexei leans close to my ear. "Someone's coming."

The corridor branches up ahead, twisting into shadow and out of sight, and that is where Alexei pulls me. He presses me into the corner and squeezes in beside me, the two of us huddling together in the darkness.

Voices carry in these long stone halls. Footsteps echo. So I hear them long before I see them. And judging by the look in Alexei's eyes, there's no doubt he hears them, too. He's listening to every word.

"The girl is a problem." The woman's voice is faint but familiar.

"The girl is a child!"

The second woman is Ms. Chancellor, I'm sure of it. And as the two women come into view around the corner, Alexei and I squeeze farther into the shadows, and I realize why the other voice sounds so familiar.

Here, deep beneath the city, the acting prime minister's accent is a bit thicker. Her tone a little more severe. She isn't trying to charm the US ambassador into making her problems go away. No. She's arguing with the woman who, two days ago, she treated like a virtual stranger.

They were lying. Of course they were lying. For three years, people lied to me about what happened to my mom. About what I did. About who really, truly was to blame. And they're still lying. My whole life is a game of make-believe and no one has ever had the courtesy to tell me.

I'm tired of everyone talking about me, worrying about me, lying about me. I'm just so tired.

I lean against Alexei.

"She was interested, but I talked to her, and I believe she will move on now. We have no reason to believe that she'll cause a problem," Ms. Chancellor says.

"No," Prime Minister Petrovic corrects her. "The American boy was *interested*. Caroline was *obsessed*. And her daughter will become obsessed, too. She won't stop her digging, you know."

"Let her dig." I can practically hear Ms. Chancellor's impatience. "What harm will it do?"

"I don't know, Eleanor. What harm did it do Caroline?"

It's not a question. It's a threat. I can hear it in the woman's tone. I can feel it in the silence that follows. Alexei's arms tighten around me, and when I start to shake, his hands steady me. Is this rage or terror that I'm feeling? I don't know.

I don't know anything.

My blood is pounding so hard I almost miss the sound of Ms. Chancellor's high heels clicking across the stone floor, walking away.

"What is this place?" I can feel Alexei's breath on my skin. I know he's right beside me, and yet he feels a million miles away. "Grace, what is all this?"

Slowly, I shake my head. A fog fills my mind. "Honestly? I have no idea."

It's maybe the most truthful thing I've said in weeks.

"Come on," Alexei says, taking my hand again and leading me in the direction Ms. Chancellor disappeared.

It's not the way she brought me. This must be the back door, but that's okay. In fact, it's better. Alexei and I creep silently behind her, far enough back that she likely won't hear us, but close enough that I can still hear the clicking of her high heels.

Eventually, though, the clicking stops. And from a distance I see her go through a large door and into one of the tunnels. I know that's our way out.

"Was that your grandfather's chief of staff?" Alexei asks. I try to meet his gaze. "Gracie, what aren't you telling me?"

He doesn't sound angry; he sounds afraid, and I can't blame him. If I had good sense — if I were a normal girl — I'd be terrified right now, but fear is a luxury I no longer have.

I want Alexei to be okay. I want Spence's killer found and for Jamie to be able to rest. But I'm not concerned for myself anymore. I learned a long time ago that there's really not much use in that. I'm far too lost for saving.

But it's not too late for Alexei, so I open the exit and listen. The sound of Ms. Chancellor's heels are fading into nothing, so I grab Alexei's hand and start dragging him down the tunnel that lies beneath Valancia's streets.

"Gracie!" Alexei pulls me to a stop. "Do you know who that was?"

Slowly, almost numbly, I nod. But I don't tell him that the woman Ms. Chancellor was talking to is currently the most powerful politician in Adria. I don't dare mention that the reason that she has the job is because Ms. Chancellor shot her predecessor, or that the world is living a lie. I don't want to say the words *society* or *conspiracy* or *treasure*. No. I'm not going to give anyone else any more reason to think I'm crazy, because I know how it sounds — I know how it feels. And right now I don't know which is more dangerous: what Ms. Chancellor did to protect me, or what these women might do to protect something else.

I won't tell Alexei any of the things I can't figure out, so I just stand there. Because when you can't lie, sometimes that means you can't say anything at all.

But Alexei, being Alexei, reads my silence.

"Wasn't your mother's name Caroline?" he asks.

The words are too much, too loud, too clear.

What harm did it do Caroline?

I'm sweating again, too hot and tired. The air around me feels like steam, and my side burns, a pain so intense that I'm afraid the fire of three years ago might still be raging, burning me from the inside out.

"Gracie —"

"Noah and the others are going to be looking for us. They're going to be terrified. Now, please. Let's go. Let's just get out of here. Let's —"

"Okay, Gracie." Alexei takes my hand again. "Okay."

A summer shower must have started while we were gone because water runs down the sides of the tunnel in places. Rain trickles down the corridor. I can actually see Ms. Chancellor's wet footsteps up ahead, leading the way.

"This can get you back to Iran," I tell him.

"I'm not leaving you. After what we just heard, I'm never letting you out of my sight ever again."

"I'm okay, Alexei. I'm fine," I say, pulling him along.

"No. You're not. You're . . . beeping?" Alexei looks as confused as I feel.

"I'm what?" But then I feel the vibration coming from my pocket. I'd almost forgotten about my brother's phone until I reach inside and pull it out, look down at the screen. We must be inside cell range now, because the phone is vibrating constantly, downloading text after text. Notice after notice of voice mails and missed calls.

"They're from Spence, the night of the murder," I say as the texts keep coming. Over and over and over. Dozens of them. "They're *all* from Spence."

You're not gonna believe this.

Bro, call me.

Where R U?

Call me ASAP.

I think I'm in trubl.

"I thought you weren't supposed to be able to make calls from the island," Alexei says, and a cold realization dawns.

"You can't."

Finally, Alexei raises an eyebrow. "So if Spence was calling and texting your brother after the party but before he died, then . . ."

"Spence didn't die on the island."

CHAPTER TWENTY-FOUR

By the time I reach Embassy Row I am absolutely drenched. But at least Alexei isn't behind me — or at least, he's not supposed to be. He should be back in Iran by now. He should be dry. He should be safe, invisible and protected from the manhunt that no doubt still blankets the city. I look back, but with the fog and the rain I can't be sure that I'm not being followed.

Rain has driven the protestors back, and the mob is smaller, but police barricades still line the streets. At the newsstands, headlines blare in three languages about the vicious fugitive who is still on the run. The rain is heavy and the sky that was utterly cloudless a few hours ago is now dark and gray. It matches my mood.

And yet, I can almost swear that I hear music. In the distance, there's a procession of people dancing in the street, and I know it's part of the festival. The War of the Fortnight ended when the sky decided to rain and end the drought that plagued Adria. I'd almost forgotten this tradition — that the people will dance in the rain as long as it lasts. Longer.

But not me. I've got better things to do.

I'm not certain how much time has passed, but I know that Alexei and I have been separated from our friends for hours. I have to find a boat and go back to the island, to tell Noah, Rosie, Megan, and Lila where we've been — that we're okay. But first I have to go to the embassy. I have to see Grandpa and Jamie. I have to give them Jamie's phone and tell them that Spence made it to the mainland. I have to make sure that they know I'm okay.

But when I burst through the gate and onto US soil, no one notices. No one cares. And that's when I realize that absolutely no one in this building has had time to miss me, time to worry. *It's almost anticlimactic*, I think as I rush inside and up the stairs toward Grandpa's office.

Jamie's phone is in my hand, and my brain swirls with Spence's final words, with the fact that he didn't die on the island. I feel vindicated and alive and nothing can make me stop.

Well, almost nothing.

As it is, I only stumble a little when I realize that my grandfather isn't alone.

"I'm afraid I fail to follow, young man." Grandpa sounds confused and annoyed and maybe a tiny bit concerned. "What, exactly, is wrong with Grace?"

Noah, Megan, Rosie, and Lila stand before him, all of them drenched. All of them terrified. They have towels thrown around their shoulders, but Rosie still shakes.

"Sir, we hate to bother you, but time is important in these situations and it seems that Grace is . . ."

"Hey, what's going on?" I call from the doorway, my voice too bright, too happy.

Instantly, Noah spins. Rosie drops her towel and Megan visibly exhales. Lila just looks at me with cool indifference, as if I've already messed up her schedule enough for one day.

"Gracie?" someone says, and for the first time I realize my brother is here, too, on the far side of the room. "Where have you been?"

But Grandpa keeps his attention on Noah. "You were saying, young man?"

"Oh." Noah's mouth hangs open and I can't tell if he's furious or relieved. Probably a combination of both, I realize, as he has to mentally rewrite whatever speech he'd probably started composing on the island. "Well, sir, Grace is not spending enough time with her friends, you see. We're worried about her. She's new and we want to make sure she experiences all that Adria has to offer."

Grandpa goes from annoyed to merely befuddled. "Okay. Go. Leave. Experience with my blessing." Grandpa stands and slaps Noah on the back. "Before you drip all over the floor and Ms. Chancellor yells at us."

Ms. Chancellor, I think with a pang.

What harm did it do Caroline?

232

"I take it you've been out enjoying the rain festival?" Grandpa's voice pulls me back, but it takes a while to realize he's talking about me and that I'm as drenched as my friends. But, as usual, Grandpa isn't really concerned about my answer. "How they get it to rain every year at least once during these two weeks I'll never know. But somehow they do."

Then Grandpa shakes his head, as if in wonder.

My brother isn't as easily distracted. "Where have you been?" he asks.

Noah cocks his head. "Yeah, *where have you been*?"

I give my friends an *I'll fill you in later* nod and move toward my grandpa's desk.

"The theory has always been that Alexei had to have killed Spence because he died on the island and no one else there had a motive to kill him, right?" I don't bother to wait for their replies. "But what if Spence *didn't* die on the island?"

If my change of subject surprises them, it doesn't last long.

"You can't know that, Gracie," Jamie says.

"Yes. I can." I pull Jamie's phone from my pocket and hold it out to him. "I found this. And it's full of messages from Spence. From *after* the party."

"Is that mine?" Jamie asks.

"Yes."

My brother comes toward me, takes the phone. "Where did you find it?"

If I tell him, we'll fight, and, for once, I'm not in the mood, so I take a step back.

"The police think Alexei did it because Spence never left the island. Well, they're wrong. There's no cell service on the island. If Spence called and texted Jamie after the party, then he must have made it back. And if he made it back, then Alexei wasn't the only person who could have killed him."

I'm right, and I know it. They know it. But there is something else on Jamie's mind as he leans toward me, his voice like ice.

"Where did you find the phone, Gracie?"

"Where did you lose your phone, Jamie?"

"I don't know. That's kind of what people mean when they say things are *lost*."

"Where did you last see it?"

"I don't know. Here, I guess. I remember putting it in my jacket pocket and then . . ."

"Spence was wearing your jacket," I say, but Jamie only looks at me, confused. "When he washed ashore, he was in your jacket. That's why I thought he was you."

I regret the words as soon as I say them.

"Oh, Gracie." Jamie moves to hug me, but I don't need his comfort or his pity. I want his trust.

So I lie.

"The phone was downstairs. In the dining room under the table. You probably turned it off for dinner, and then it fell out of your pocket, but how I found the phone doesn't matter. What does matter is that Spence made it back to the mainland."

"No." Grandpa shakes his head, walks around his desk. "Impossible. The police questioned everyone, and no one admitted to giving him a ride off the island, Gracie. It's too far to swim. There's no way."

"There is a way! I know because it happened." I reach for the phone again, shove it toward my brother. "Here. Play them. Play your messages."

When Jamie reaches for his phone, it's almost like he's afraid that it might bite him, so I press the buttons myself, and soon there's a voice in my grandfather's office. A ghost on speakerphone, calling from the grave.

"Blake! Man, you're not going to believe this. Call me back."

Slowly, my brother reaches down to play the next message.

"Blake! Pick up the phone, man. I've got to . . . Just call me. As soon as you get this, call me!"

At first, Spence sounds excited, intrigued. But by the next message he's out of breath. It's like he's been running and is winded. His voice is barely a whisper.

"Blake. It's me again, man. I'm trying to get back to the embassy, but if I don't, you have to know —"

Spence never speaks again. I hear a crash, like his phone falling to the street. There are mumbles and scuffling sounds. A hit. And then there's nothing but silence and a cold chill of dread that comes with the knowledge that we've just heard the last moments of John Spencer's life.

For a long moment, my brother just stands, looking at the phone, guilt and grief spreading across his face.

His friend called him, but Jamie wasn't there. Not for our mother. Not for Spence. And now it's way too late to save either one.

"He made it back to the mainland," I say again, hoping that this time they'll believe me. "He made it back, and he saw something. And they killed him."

No one says, *There is no "they."* My grandfather and brother have already spent years telling me there is no Scarred Man. But there is. Dominic is real. His scar is real. It's just the details of that night that my mind always managed to forget and confuse.

This time, it's the details I don't know.

"He made it off the island," I say again.

"How?" Jamie asks, and for a second, I think I might do something crazy. I think I might just tell the truth. But then I hear my name.

"Grace?" Ms. Chancellor is at the door. She looks at my friends and then at me. Once upon a time I might have thought I could read her bemused expression, but not now. Now I have no idea what she's thinking when she says, "Well, isn't this the party?"

In a flash, I see the future. Spence's phone is right here, not quite proof, but something. And I could tell them about the tunnel and the Society and the cryptic, nagging doubts that plague my mind. I could tell them about Spence's search, my mother's obsession, and maybe I could make somebody understand that this is so much bigger than two boys fighting at a party.

I could do that. And I could also end up back in a psych ward. Or worse.

Whoever did this killed a US citizen, framed an ambassador's son, and planted a bomb on a diplomatic vehicle.

There are things that are far, far worse.

"Did I hear that you all are going out to dance in the rain?" Ms. Chancellor says. Her smile doesn't quite reach her brown eyes, though. I'm almost terrified of what she might mean when she says, "Do be careful. I'd hate to see anyone else get hurt."

CHAPTER TWENTY-FIVE

Where were you?"

That we make it all the way to the street before Noah spins on me is something of a miracle. It's still raining — not a downpour, but the kind of heavy, lingering drizzle that clings to your hair and your clothes until it feels like you'll never be truly warm or dry again.

But that doesn't stop the festival. According to legend, when the rains came two hundred years ago, musicians filled the streets and the people danced, so now everyone who has ever played an instrument is outside in the rain, leading the nonstop procession. Tourists and natives alike are dancing in the streets now, carrying umbrellas that they don't even hold overhead as they spin and spin, following the circle that rims the city, dancing down Embassy Row.

Noah glances in their direction then shakes his head. "Ignore them."

"Noah, I —"

"Where were you?" he says again, not teasing. And for the first time I really let myself consider today's events from his perspective. We all went to a place where someone died and then Alexei and I disappeared without a trace. We were gone for hours, and Noah's right to be angry. They're all right to be terrified.

"We got stuck," I say, as if that makes any sense.

"Stuck how?" Noah asks through gritted teeth. "And how did you get back here? We had the only boat."

"There was a tunnel," I say. "Or really more like catacombs or caverns or something. Anyway, there are these big ruins in the center of the island. It looks like it was some kind of temple or fortress or something once. I think Spence went in there. That night. I think he got stuck in the same room we got stuck in and then he found the same tunnel we found and took that back to the mainland."

"I don't understand," Megan says. "What kind of tunnel? You mean like the ones that are under the city?"

"Yes," I say, then reconsider. "No. I mean . . . I don't know. It hooks up with the city tunnels, though. That's how Alexei and I got out."

"Hooks up where?" Rosie asks, and I can't help myself. I look at Lila.

"No!" Noah yells. He points between me and his twin sister. "Don't think I don't see you two. Whispering and giving each

239

other looks. You're working together now? You two? In case you have forgotten, you don't like each other! You barely know each other. And now you're acting like best friends and I don't like it. I know something is going on, and I want to know what it is. Now."

I think about what Noah's asking me to do — what I want to do. If Ms. Chancellor was right, the Society has existed for a thousand years; I've been a member for less than a week, and already I'm about to crumble.

"Grace." I can hear the worry in Megan's voice. "What's wrong?"

When I start to shake, I tell myself it's because of the rain, so I push my wet hair out of my face. Water runs down my cheeks, and I remind myself that I'm not crying — that crying is a luxury I'll never have again.

No. It's a luxury that *Spence* will never have again. And Mikhail, the Russian driver. And maybe Alexei if we can't make this stop.

What harm would it do to tell my friends? I wonder. Then another thought cuts through me:

What harm did it do Caroline?

The words chill me like the wind, and only one thought remains: *This is happening.* I'm going to have to face it one way or another. The only question now is whether or not I'm going to face it alone.

"We need to go inside. Let's go meet Alexei, and then I'll tell you." I look at Lila, but I can't read her eyes. "I'll tell you everything."

It's not hard to find a tunnel entrance and, from there, to make it to the north end of Embassy Row. As soon as I push open the doors into the basement of Iran it feels, shockingly, like home. This dingy basement with its hot springs–fueled swimming pool and ornately tiled ceiling is as comforting as anyplace else. For the first time since I heard the temple door closing behind us, I let myself relax.

"Where are we?" Lila asks, stepping inside.

She's taking in the long room with its domed ceiling, the moldy lounge chairs and water-stained walls when Rosie says, "Iran."

Lila almost knocks her down as she spins. "Where?" she shouts, and I remember.

"Oh. Yeah. I forgot you didn't know. Sometimes we hang out in Iran." I'm so matter-of-fact that it takes a moment for her to hear what I'm saying.

Lila is a blur as she whirls on her brother and starts shouting at him in a steady stream of Hebrew. But Noah throws his hands in the air — the universal signal for *don't blame me* — and fires off a reply.

It might go on forever if not for the dark shadow that appears in the stairway, the deep voice that says, "Is someone going to tell me what has happened?"

And just that quickly Lila forgets all about her brother and runs to Alexei as fast as she can. He throws open his arms and practically swallows her whole.

"I was so worried," she says as Alexei speaks softly near her ear, his voice so low that I can't hear it. And the whole scene makes me feel . . . angry. And sad. And guilty.

But mostly it makes me want to pull Lila out of Alexei's arms and toss her in the pool.

I have no right to feel this way, but that's the thing about feelings. You never get what you deserve.

When Megan clears her voice, "*Ahem!*" Lila peels herself off of Alexei and turns back to us. Her mascara is smudged and her cheeks are too red.

"Now, will someone explain where the two of you went?" Noah points to Alexei and then to me. "And what the two of you" — this time he points between me and his sister — "have been keeping from us?"

"Grace," Lila starts, my name a warning. *We should talk about this*, it says. *We should think. We shouldn't throw a thousand years of secret sisterhood out the window just because one of us is having a really messed-up summer.*

But this isn't my summer. It's my life. And I don't know how much more I can take.

"You can leave if you want to, Lila. You can go tell your mom or Ms. Chancellor what I'm doing right now. You can. It's your right, and I won't try to stop you. But don't try to stop me." I look at my friends. "They're already involved with this, one way or another. They have the right to know."

My mom was obsessed with something once, if Ms. Chancellor and the prime minister are to be believed. Just a few weeks ago I

242

was obsessed with the Scarred Man and justice and proving to the world that I'm not crazy. I was wrong, of course, about so many things. And I may be wrong about this. But if there's something worse than knowing an awful thing, it's knowing nothing at all.

I look at my friends and then to Lila.

"Go ahead," she says. "I won't stop you."

Maybe this means she believes me. Maybe she trusts me. Or maybe Lila is just smart enough to know that, given enough rope, eventually, I am bound to hang myself.

"Okay," I say. "Get comfortable, and I'll explain."

It's chilly in the basement, and we're all still wet, but we settle on the hard tiled floor. We wrap towels around our shoulders and huddle around like there's an old-fashioned campfire. Then it's time for me to tell the story.

"A thousand years ago, the knights of the Crusades settled Adria."

"Feel free to skip ahead a millennium," Noah tells me, but I shake my head.

"No. I can't. Because a thousand years ago men founded this country, but their wives and their daughters and their granddaughters formed a sort of . . . society. Or so they tell me. And that society still exists today."

"I've never heard of it," Megan says.

"It's a secret," I say, not realizing how foolish it sounds until the words are out of my mouth.

Noah doesn't look impressed. "What do they do?"

"I don't know," I say. My towel is fraying and I pick at the edges. If I pick long enough and hard enough, eventually I might find the thread that makes it all unravel. "Ms. Chancellor said that my grandmother was a part of it, and my mother, and that that might be why someone wanted to kill her."

Noah glares at his sister. "You knew about this?"

Lila shrugs. "Mom told me a few —"

"*Mom* is a part of this?" Noah stands up and starts to pace.

"Yes!" Lila says. "It's why she wanted to be posted in Adria. She wanted me raised as her grandmother was raised. She wanted me to know my birthright."

"*Your* birthright?" Noah asks, indignant.

"It's a girls-only kind of thing," I explain, but I'm not helping.

"I don't get it." Rosie leans back, totally unimpressed. "So there's a really-old-lady society. That doesn't seem like such a big thing."

"To be fair," Megan corrects, "I don't think it's a club *of* old ladies, merely —"

"The Society is a thousand years old," I blurt. "*A thousand years.* The Society is as old as Adria itself. It's older than the wall." I let that fact sink in. "In fact, they're the ones who decided to build the wall. This thing is ancient and powerful. We don't even know how powerful."

"So there's a club," Megan says. "That's nice. I'm sure it's —"

"It's not a club," I say. "It's bigger than that."

"Okay. Of course. I'm sure it's very prestigious and —"

"Ms. Chancellor shot the prime minister!"

The only sound is the steady plop, plop, plop of the rainwater that leaks through the ceiling and drops into the pool. I can't tell if they don't believe me or if they're just too shocked to argue. I no longer care. I just start talking.

I tell them about Spence and his grandmother, about the rebellion and the treasure. I tell them everything from the moment the former prime minister cornered me in the shadows and Ms. Chancellor picked up a gun. Never before have I felt so many secrets tumble out of me. I can't stop. I might as well try to hold back the tide.

But as fast as I spill the Society's secrets, I still can't bear to tell my own. Maybe that makes me a hypocrite. But I'm a hypocrite who doesn't want her friends to know she shot and killed her own mother. And, honestly, I'm okay with that.

"And that's it," I say when I'm finished. I sit back and wait for them to laugh, to tell me I must be joking. Or — worse — that I must be hearing things, misremembering things. Crazy.

But before anyone can argue, Alexei says, "It's true. We saw Ms. Chancellor. She was with the new prime minister. They spoke of the cadet and of Grace." Alexei cuts his gaze toward me, as if asking permission. "And of Grace's mother."

I shiver beneath the towel I have thrown over my shoulders. But none of my friends move to comfort me. It's like they already know me too well.

"Wait. No. This is Ms. Chancellor we're talking about?" Even Megan sounds confused. "*Eleanor Chancellor?*"

"Yes," I say.

"She shot the prime minister and this *society* or whatever covered it up?" Megan says.

"Yes! I know how it sounds, okay? And I know how it looks, but it's true. This time, I swear that I'm not wrong." I'd give anything to be wrong. "It's true, and . . ."

My voice cracks. My vision blurs.

"Say it," Noah demands. "Come on, Grace — say whatever it is you're afraid to say."

"I think Spence got stuck in that tunnel on the island and then came out the other side. I think he ended up inside the Society — someplace he was never meant to be."

"And what else?" Noah prompts.

There are truths you think and truths you feel and truths that, deep down, you know but pray you'll never have to bring to the surface. So I dig deep and look Noah in the eye and whisper the words I've been too afraid to voice for days.

"And I think they killed him."

CHAPTER TWENTY-SIX

It's not hard to make a to-do list. We've been here before and we know how this goes. It's just that, this time, I hope it goes better.

"Check every camera you can find," I tell Megan. "I don't think the police ever considered the possibility he wasn't murdered on the island. It's possible they missed something big."

"On it!" she says.

"We need to find some other suspect. Any other suspect," I say.

Lila considers this a moment, then asks, "What about that creepy guy? He seems like he could break somebody's neck."

"What creepy guy?"

"*Scar Guy*. You know, the one who was following you," Lila says, and I can feel the room shift.

"The Scarred Man is following you?" Noah asks me.

"No. Yes. I mean, I've seen him around."

"He's *following you?*"

"It's nothing, Noah," I say.

"Do I need to remind you that two weeks ago you swore that the Scarred Man killed your mother?"

"And do I have to remind you that I just told the story of how Dominic saved my life?"

"But what if he *did* kill your mom?" Rosie asks.

"He didn't. I know for a fact he didn't." I don't even try to tell them why I am so certain.

"And yet you're convinced that Ms. Chancellor and *my mom* are criminal masterminds now?"

Noah has a point, but I don't say so. "I think they're hiding something. I think we need to find out what. Now, do you have a problem with that?"

Noah shakes his head and backs away. I know he wants to fix this — fix me. He doesn't yet know that his best friend was broken long before he met her — that I'll never really be okay again.

"Can I follow the new prime minister?" Rosie asks. "Please. I'm really good at following prime ministers."

Megan and I share a look before I cautiously say, "Okay. But be careful. And . . . take Noah with you." Noah looks less than excited about this prospect, but he doesn't bother to protest. "Don't approach her. And don't follow her anywhere that isn't totally public. Okay?" I ask, but Rosie says nothing. "Rosie, okay?"

"Okay." She sulks like I never let her have any fun.

"You almost act as if you've done this before." Lila laughs, but Noah shrugs. Instantly, Lila registers the truth. *"You've done this before?"*

But we don't have time for Lila's shock or outrage.

Megan gives her a *that's old news* hand wave and starts making notes for what she has to do.

"And I guess that leaves us," I say, looking at Lila. "I mean, if you want to help."

"That depends. What are you going to do?" Lila sounds more than a little skeptical.

"We're going to the Society," I say. "We're going to claim our birthrights."

Slowly, we all stand and gather our things. Once we've cleared away any evidence that someone has been inside Iran, Alexei takes my hand and pulls me aside.

"I believe you forgot to give me a job." He's smiling, trying to tease. To flirt. He doesn't want to hear what I have to say and, already, he knows it.

"You can't stay here, Alexei."

"No." He's shaking his head. "I'll not leave you to take chances because of me. I'll not sit on my hands while you and our friends place yourselves in danger *because of me*," he says again.

"We won't be in any danger! Megan's going to be on her computer. Noah and Rosie are going to be walking down public streets. And Lila and I are just going to go look around a place we've already been invited to look around. It's not dangerous."

"Digging up secrets is always dangerous."

"Alexei, you're still the most wanted man in Adria. We need you to go back to the cave."

"No. These are dangerous people. I don't want you sticking your noses where they do not belong."

"Why?" I ask. "It's not like *you've* got anything to hide," I say in the manner of someone who knows too much about secrets.

Alexei catches my arm and doesn't let me pass. When he speaks again his voice is low and his accent is thick. "We all have things to hide."

It's late in the day when I return to the embassy and find a suitcase on Jamie's bed. Rows of neatly folded clothes sit in orderly stacks. Some books. A few toiletries. For a second, I panic. Jamie just got here. I just got him back. But another part of me has to wonder if this isn't what I want — for Jamie to leave Adria, to go back to West Point. For my brother to get far, far away from me.

"Jamie? Are you leaving?" I step farther into the room, but Jamie just keeps folding and refolding clothes, trying to bring order to our messy world.

He doesn't even look me in the eye when he says, "No. Not yet."

"But —"

"These are Spence's things. His parents asked me to ship them home."

Suddenly, the feeling in the room makes sense. Jamie isn't packing. He's mourning. And as usual I'm in the way. I should slip back through the door, but my legs don't move. I stand, frozen.

"I'm really, really sorry about your friend, Jamie. I don't know if I told you that. But I am."

"Thanks," Jamie says, then finally glances up. I'm filthy from walking through tunnels and sitting on the floor in Iran, and my rain-drenched hair has no doubt dried funny. I probably look as awful as I feel, and my brother sees it. "Where have you been?"

That's all it takes to make me want to crumble, to break down and tell him everything. Jamie is older. He's supposed to be wiser. He had years more with our mother than I will ever have, and I want to ask him if he ever heard her talk about a treasure or a society or any reason someone might want her dead. Mom was obsessed with something, I want to say. It's like I never knew her, and now I know I never will.

A week ago I thought I'd spent the last three years living a lie, but now I know that it's actually been much longer. I want to go back to being the little girl who was on the outside of the secret.

"Grace, what is it? What's wrong?"

I killed our mother and someone killed Spence — someone is trying to kill Alexei. A better question might be *what's right?*

So I tell him, "Alexei's okay," because right now it's the only thing that matters. "I mean, I don't know where he is exactly, but I know he's fine."

I'm lying, but that's not the look that Jamie gives me. If anything, he looks like someone who would give anything not to be the bearer of bad news.

"Oh, gosh," my brother says. "You don't know."

251

"Know what?"

"Russia blew up their own car, Gracie."

For a second, I'm sure I must have misheard him.

"No. I told you. Alexei was supposed to be *in* the car. He was turning himself in. And, besides, Spence made it back to the mainland!"

"Oh, Gracie." Jamie sounds like he'd give anything to keep me young and naïve and stupid. But we both know it's far too late for that. "There's proof. Adrian officials finally got eyes on the car. And, besides, there's a witness. The cops just briefed Grandpa. There's a witness who saw Spence on the mainland after the party. And he was *with* Alexei."

Jamie sounds as if this makes it real, but I know all about witnesses, how they appear and disappear to suit the needs of some kind of higher calling. I know medical records can be altered and even gunshot wounds can morph into something else. Jamie's older and no doubt wiser, but on this topic I am the expert, and my brother has no idea.

"No." I shake my head. "Witnesses lie. They get confused."

"This one isn't confused."

"Alexei's not a murderer."

"But Spence was a hothead!"

For a second, Jamie's as stunned as I am to hear him shout, but he's so angry now. Not with me. Not even with himself. He's angry with the thoughts that he's obviously been carrying for days. Gone is his cool logic, and what remains is guilt and dread. It rolls off of him in waves.

"Okay, Gracie? I know that. And *that's* what worries me."

The rage fades, and in its place grows something so much darker, sadder.

"Spence wasn't the type to let go of what happened on the beach — to take it. Not from some high school kid. Not from some Russian. He could have picked a fight, and in the heat of the moment, in the dark . . . it could have gotten out of hand. It could have gotten out of hand real fast. Don't you get it, Gracie? I'm not afraid Alexei started something." His voice cracks. He can't meet my gaze. "I'm afraid that Alexei finished it."

Jamie's really scared, I can see it now. This isn't the by-product of grief or guilt. He actually doubts Alexei. And that makes me doubt myself.

"But if Spence made it back to the island, then anyone could have done it," I say.

Jamie laughs softly, as if it would be nice to be so innocent. "Do you know how hard it is to break a man's neck with your bare hands — how hard it would be to do it to someone like Spence, who was big and strong and trained? Dad could do it. It would have to be someone like Dad."

"Exactly! Alexei doesn't have that kind of training!"

It's supposed to be the perfect argument. This is supposed to be the moment that changes his mind. But, instead, my brother gives me a look that makes my blood go cold.

"Did Alexei ever tell you what his dad did before he came to the embassy?"

"No."

"Well, I don't know what it was exactly. KGB? Russian special forces? I don't really know. I just know that . . . You know how, growing up, boys say things like *my dad could beat up your dad?*"

"Yeah."

"Well, Alexei's the only kid I never said that to."

I try to remember the boys they were, how they used to laugh and play and run wild through the halls and down the streets, but no matter how hard I try I just can't reconcile who they were against who they are.

"What are you saying?"

"I'm saying Alexei doesn't have to be a murderer to be a killer. I'm saying that if he ran into Spence on the mainland that night . . ."

Slowly, my brother turns back to Spence's things. He's still trying to make them straight and even.

He can't look at me as he says, "I don't want you to tell me where he is, so I'm not asking. And don't bother telling me you don't know, because I don't want you to lie to me and I don't want to have to lie to anybody else. But know this, Gracie — you're right. Alexei is the best friend I have ever had. And I don't want to think this. If there were any way to convince myself otherwise I would have done it days ago, but — right now — I'm pretty sure he did it. I want to be wrong. But, Gracie" — Jamie looks at me — "I'm probably not."

CHAPTER TWENTY-SEVEN

When I leave my brother, I can't go to my room. There's no way I can sleep. I leave the embassy, but Noah and Megan and Rosie are no doubt sick of me and all of my drama. They've earned a night off, and so I'm not really sure where I'm going until I feel the cobblestone streets give way to soft dirt. I check to make sure I'm not being followed, and then I'm climbing. Pebbles shift and muddy earth crumbles beneath my feet, but I climb faster. My breath comes harder than it should. I'm still too thin and too weak. My side is still tender, and I know that I am fragile, but that makes me move faster, careless on the uneven ground. I don't care. I'd run if I could. And I'd keep running. Until I ran out of land.

When I see the clearing and the rocks I know exactly where my feet have led me. When Alexei emerges from the small crack in the stone, I know why.

"Hi," he says. We are high in the hills that overlook the city. In the distance, the sun is setting on the far side of the sea, and I stand in the twilight, looking down on the great walled city. They call it one of the wonders of the world, but the walls I have built around myself are higher, stronger, deeper. They have kept me safe for years, but when Alexei moves toward me, I feel the stones begin to shift; the mortar starts to crack and crumble, and the walls that guard my heart grow unsteady. But I cannot turn and run away.

"What's wrong?" Alexei asks.

I shake my head but can't speak. I don't want my voice to crack. It's hard enough being vulnerable without letting anyone know it, see it, hear it. I can't let this boy know how easy it would be for him to hurt me.

"Gracie, are you okay?" Genuine worry fills Alexei's eyes, and I think that's what finally breaks me.

"Is it true?"

"Is what true?"

"Did your embassy blow up its own car? Were they going to fake your death and send you back to Russia?"

He's supposed to deny it, be outraged. But instead he says, "I don't know." It's harder than hearing him lie.

"Did you see Spence back on the mainland that night?"

"*No.*" This time he's emphatic. He takes two long strides and reaches for me, but I pull away. "Gracie, I swear to you that I got a ride home with some kids I didn't know and went straight back to the embassy. I swear it."

"Jamie says there's a witness who saw you with Spence on the mainland. *After* the party."

"There isn't. Or the witness is mistaken. Or lying. I never saw Jamie's friend again. Not after the island."

I want to believe him. Really, I do.

"Gracie, would I lie to you?"

I never thought my brother would lie to me. Or my father. Or Ms. Chancellor or Grandpa or practically everyone else I've ever known. I never thought I would spend three years lying to myself.

The ground beneath me has been shifting for too long. My world is too unsteady. So when Alexei reaches for me again, I don't try to pull away. I am looking for anything that might anchor me at last to solid ground.

"Say you believe me, Gracie. None of it matters if you don't believe me." He's forcing me to look into his eyes. "What's wrong?"

I think about Grandpa and Jamie, about the Society and the wanted posters that still blanket the city — of how high the flames were when the car exploded. I'm thinking of lost treasures and hidden rooms and of whatever obsession might have driven my mother to her grave. I've been carrying these things with me for too long, and I can feel them tumbling over and over in my mind like clothes in a dryer, warm and full of static. I keep waiting to feel a shock.

"Lila and I are going to go down to the Society tomorrow. Maybe we can find something about the treasure or Spence or . . ." I shake my head. "I don't know *what* to do."

"Then don't do anything. Please, Gracie. Please. It's too dangerous. And you're too . . . You're too important."

"I'm not important." I shake my head, but Alexei catches my hands.

"You're important to me."

The air is growing chilly, but Alexei's hands are warm. I tell myself that's why I don't pull away.

"Just don't take any chances, okay?" he says. "Don't get hurt. I don't think I could take it if you got hurt. Say you understand, Gracie."

I do understand, so much more than Alexei can ever know. I understand what it's like to feel the earth shift beneath you, to know there are people you can't trust. I understand what Dominic meant when he told me that Alexei is a pawn in a much bigger game with dangerous players who will sacrifice anyone to get whatever they want.

I understand that no one else is looking for the truth.

I understand I might be his only hope, as pathetic as that sounds.

So I look up into his eyes and force a smile. I'm not lying when I tell him, "I understand."

"You want to get out of here?" Alexei asks, tugging on one of my hands.

"You can't go back to town, Alexei. It's not safe yet."

"Then we won't go to town."

●   ●   ●

I don't know how far we walk, or for how long. I'm only aware of how big and bright the moon is as it rises over Adria, how warm Alexei's hand is and how tightly it holds on to mine.

I'm content to let him lead me. For a little while, I forget to fight. Alexei is with me, guiding me, and I am not alone anymore, watching my mother's shop burn. I'm not shaking on the street or strapped to a bed in a psych ward, screaming out my mother's name. There is someone here who is bigger, stronger, faster, and he's on my side.

I use the wall inside of me to block out those thoughts, a very brief reprieve against the worries and doubts that are in a constant siege against me. Alexei is standing guard.

I close my eyes. I take a deep, deep breath. The air is cool and fresh after the rain. When Alexei stops I come to rest beside him, and in the stillness that follows, far away from the chanting of the protestors or the crashing waves of the sea, I hear water. Not the Mediterranean. It is a rush — a steady, constant hum that fills the darkness.

"What is that?" I look up at Alexei.

"A secret," he tells me. "Come on."

A minute later he is pushing aside the undergrowth of trees and pointing down into a tiny valley. The noise is louder now, and I can see its source. Rivers run through the hills surrounding Valancia, and some of them must converge here, rushing into a great waterfall, pooling at the base of the valley. The vegetation is thicker, the air cooler. It's like Alexei has taken my hand and led me all the way to Eden.

"Jamie and I found this place when we were kids, trying to run away from you. I think the land technically belongs to the royal family — most of the land around the city does. I've never seen anyone else here, though. I'm fairly certain we are alone."

Even without Alexei's assurance I would know that it's true. We're no more than a few miles from Embassy Row, and yet it feels a world away as Alexei drags me down the hill — too fast. We stumble but keep running, in an odd kind of race. We want to leave the world away, on the far side of the ridge. We are running toward paradise, and nothing — not even common sense — can stop us.

When we reach the water's edge, Alexei drops my hand and immediately reaches for his shirt.

"What are you" — I start, but by that time, his shirt is already off, tossed to the ground — "doing?" I finish. I know I should turn away, but my feet don't agree with me, because I just stand there, staring.

"Come on, Gracie," he yells, already diving into the water. His cargo shorts are going to be soaked. I can't remember whether or not Rosie brought him a change of clothes. The nights are going to be cold in his wet things, but logic fails me, words fail me. I can think of nothing as I watch him swim out into the dark water — strong, sure strokes that carry him farther and farther from me.

"Come in!" he yells.

"I —"

I don't have a swimsuit.

I don't want my wound to get infected.

260

I really should be getting back before Jamie or my grandfather or Ms. Chancellor sends out a search party.

I have a big day of betraying my ancient sisterhood tomorrow.

I could offer up any of a dozen valid excuses, but I don't let myself think of the reasons not to do something. I try to focus on the reasons I should.

The tank top beneath my sweater is black.

My cardigan is warm.

And one of the few people in the world I actually trust is out there in the stillness, waving, yelling, "Gracie, come on!"

So I take off my shoes and my sweater.

So I follow.

"We shouldn't be doing this," I tell Alexei when I reach him.

"I smell, Gracie. And I'm tired. And every part of me hurts from sleeping on the ground last night, so yes, I *should* be doing this. I'm just glad you're doing it with me."

I tread water and look up at the moon that's rising.

"The water's warm," I finally say, dipping low to let my hair wash back away from my face.

"Yeah." Alexei's treading water, too, barely moving. We're both suspended — in the water, in time. "I think one of the hot springs must feed into it. It's like this all year long," he says, and I know it's true. The weather in Adria never varies much, but I can imagine Alexei sneaking out here in the middle of winter, taking off his shoes and shirt and diving in.

"Stop," Alexei says, pulling me back.

"Stop what?" I ask.

"Stop thinking." He's closer now, I realize. I can barely see the shore. In Valancia, the Festival of the Fortnight is in full swing. Natives and tourists no doubt fill the streets, but Alexei and I are cocooned in our own little world. And we are happy. Almost.

"I'm going to do it," Alexei warns. His smile is too bright in the moonlight.

"Do what?" I ask.

"I'm going to make you laugh."

"You're what?"

"I'm going to make you laugh," he says, grinning. "It's been a long time since I've heard you laugh, Gracie, and it's time."

I'm just opening my mouth to protest when he splashes me.

Water gushes over my head. It gets in my mouth and my eyes.

"You —"

He does it again and again.

And again.

And he's right. I do laugh. I laugh so loudly that it echoes off the hills and drowns out the sound of the rushing, falling water.

I laugh like a little girl who has finally climbed the wall and caught up with the boys.

I laugh because, for once, Alexei chose to run away with me.

When I splash him back, he lunges in the water, wrapping my arms in his own, squeezing me from behind. I squirm and kick and try to break free, but Alexei only holds me tighter, pulling me against his chest as we float, weightless, looking up at the stars.

Slowly, I stop fighting.

For a long time, we are alone and we are silent. I can feel Alexei's every breath. My head rests on his shoulder and he doesn't move to push me away. If anything, he holds me tighter.

"The people who are behind this . . ." Alexei begins, but I just keep gazing at the stars. "Someone put a bomb in a diplomatic car, Gracie. Someone killed a West Point cadet who was a personal guest of the United States ambassador. Whoever these people are, please tell me you're being careful."

He squeezes me so tightly that I can barely breathe. The last thing I want to do is stop him.

"I'm okay," I say, to the boy and to the stars. "I'll be okay," I say, praying it's true.

CHAPTER TWENTY-EIGHT

Embassy Row is dark when I reach it. It's late enough that if I'm quiet I know that I might just make it inside and up to my room before Jamie or my grandfather or Ms. Chancellor even realizes I've been missing. The rain drove most of the protestors away, and now Embassy Row is oddly silent. For the first time in days, the street is at peace.

"You have been careless, Grace Olivia."

When Dominic steps out from the small crack in the fence between the US and Russia, I almost jump out of my skin.

"You scared me!" I say while I try to force my heart back into my chest.

He doesn't ask where I've been or who I've been with. No. It's worse than that. He looks at me like he already knows.

"Valancia is a dangerous city," Dominic says, but I can't help myself. I glance down the mansion-lined street. Armed guards stand approximately every fifty feet; cameras cover every angle.

"Yeah." It's all I can do not to roll my eyes. "Clearly the neighborhood is super sketchy."

But Dominic doesn't laugh at my joke, doesn't relax. He doesn't even scold me like my dad or Jamie would. He just looks at me as if he sees something I don't. And he probably does. He was some kind of elite soldier once upon a time. It's his job to look in shadows and see ghosts. Now that there's no one he's supposed to be protecting, I guess he's decided to protect me.

For the first time in my life, I actually feel sorry for the Scarred Man.

"How are you?" I ask.

He looks stunned by the question.

"You should not be concerned about me," he says.

"But you get to worry about me? That doesn't quite sound fair."

"I . . ." He stumbles, and I know I've knocked him off guard, probably the first time that's happened in decades. He moves out of my way and gestures to the embassy. "Go inside, Grace Olivia. And do not wander the streets alone again. Especially after dark. Especially now."

The Festival of the Fortnight is just getting started, and as if on cue, some drunks stagger down Embassy Row, proving his point.

I move to the gates but at the last minute turn back and study the Scarred Man. Was he always so dark, so brooding? Did he ever go night swimming with a girl and splash her until she laughed? And did that laughter die the night my mother died? Did I kill his laughter, too, when I killed her?

"Thank you, Dominic. If I didn't say so before, thank you for saving my life."

I'm quiet on the stairs of the embassy. I'm like a ghost as I walk down the hall. The light is off in Jamie's room, but I can't tell if he's asleep or out somewhere, wandering through the city. I don't know, and I tell myself it doesn't matter. I just ease open my door and step inside, closing it softly behind me, thankful for the dark.

"It's about time," a voice says, and I can't help myself: I scream and spin.

"Lila!" I try to catch my breath and glare at the girl who is lounging atop my covers, a smug smirk on her perfect face.

"Members of your family really need to learn to knock," I say, remembering the night when I met Noah.

"I *did* knock." Lila stretches and twists across my bed like a very shiny cat. "You weren't here."

"And you came in anyway?"

"Oh. I'm sorry. You're so right. I should have knocked on every door in the embassy looking for you, asking if anyone knew where I could find you. Would you have preferred that?"

She has me and she knows it. When I flip on the light she eyes me, and I see that Megan is asleep in my chair.

"Nice sweater," Lila says as I strip off my cardigan. That's also when I realize that I must have put it on inside out.

I could say something, retreat. But I am far more comfortable on the offensive.

"What do you want, Lila?"

I think maybe she's going to tell me that it's over, that she's told her mom or Ms. Chancellor and any moment now an army of lady librarian assassins is going to storm the embassy's walls and take me away for my betrayal.

But Lila just crosses her arms and studies me. "So how was Alexei?"

I could deny it. I could fight it. But I have learned to pick my battles wisely, and under any circumstances, Lila is a worthy foe, so I say, "Fine."

"What is it?" Megan is still half asleep, but she's pulling herself together.

"Also, your hair is wet," Lila tells me, then looks at Megan. "Grace came home."

"Was there something the two of you needed?" I don't mean to snap, really I don't. But I'm too tired and it's too late. I'm too hungry and worried and I don't know what just happened between Alexei and me, but I know that something's different now. *We* are different. Lila and Megan would probably know about boys. They could probably tell me what happened, but that would be betraying Alexei and whatever our private moment meant.

If Megan and I were alone, I might ask, but Lila and I aren't friends. I know it. She knows it. If it weren't for the Society and Alexei and all the drama of our lives, we would exist in completely separate social spheres.

But I can see something changing inside of Lila. Her features shift as she climbs off the bed and walks to the window. The moon is bright and full, and its light slashes across her pretty face. There was a time, not long ago, when that would have reminded me of a scar. But Lila's skin is perfect. It's what's in her eyes that scares me.

"What's wrong?" I ask.

Lila turns to Megan, and something passes between them. Megan's fully awake now, and I can tell that she's almost afraid.

"You two are scaring me," I say.

Megan reaches down and picks up her laptop. "You know how you told me to — and I quote — do my computer thing and find out all I can about that night?"

"Yeah."

"Well, I did."

"That was fast. What did you find?"

"This." Megan sounds like she'd give anything to take it back, but it's too late. For a lot of things.

She turns the laptop around. It takes a moment to recognize the scene that's playing out in black and white. The footage is from one of the embassies. I can tell by the fences that line the street. It's dark and the night is clear.

"It's from the night of the party," Megan says. "Most of us were still on the island — it wasn't that late. And then . . ." Megan trails off but gestures to the screen, where Spence is walking down an alley that's just off Embassy Row. He's covered in dust and his hat is missing, but it's definitely him, and he's definitely 100 percent alive.

"Isn't there a tunnel entrance around that corner?" I ask. Megan nods.

"Yeah, but —"

"Well, that's good, right? This is more proof that he made it back to the mainland alive?"

"Keep watching," Lila says.

On the screen, Spence turns, walks out of sight.

Then, ten seconds later, Alexei appears as well.

And follows.

CHAPTER TWENTY-NINE

I've been wrong, and I've been crazy. But this is the first time I've ever truly felt like a fool.

I keep thinking about the way Alexei held me and looked into my eyes while he lied. It makes me want to take a hot shower, scrub off every inch of skin he might have touched. It makes me wonder how a person can be so wrong so often. It makes me realize I'm the last person on earth anyone should ever trust.

That's what keeps me up all night.

That's why I can't relax long enough to close my eyes or sleep or eat or do anything but stare at the walls of my mother's bedroom, rocking and wondering exactly when and how everything went so wrong.

That's why, when morning comes, I know exactly what I have to do.

There's no answer when I knock on the door, but it's unlocked, and as I push it open just a crack I can hear the water running in the bathroom. I let myself in and stand at the window.

You can see Russia from here. I'd almost forgotten that. But now I remember stories about flashlights and Morse code, a long-running debate about the wisdom of stringing a laundry line between the two embassies so that no matter what — day or night — messages could be passed in between.

I hear my mother's laugh when I think about it. I can almost see her close this window, blocking out the rain and the sun and the boy next door.

When the bathroom door swings open, the small bedroom floods with steam, and I hear my brother gasp. "Gracie! You scared me half to death!"

Jamie's hair is wet, and he's not wearing a shirt. He's always been my big brother, but it's hard to disguise the fact that, now, he's even bigger. His arms are huge and his chest is broad, and it feels like he's grown a foot. Or maybe I'm just smaller. It feels like I shrink a little more every day.

"You're up early," my brother says. He digs around in his dresser and pulls out an *ARMY* T-shirt, pulls it over his head. It wouldn't do any good to tell him that I never went to sleep.

"How far did you run?" I ask instead.

"I did the circle," he says. I don't have to ask which circle. He means he looped the city, ran all the way around Embassy Row. Five miles. It's barely six a.m.

"Is that all?" I tease.

Jamie shrugs. "I did it twice."

Of course he did. It used to bother me, having a sibling who was so perfect. But now I'm glad Dad has him. I'm glad not all of our family's expectations have to land on me.

"Gracie?" Jamie's closer than I remember. I can see his reflection in the window as I look out at Russia. The sun's just coming up.

"I'm sorry, Jamie."

He turns to me. "For what?"

"For killing your mother."

The wall that runs around Valancia is high and wide and strong enough to stand for a thousand years, but it's nothing compared to the one I've built inside me. In the haze of early morning, though, I can hear it start to crack. I can feel my defenses crumble. And when the tears come they don't slide down my face in slow motion. No, my grief comes out in wails and sobs.

I know Jamie's arms are around me. I know that's the reason I haven't already fallen, broken, to the floor.

"I did it," I say. "It was me. I did it. I . . ."

"Shhh, Gracie. Shhh. It's okay."

"I killed her. I killed Mom. I shot her, Jamie."

"You didn't mean to. It was an —" He stops himself before he says the word *accident*. "You didn't mean to do it. It's okay," my

272

brother says, like that will make it better. He doesn't know that that's maybe my least favorite lie of all.

Jamie drags me to the bed and makes me sit on the edge, his arms around me like a vise. He's not going to let me split into a thousand pieces no matter how much I want to. He is going to hold me together.

"I was wrong," I say.

"It's okay," he tells me. He has no idea I'm talking about Alexei.

"I was so stupid!" I say, then my anger shatters, fractures into tears. I'm not really mad, I realize. I'm betrayed. Like it or not, I know I'll never trust again.

I've been quiet for a while now. Jamie must think it's safe to speak again because he presses a kiss to the top of my head just like Mom used to do.

"Did you sleep at all last night?"

I can hear the tension in Jamie's voice, the worry. He's already wondering if he should call Dad, what he's supposed to say to Grandpa. He wants to know how bad I am. He doesn't even know the half of it.

"No."

"I didn't think so." He rubs my back, mutters, "Man, you're thin," and I know it's not a compliment. My brother is worried about me. It's not his fault he isn't a fool.

My sobs have turned to silent tears. The only motion is the feel of my brother rocking me as if I were still a little girl who's had a bad dream. But this is one nightmare from which I will never, ever wake.

"Is this the part where I sing?" he asks me. "Mom always sang."

"*Hush, little princes, dead and gone* —" I start softly, but Jamie pulls back and looks at me. He's smiling.

"What?" I ask.

"You. You always get the words wrong."

"No, I don't."

"Yes," he says in that tone that must come standard in the Big Brother package. "You do."

"No. I . . . never mind."

"Fine," Jamie says, and for a long time, he just hugs me. But I can hear him humming under his breath. And when the humming stops, his words are almost a whisper.

"What if I stay?"

"No."

I push away and rub my nose with my sleeve as he tells me, "I could defer. Go back in a semester or two."

"No!" I'm shouting now. Grandpa might hear us, get worried. Come to see what has become of his only grandchildren. But that's not likely, and we both know it. "I'm not going to let you throw West Point away."

"West Point isn't going anywhere."

"I'm not going to be responsible for ruining anybody else's life. I can't . . . I won't do that."

There's nothing my brother can say to that so, to his credit, he doesn't say a thing.

"Get some sleep, Gracie." He pulls me to my feet and pushes me toward the door.

"I'm not tired."

274

"You're exhausted," he says, and a part of me has to admit he might be right because, when I reach the door, I sway a little. I have to hold on to the frame when I turn.

"Jamie?"

My brother looks up at me.

"Alexei is in a cave in the hills, three clicks north of the Iranian embassy."

It takes a moment for the words to register, for their meaning to land. I can't tell if he's relieved or disappointed when he shakes his head.

"You don't want to tell me that."

"He's not far from the hot springs where the two of you used to sneak off and swim. The cave's pretty well hidden. There's just a narrow crack. But you can find it if you're looking."

"Why are you telling me this?"

"Tell the cops. Don't tell the cops. Tell Grandpa. Swarm the place with a SWAT team, I don't care anymore. It's your choice. I'm through."

With Alexei?

With drama?

With taking foolish chances all on my own?

I don't stop to specify because, in truth, I really don't know. I'm just through. With all of it. Most of all, I'm through with trusting my own judgment because, clearly, it's as messed up as my mind.

•　　•　　•

275

Lila and I aren't going to storm the Society. They are welcome to their secrets, and as far as I'm concerned it can stand for another thousand years. When I go back to my room I fall onto my bed and deep into sleep. I don't even dream. The embassy could go up in flames around me, the neighbors could start World War III . . . I wouldn't notice anything. I'm dead to the world.

Or at least it feels that way. I tell myself that's why I don't notice when my door opens. I don't feel the mattress sag. And when a hand presses against my mouth it's why it takes a moment for me to swallow down the instinct to scream.

"Wake up, you little traitor."

I bolt awake and realize Alexei's blue eyes are staring into mine. His face is inches away. "We need to talk."

CHAPTER THIRTY

I'm not afraid.

That's the first thing I realize, aside from the obvious. That Alexei is in my room. That Alexei is in the US embassy. That Alexei knows I told someone his location, and now Alexei has fled his hiding place and come to me.

And Alexei isn't smiling.

It's been days since he's shaved, and dark stubble covers his strong jaw. But his blue eyes are clear and alert as they stare into mine. Alexei is wide awake, but he's not wild. His breathing is slow and even. He's almost the boy I know. Or, at least, the boy I thought I knew.

"If I take my hand away, are you going to scream?" he asks, and, slowly, I shake my head.

"Don't lie to me, Gracie."

And that does it. I wrench myself away from him and roll off the other side of the bed.

"You're telling *me* not to lie to *you*?!"

"You said you would not scream."

"Oh, I can show you screaming . . ."

But Alexei is on me in a flash. "You might want to lower your voice if you don't want your grandfather and a whole host of your American marines to find a killer in your bedroom."

"Maybe that's exactly what I want," I bite out.

Alexei grins. "Once upon a time that would have meant we'd have to marry, you know. It would have been the only honorable thing to do."

"Don't!"

"Don't what?"

"Don't flirt with me. Don't tease me. Don't lie to me."

I'm mad and I don't trust him — not to tell me the truth, not to do anything but hypnotize me with a touch. Mainly, I don't want the reminder of how weak I was, how easily fooled. I don't want to remember being used.

"You've been busy, Gracie."

"You can't call me that anymore," I tell him. "I revoke the privilege."

"Jamie came to see me," Alexei says.

"Did he bring the police with him?" I ask, even though I'm almost afraid of the answer.

He glares at me, betrayed. "I didn't wait around to find out."

He releases me then, moves around my mother's room. When he stops at the window he draws the curtains and blocks out the light. I'd almost forgotten it's still the middle of the day. Time doesn't mean anything to me anymore.

"Why are you here, Alexei?"

"Isn't it obvious? I'm a dangerous murderer and there is a nationwide manhunt. I have more Americans to kill."

"Why are you *here*?" I practically shout. "If you can break into the US you can break into Russia. You'd be safer there. Why are you in my room?"

"Because you and I have unfinished business."

I expect him to grab me or tease me or . . . kiss me. I expect him to shout from the rafters about my betrayal or throw me over his shoulder and drag me away.

But Alexei just stalks into the bathroom and starts pulling out drawers, throwing open cabinets. There's a pack of toothbrushes, and he grabs one, wheels on me.

"This is mine now," he announces. I don't say a thing to protest as Alexei starts to brush his teeth.

I sleep in Dad's old T-shirts, and one is lying on top of my dresser. Alexei grabs it. "This, too!" he says, toothbrush sticking out the side of his mouth, toothpaste foaming on his lips. He looks like a rabid dog.

"Okay." I sit down on the edge of the bed and wait silently as he brushes his teeth and rips off his stained and sweaty shirt. He wets a washcloth and rubs it over his chest, then pulls on my clean shirt. Finally, he leans over the sink and splashes water on his face. When he looks up again, our gazes meet in the mirror.

"You don't look scared," he tells me.

"I'm not."

The look that crosses his face next is one I've seen before: *Maybe she really is crazy.*

"I thought you believed I was a killer."

"And I thought you got a ride home with some kids you didn't know and went straight back to Russia. We've both been disappointed."

Alexei huffs and slowly turns. As he leans against the sink I can feel him studying me. It's not the first time I've watched someone wonder, *What am I going to do with Grace?*

"Jamie probably has shaving stuff," I tell him, but he shakes his head.

"You're not running to Big Brother. Not this time, Gracie. This time you will sit right there. And I'm going to tell you a story."

Alexei doesn't move toward me. I'm happy for that, I think. When he touches me I get stupid, so I vow to never, ever let him touch me again.

He crosses his arms and studies me, as if we have all day, as if this is the most natural thing in the world.

"My mother was Adrian."

It takes a moment for me to register what Alexei's just said, for me to realize that I have never heard him mention his mother before.

"I didn't know that."

"There is no reason you should know. I doubt you ever saw her. She has not been seen by anyone in ten years. Not since she went missing."

"Your mother's missing?"

Alexei looks away for a moment. It's like he doesn't want to face what comes next.

"I know, Gracie. I've always known. About the Society."

"Your mother was a member?" I ask. Alexei nods.

"She . . . and her friends. I used to see them together, meeting in secret, talking in whispers. I watched them obsess over things that disappeared hundreds of years ago. It is rather ironic, is it not? That now she is the thing that is missing?"

"Who exactly were her friends?" I ask, even though I already know at least part of the answer. Alexei must see it in my eyes, because he nods.

"Yes. Your mother was one of them. How do you think Jamie and I became so close? The two of us were pushed together practically in the cradle, told to go play while the three of them did whatever it is they would do."

Alexei reaches into his pocket, pulls out his wallet, and tosses it in my direction. I catch it as he says, "Look." There among the euros is an old snapshot of three women. No, three girls. They're laughing and smiling, so happy as they stand atop the wall with the blue sea stretching to the horizon beyond their shoulders. I stare into my mother's eyes and know I never knew her at all.

"My mother carried that photo with her," he says. "Almost always."

"Alexei . . ." I start to stand, to reach for him, but I'm rooted to the spot. I'm half afraid that if I get any closer he'll jump out the window, never to be seen again.

"What happened the night Spence died?" I ask instead.

"We fought." Alexei shrugs. "And I saw the medallion around his neck and knew it had to do with the Society, so when he went to search the ruins I followed him. I wasn't going to stay behind just because I did not care for the company."

"So you came back via the tunnel? With Spence?"

"Yes."

"The last time I saw the two of you, you were trying to claw each other's eyes out."

"The enemy of my enemy is my friend," Alexei tells me, and in a strange way it makes sense. I can see it. "I did not kill John Spencer."

I think it might be the first time I've heard him say it. And even ten feet away, with his arms crossed and his gaze down, I have to admit that I believe him.

"Did you see anyone when you were down in the Society?"

"No."

"Did anyone see *you*?"

Alexei shakes his head. "I cannot be sure."

282

"Was anyone on the street with you? Were you being followed?"

"No!" Alexei pushes away from the sink and bolts toward me. "I don't know who killed him. I wish I did. I wish I had been there because then . . . It was late, but he was still on American time and wasn't tired. He wanted to look around the city more, and I wanted to come home, so I left him. I did not see him again until the next morning. With you."

I must sit in silence for longer than I realize because eventually Alexei says, "Say something."

"Stay here."

"I can't."

"You're the most wanted man in Adria. This is the US embassy. Can you think of someplace they are *less* likely to look for you? Stay here. In this room. I'll be back."

I'm grabbing my sweater and walking toward the door when Alexei gently takes me by both arms and pulls me closer.

"It's not safe out there," he says, too close to my ear.

"Yeah, well . . ." I look up at him. "Maybe it's not safe in here either."

CHAPTER
THIRTY-ONE

Once, when I was little, my mom took me on a tour of the city.

It wasn't like the tours the real tourists do. No. It was *My Mom's Valancia*, and we spent a whole day, just the two of us, eating gelato from her favorite stands and riding bikes down her favorite streets.

We browsed in the store where she bought her first fancy party dress.

We took charcoal and palettes and tried to sketch her favorite view of the city from high up in the hills.

As the sun set that evening, I held my mother's hand and walked back down Embassy Row, knowing there was no place else in Adria that I ever really needed to visit — that I'd seen everything worth seeing.

I was wrong.

Because now I'm walking into a room that no tourist — no mere mortal — is supposed to ever see.

"Hello, Grace." Princess Ann stretches her arms out as she greets me. "I was so glad to get your call."

The man who escorted me up from the private entrance leaves us and closes the big double doors behind him. I'm filled with a kind of nervous energy that I can't quite hold in.

"I can't believe the phone number my mom had for you was your actual phone number."

At this, the princess laughs, and that makes me remember that she really was my mother's best friend, that once upon a time she was just a regular girl.

Before she married the crown prince of Adria.

Before she gave birth to a future king.

Before my mother died.

Long before I became a killer.

"I'm sorry," I say. "I don't know how I got here exactly, I just . . . You're part of it, aren't you? You're one of them."

Princess Ann considers answering, I can tell. But instead she turns toward the staircase that curves along the edge of the great room, lush red carpet running down its center. It's a staircase meant for a queen.

"Come, Grace, you must be thirsty. I've already rung for tea."

I'm not the kind of girl who has tea parties. Not when I was little. And certainly not now. I was the kind of girl who might set her teacups up along a fence, use them for target practice with her slingshot. But I don't say any of that to the princess of Adria.

She leads me to the massive staircase, then up and up to the fourth floor of the palace.

These are the family rooms, I can tell. The paintings on the walls are all less than three hundred years old. The cheap ones. And the ceilings are lower than in the grand staterooms and ballrooms below. But when she pushes open a wide set of double doors, the room she leads me into is still maybe the most beautiful that I have ever seen. It's smaller than the ballroom, less stately than the entrance where just a few weeks ago I curtsied before the king. No, this room isn't quite that formal, but everything inside it is equally majestic.

Two fireplaces flank it on either end, surrounded by deep chairs covered in soft brown leather. There are plush couches, and tables covered with beautiful pots of orchids and family photos in silver frames. But there is also a soft blanket, an overturned book. Beneath one of the sofas there is a pair of discarded tennis shoes. This isn't where Princess Ann entertains, I realize. It's where she *lives*, and I know it is some great honor just to be here.

But perhaps the most striking thing about this room is the four large windows that dominate the far wall. Black silk curtains run from floor to ceiling and, wordlessly, I'm drawn toward them. When I look outside I see that we are exactly in the palace's center — the gates are right outside — and I remember standing right there, looking up at this very spot while Ms. Chancellor told me a story.

"Is this . . ."

"Yes, Grace," the princess says. "This is where they hung the bodies."

Behind me, doors open and a maid delivers an elegant tray covered with the things for tea. But even the splendor of this room and all the trappings of the palace can't keep me from the windows and the scene that is playing out down below.

"They're setting up for tonight," the princess says. I hadn't realized she'd come so close.

"What's tonight?" I ask.

Princess Ann looks at me, surprise all over her face. "You don't know?"

I shake my head, stare back at the window. "Mom didn't like the festival. She always kept us away from it. She said it was dangerous."

Gently, Ann reaches out and touches the glass. "It is."

Down below, workers are stringing lights throughout the square and over the sidewalks. Vendors are setting up carts draped with fabrics in white and red. And in the center of it all, the fire still burns.

For the first time, I see it all through the eyes of the woman beside me. When a group of tourists look up at the palace and start taking pictures, I expect her to step away, but she just shakes her head, reading my mind.

"The glass is one-way," she says. "And bulletproof."

Every girl thinks about growing up in a palace. Few ever ponder living in a cage.

"What's tonight?" I ask.

"It's the fourth night," Princess Ann tells me. "The Night of a Thousand Amelias."

"What does that mean?" I ask.

She looks at me. "Your mother *really* never told you?"

"No." I shake my head. "She didn't want us anywhere near here during the festival. We weren't even allowed out after dark."

"I'm not surprised," Princess Ann says. "Caroline knew what this really is."

"What is it?" I ask, even though I'm half afraid of the answer.

"It is a fourteen-day celebration of a time when people like them killed people like me."

I've never thought of it like that — how it must feel to look out every night onto that scene, knowing.

"The royal family is very popular now," I say, but Princess Ann just laughs.

"You are sweet to say so, Grace. Just like your mother."

It is the perfect time to change the topic, to ask her what she knows about my mother's death and my mother's work and all the ways the two things are intertwined. But for some reason I can't. Not yet.

"Why does the royal family allow it?" I ask instead.

"Because perhaps allowing people to remember history will help us all be less anxious to repeat it."

"I see," I say, even though I don't. Not really.

"Come, Grace," the princess says. "Your tea is getting cold."

I follow Princess Ann around to sit on one of the straight-backed chairs that face the window. She pours me a cup and adds a generous dose of honey without asking how I take it.

"You knew," I say as she hands me the cup.

The princess smiles. "You are very like your mother. I couldn't imagine you would take it in any other way."

"Thank you," I say, but I'm not talking about the tea. I am grateful for the compliment, until I remember all of my mother's secrets. Maybe being just like her is not such a great way to be after all.

"This is the worst night," Princess Ann volunteers after a moment. She sips her own tea, places the cup gently on her saucer. "I always sit in this room — in this chair — on the fourth night."

"Why?" I ask.

"Ms. Chancellor should tell you," she says, as if I've just asked where babies come from and she wants nothing more than to avoid an awkward conversation.

"Please. What happened on the fourth night?" Suddenly, the room is cold even here, on the Mediterranean in the middle of summer.

I watch the princess weigh her options, contemplate what she should and should not say.

"You say your mother never allowed you to attend the festival, but you know the reason for it, don't you?"

"I know the royal family was murdered, and that it started a war." I study Princess Ann. "And I know about the treasure."

For a while, the moment stretches out, the silence hangs heavy between us. "What do you know about it?"

"Ms. Chancellor told me everything," I try.

"I doubt that, Grace, because no one knows everything. Three elders came to the palace the night of the coup. They salvaged what they could, but died before they could tell anyone the details."

I nod.

"It must have been chaos," Ann says. For a moment I wonder if she's even really talking to me. "They say it was an angry mob, but it wasn't, you know. In truth it was no more than a dozen people who stormed the palace. At first. Did they come intent on murder? I don't know. I've often wondered, though. Maybe all they wanted was food for their families? Maybe it simply got out of hand? Or did they come up those stairs intending to kill? Does it make me a bad person if I think it was the latter?" She doesn't really wait for an answer. "Because I do, Grace. I really do. I think they came to kill."

Ann holds her teacup in her hand, but she doesn't sip, doesn't move. It's almost like she's frozen, looking back in time.

"Those windows," she says after a long moment. Then her cup begins to shake. Hurriedly, she places it back on the table. "They hung the bodies from those windows, like trophies. Like a warning. They hung their bodies from those windows," Princess Ann says, stronger now, "until the fourth night, when the Society came and cut them down."

I can't help myself. I look at the windows before me, now tinted and bulletproof and bordered by black silk. There's no way to see what actually happened, but this room carries the truth inside it still. And maybe it's just the sadness radiating off of Princess Ann, but I swear I can feel it.

"The Society did that?" I ask.

Princess Ann nods. "They came through a passageway and smuggled the bodies out of the palace. They took them and buried them. I don't know where. No one knows, and that's probably for the best. They deserve to rest in peace."

My tea has gone cold in front of me. I've lost all desire to drink it. So I just sit here, thinking about how the king and his family are just people, and for two weeks every year an entire nation celebrates the moment their ancestors died.

"I'm surprised your mother never told you," Princess Ann says.

Now my teacup is shaking too. "There were a lot of things my mother never told me."

She must hear the bitterness in my voice. She has no trouble guessing why.

"She never told you about the Society?"

"She never told me about *anything*."

"You mustn't blame your mother, Grace. She loved you so. She just wanted to protect you."

"From what?" I snap. Ann is not the princess of Adria now. She is my mother's first and best friend.

She is someone who might have answers.

"Tell me," I demand.

Ann smiles. I suppose very few people ever make demands of princesses. "Tell you what, Grace?"

"Tell me everything. About the Society. And the treasure. And your other friend — my friend Alexei's mother. Do you know what happened to her? Why did someone want my mother to die?"

Ann stands. "We found out when we were about your age, I suppose. Your grandmother had passed away, but one day Ms. Chancellor and my mother came to us. Caroline and I had always been friends, but when we learned that we were descended from the daughters of the founders . . . when we learned we had that in common — that in that way we were more like sisters than friends — then we became much, much closer. I suppose you might even say we grew obsessed."

"With the Society?" I ask.

Slowly, Ann shakes her head. "With *history*."

It's such a strange response it takes me a moment to truly hear it.

"What did she find? Why did someone want her dead?"

"Grace —"

"Don't deny it!" I stand too, unable to sit corralled inside some fancy chair. "I know she was obsessed with something."

At last, Ann looks surprised. "You do?"

"Was it the treasure the Society smuggled out of the palace the night of the coup? Was it something else? Did she find it? Is that why they tried to kill her?"

I watch Princess Ann's brown eyes, wait for her to carefully word her denial. But the denial doesn't come.

"Oh, Grace," Ann says instead. "Your mother loved antiques, and she loved secrets. I think perhaps she did find . . . something. But I don't know what."

"What was she working on?"

"You have to understand, your mother and I hadn't been truly close in years. When I married, it was difficult to maintain ties to my old life — my life before *this*." She gestures at the palace and all its trappings, but also its loneliness. It feels like we must be the only people here.

"But you know she was still looking for it, don't you? You know about the treasure."

I'm deadly serious, but Princess Ann almost laughs. "The treasure, if you want to call it that, disappeared two centuries ago. It won't be found now. When we were girls we thought it exciting and fanciful. It was our own little adventure. But we grew up, Grace."

"I know you got together as grown-ups. I know you were still looking after Jamie was born."

"After Jamie was born we would get together as friends."

"What happened to Alexei's mother?"

"I don't know," Ann says. "Karina was always a bit . . . wild. She had an unhappy marriage. When she went away, Caroline and I did not ask too many questions."

"You think she abandoned her child?"

"We didn't know what to think. But a part of me did wonder. I saw less and less of my friends in those days. I was desperate to have my own child, and I was selfish. I forgot about my friends. But after Karina disappeared, your mother told me she still searched for the treasure — that that had become her job within the Society — and I grew worried. I told your mother to forget it. To be honest, I thought she had."

Slowly, the princess turns to me, a sad smile on her face. "Oh, how I wish she had." Princess Ann is one of the most beautiful women in the world, but right now she looks like she wants to cry. I know the feeling. There is nothing worse than remembering.

"Now, Grace. I need you to tell me the truth: Are you here with your grandfather's permission?"

"Yes." The lie is automatic now.

"*Grace.*" Princess Ann's voice is a warning. She sounds just like . . . a mother. "If your grandfather is at the embassy right now, worrying about where you might be —"

"He's not." This much, at least, is true. "He's not worried. I promise. I told someone where I was going." If Princess Ann doubts my lie she doesn't say so.

"Forgive me," she says. "Motherhood has this effect on a person. I worry about my son every day."

"Oh. Yeah. I'm sure you do."

"Your mother said that someday we would make the two of you get married and then we'd truly be family. Did she tell you?"

I choke on my tea, and Ann laughs.

"Don't worry, darling. We never actually signed the betrothal contracts."

The look on my face makes her laugh even harder.

"Oh, Grace. I am so glad you called."

It's funny how, until this summer, I'd never really realized that my mother was a girl once. Sure, I always knew that she'd grown up in Valancia, that the embassy was her childhood home, and yet I'd never thought about the fact that my mother had once been a *child*.

Like me.

No wonder someone tried to kill her.

"Excuse me, Your Highness." I turn and see a man in full livery standing by the doors. "I am sorry to interrupt, but the young lady's escort is here to return her to the embassy."

"I don't have an escort," I say, but then Dominic appears over the footman's shoulder.

"Please excuse the interruption, Your Highness, but the ambassador has asked me to bring Grace home," the Scarred Man says. "It is no night for her to be out alone."

I could argue, but then I remember the bonfires and the crowds and the chaos. I remember bodies hanging from four beautiful windows, and that, no matter how high your walls are, no one is ever truly safe. It's no wonder my grandfather has sent Dominic to find me.

I turn back to Princess Ann one final time. An hour ago I'd hoped that someone who knew the girl my mother was might be able to explain what happened to the woman she became. But that's not meant to be, I guess.

"Thank you for the tea," I say, because I can't thank her for the answers.

"It was my pleasure, dear." Ann pulls me into a hug too tight to be anything but real. When she pulls away she actually pauses for a moment, pushes a stray bit of hair out of my face and tucks it behind my ear. A motherly gesture.

It makes me want to cry.

CHAPTER
THIRTY-TWO

Dominic doesn't speak. Doesn't smile. I'm walking beside him, trying to keep up. When he leads me through the palace gates I look for a black car with the little US flags flying near the head-lights, but the circle drive is empty. I guess we're going to walk.

The sun is nearly down, and soon the streets will be black and lit by fire. We're walking quickly through the crowds that are fil-ing toward the palace, over cobblestones and curbs. Tonight, the crowd is different. Most of the men wear long black capes and ornate masks. Women and young girls dance in flowing white dresses with red sashes. Most have flowers in their hair.

It's beautiful.

And it's insanely creepy.

Dominic holds me tight, pulling me against the tide of people flowing toward the palace. I should be happy to have his arm around my shoulder, to feel his big, steady, and intimidating presence beside me. I stumble once, but he holds me so firmly I don't even start to fall.

"Grandpa sent you?" I ask.

He grunts something that sounds like *yes*, and we keep walking.

"He didn't know where I was," I tell him, but Dominic shakes his head.

"*I* knew where you were, Grace Olivia."

Of course he did.

"How is your injury?" Dominic asks.

"My what?" It says a lot about me that I don't even notice the ache of a stab wound anymore, that a part of me is so utterly immune to pain. "It's fine. I mean, it hurts. But I'm used to that."

Then, as if on cue, a wave of tourists passes by us, jostling me closer to him. "You should never have left the embassy. It was foolish to come."

Now that Dominic has mentioned it, my side starts to ache. I feel out of breath. Aware.

"What were you thinking, leaving the embassy tonight of all nights? Are you listening to me? You aren't safe here!"

"I am safe! I'm fine."

I'm not fine, and standing before me is one of the few people on the planet who really knows it — who will ever know why.

As the sky grows darker, the crowds grow thicker. People push recklessly toward the palace, too close. Too strong. It's different from the first night somehow, and I'm not the only one who feels it, because Dominic reaches for me, tucks me protectively under his arm.

"Masks are dangerous things," he says. "They make people feel anonymous, immune. They give people license to act as they otherwise wouldn't dare. This is no time to be out of the embassy."

"That's okay," I say, "you're here to protect me."

I'm not being flippant. This isn't my idea of a joke. It is the truth, and I know it. I watch him move — see how strong he is — and even as I know that I am safe, another thought is coming to me. My brother's words come rushing back.

It's hard to break somebody's neck, Jamie said. It would take someone strong. And fast. And trained.

It would take someone like Dad.

The Scarred Man is about as much like my father as one man could possibly be. I suppose my mother had a type.

And with that realization, a cold sense of dread bubbles up within me. A realization dawns.

"You."

It's easier than it should be for me to pull myself free of the Scarred Man's grasp. I think he's too shocked. But he, of all people, should know better than to underestimate me and all of my crazy.

"You were there. You saw us that night, when Jamie and I got back from the island."

"Grace, this isn't the time."

When he reaches for me I pull away. "No. I saw you! And you heard us fighting about Spence, didn't you? You knew he tried something. You said you'd always keep me safe."

"I will."

"Did you kill him?"

The look on the Scarred Man's face chills me to the bone. "If *I* had killed a man who hurt you, Grace Olivia, they would have never found the body."

He's not joking, and that's what scares me. Dominic could kill, would kill — no doubt has killed. But he wouldn't hurt me, I know it in my soul, and I realize something strange: I'm the only person in Adria who actually trusts the Scarred Man.

Maybe this makes me even more of a fool.

Or maybe it just makes me safe.

"You belong in your embassy," Dominic says, and nudges me forward.

The crowds are growing thicker, the sky darker. Someone must have lit more bonfires because the smell of smoke carries on the wind.

"I'm going to get you to tell me, you know," I say, but I don't glance back as I start down the hill. "About my mom and the island and whatever it is you think you can't tell me. I'm going to get it out of you. I'm . . ."

The Scarred Man is silent. Too silent.

And when I turn back, he's already gone.

CHAPTER
THIRTY-THREE

I stand for a moment, wondering what to do. But the current is too strong, and soon I'm pushed with the crowd. Even though the embassy is in the other direction, I can't fight it. I am surrounded by people in masks and capes and long white dresses draped in red.

The sun is down, but it's not dark. Not exactly. Not yet. The gaslights are growing brighter, though, and the bonfire still burns.

Firecrackers erupt in the street, and I jump. It sounds like gunfire, and I find myself pressed against the brick of one of the buildings, rocking.

"Hush, little princess . . ."

Maybe it's the smoke, but I feel my eyes begin to water. I will not allow myself to cry. I will not crumble. I will not turn to ash and blow away like the tiny sparks and embers that fly up from the bonfire and float like fireflies out to sea.

"Dead and gone . . ."

The words come to me through the darkness, and I want to scream.

"No one's gonna know you're coming home . . ."

"Grace!" I hear my mother's cries.

"Grace!" my mother screams, and I find it harder and harder to breathe because I'm surrounded by smoke and masks and the sky is the color of fire.

"Hush, little princess, wait and see . . ."

"Grace!" the word comes again, and I know these women in white dresses are each my mother's ghost.

When I feel a hand on my arm I want to fight and run, but the man in the mask is gripping me too hard. It's too dark and I'm too tired. I lash out, pushing and fighting with all that I have. I grab the offending hand and step to the side, spinning. But then the voice calls again, "Grace!"

With his free hand, Noah removes his mask. He leans down and looks into my eyes.

"Grace, it's me!"

I'm breathing so hard now the air doesn't actually reach my lungs.

Noah frees himself of my grasp and reaches for me again. Then he seems to think better of it.

Another man in a mask bangs into me, his elbow landing in my side, and I cry out. I think about another day, another mob. The knife wound in my side. The mob that was after Alexei. After me.

And just that quickly I can feel the panic take me, the air being pulled from my lungs. There are just too many people — just too much smoke.

"Jamie," I tell Noah. "I need Jamie."

When Megan appears at Noah's side, she's breathing hard, laughing. I can tell she's been dancing around the fire. Her long black hair is swept back and tied with a red bow at the base of her neck. Her white dress is long and flowing, old-fashioned and high-waisted. It's like she's danced here from a dream.

"Grace!" she exclaims, breathless. "You came!"

"Was Jamie at the embassy when you left?"

It's loud, and Megan can't hear me, so I yell again.

"Was Jamie at the embassy?"

"I don't know," Megan says, shaking her head. "I haven't seen him. Grace, what's wrong?"

"I have to get back to the embassy," I say, even though I have no idea what will come next. I can't think that far ahead. This is no chess game. It's my life. And it is spiraling out of control.

"Hush, little princess . . ."

"Stop it!" I yell, putting my hands over my ears, trying to block out the song that is echoing over and over in my mind. "Stop it!"

"Stop what?" Noah asks.

"That singing. It's —"

In my mind, I start to say. But Noah is shaking his head and rolling his eyes.

"They'll sing it all night," he says, as if he is annoyed, too. He has no right to be bothered, I think. The song's not inside *his* head.

But then I realize that if it's not in Noah's head, then it isn't in mine either. Noah gestures at the crowd, at the men in their capes and masks and the women and girls in their dresses. I catch glimpses of red sashes waving in the firelight. It's like seeing splashes of blood.

"They always sing it on the Night of a Thousand Amelias," Noah says, as if it's a simple fact, common knowledge, as obvious as the sun rising in the east.

"The what?" I think Princess Ann said something like that too, but she didn't explain it.

"The Night of a Thousand Amelias," Noah says. "You know how on the fourth night the masked men came and cut down the bodies of the royal family? The king and queen and the children were all wearing these white nightgowns or sleep shirts or whatever, but they'd been stabbed so many times there were big red streaks like —"

"I get it, Noah."

I recall Ms. Chancellor's words, the image of white muslin glowing in the moonlight except where it was stained with blood, and I think I'm going to be sick.

"Well" — Noah is getting into it now — "legend has it the royal family comes back every year and haunts the mob who killed them. So every year the women pretend to be little Amelia, all grown up and out for revenge."

He gives me his Evil Laugh, but I just think about Princess Ann watching from her window. Noah doesn't know his story is terrifying in a totally different way.

"The men dress in masks and capes like the men who came on the fourth night to cut the bodies down," he finishes.

"They weren't men," I say, but the crowd is so loud that no one hears me. In fact, if anything, the song grows even louder. My mother's voice is singing.

"Hush, little princess . . ."

"Grace, are you okay?" Megan asks from beside me.

I shake my head slowly. "My mother used to sing this song."

"Everybody in Adria sings this song."

The firecrackers erupt again, their sparks flying up and filling the small side street that stretches up the hill. The gaslights are brighter now in the darkness; the street almost glows with an eerie, smoky haze.

This isn't right. I shouldn't be here. Dominic was right, but now Dominic is gone. In my head, my mother sings and I smell smoke, and I'm afraid I'm going to be sick all over Megan and her pretty white dress.

Something is wrong, I know it.

When I see the dark figure striding through the smoke, back-lit by the glow of the torches, I can't help myself. I start to shake.

"Spence," I say. I could swear I'm talking to a ghost.

Even when the smoke fades and the figure becomes clear, the words on his jacket support the lie. "Spence." I read the name and struggle to breathe.

"Gracie!" It's Jamie's voice, but I'm still shaking as my brother draws closer and pulls off his mask. "You're here," he says, but I'm grabbing him, clawing, as he asks, "What's wrong?"

"I thought you were Spence. I thought . . . *Spence*," I mutter. My gaze goes to the words embroidered on the jacket my brother wears.

"It's his." Jamie's voice is solemn, and he doesn't look me in the eye. "They got swapped and —"

"He was wearing your jacket."

Suddenly it all makes sense, but I'd give anything for it to go back to being a mystery. Sometimes the answer is far worse than the question.

"They thought it was you," I say, the words lost amid the firecrackers and the singing, the roar of the flames and the people dancing in the streets.

"Grace!" Jamie grabs my arms and shakes me. He makes me look into his eyes. But all I can remember are Dominic's words.

You're not safe.

There is no one on earth who knows all of my secrets. I've dug too deep, hidden them too well. But Jamie comes the closest. He knew the girl who jumped from the wall and the monster that lay strapped to a bed, out of her head with grief and guilt and terror. My brother has seen my demons and he knows my ghosts, but the specter that is after me now haunts us both.

"Jamie, listen to me!" I yell, but my brother has a death grip on my arm; he's trying to drag me away from the crowds. I'm happy to let him steer me, but I also have to make him see.

"Jamie, listen to me! Spence was wearing your coat."

Noah and Megan are fading away. People push between us.

They must know this is sibling stuff — family drama. They don't even try to follow.

"Jamie, stop!" I yell, and pull free of his grasp. "Listen to me!" I grab his arms then, hold him still and make him look into my eyes.

"Are you feeling okay?" he asks.

"Jamie," I say again. "Spence was in your coat when he died. What if they thought they were killing you?"

But Jamie doesn't see. Of course he doesn't.

My brother scoffs and looks away. He can't face me. But then he turns back, and the look in his eyes is even worse than his scorn or my shame. It is worry. My brother is so worried about me that even James Blakely Jr. of West Point is about to cry.

"Gracie," he says, reaching for my face.

A part of me wants to sink into his touch, to be a little girl again, safe within the reach of my big brother. But I can't be Gracie the screwup right now, not the daredevil and not the freak. I can't be the girl who got strapped to the bed. I have to be the one who was brave enough to jump from the wall. I have to make him notice.

"The man wasn't a burglar!" I snap, and push his hand away.

"What man?" Jamie asks, and I can tell he honestly doesn't know.

"The intruder, the one in Mom's shop. When she died, he wasn't there to rob her; he was there to kill her. I thought he *had* killed her."

"Don't think about that, Gracie —"

307

"Someone wanted our mother dead, Jamie! They sent a man to murder her, and I —"

I killed her.

I killed her.

I killed her.

"Someone wanted her dead!" I shout, because I have to do something besides remember the truth — that she wouldn't actually be dead if it weren't for me.

"Gracie, let's get you back to the embassy."

"Don't." I push away from my brother's grasp. "Jamie, you have to listen to me. Will you listen? When Mom was a girl, she got involved in something. She found out something. Someone tried to have her killed, but the Scarred Man came, and —"

They're the wrong words.

For too long, Jamie heard me rant and scream about the Scarred Man. For years, Dominic was the thing that went bump in the night, the monster under my bed. My brother can't possibly know that he's my friend now.

"Don't look at me that way."

"What way?" Jamie asks. "Come on, Gracie. Let's just go home. I want to go home. Don't you?"

I don't have a home.

"They tried to kill her, Jamie! And then . . . What if they tried to kill you?"

I say it as clearly, as plainly, as I can. I don't rush, and I look him squarely in the eye.

I do my best not to sound crazy.

All around us, the crowd swells and crashes closer, jarring Jamie and pushing him against me.

"Gracie, I —"

But the words don't come. He doesn't chastise or patronize. I'd give anything to hear my brother say there is no Scarred Man. I'd even give anything for it to be true.

Because what happens next is worse. So, so much worse.

Jamie looks at me, surprise etched on his face. It's like he's dragged his feet across the carpet and gotten a shock, stubbed his toe. Then the look morphs into dread and understanding.

It's the look of someone who — at last — believes me.

"Gracie?" He opens Spence's jacket, then stumbles forward.

My brother is falling. I see the red splash of blood that is spreading across his white T-shirt, covering his side. A scream rises in my throat, but the sound is lost amid the chaos of the festival.

Was he stabbed? Was he shot? No one is screaming and running away. So it's almost peaceful as I watch my brother crumble.

I'm reaching for him, but he's so much bigger than I am, too heavy for me. I feel him slip through my grasp, dead weight.

Dead.

I scream, "Jamie!" But then he stops falling. His arm is dragged around a man's neck as the dark figure takes Jamie's weight. The man's mask covers his face, but I know the blue eyes that stare back at me.

My heart pounds as Alexei yells, "Run!"

CHAPTER
THIRTY-FOUR

My brother isn't dead, but he's still bleeding. Even in the dark, I can see the color fading from his face. And yet he stays upright, his arm slung around Alexei's broad shoulders. His feet move, but I know it's only because Alexei refuses to let him slip away. I push ahead through the crowd, trying to make room, blaze a path, but to where I have no clue.

"They shot him," I say, glancing back toward Alexei. "Or they stabbed him. I don't know!"

Alexei's mask is gone, forgotten. And Jamie looks up at his oldest friend and says, "I'm okay . . ."

"Shut up," Alexei snaps. "Save your strength."

"I'm fine." Jamie struggles to pull his arm from around Alexei's shoulders, but when he does he stumbles, and Alexei catches him.

"I've got you," Alexei says.

"I know," Jamie replies.

This is how boys make up, I decide. Some bloodshed, a mob, and a few terse words, not a single one of which is *sorry*.

"Can we save the man hugging for later?" I snap. For once, it seems, I am the mature one.

When I look back, I see the blood that covers Jamie's shirt. He's trying to press against the wound with his free hand, but it's not working. My brother is going to bleed to death, die right in front of me. And I can't watch that happen. Not again. Not to somebody else I love.

"Stop!" I tell Alexei, and rush to press against Jamie's side. His wound isn't like mine. It's deeper. The blood is almost black, and the harder my brother's heart pumps, the more it tries to kill him.

"We cannot stop here," Alexei says. I'm not sure Jamie even hears us. Sweat beads on his brow and his skin looks like ashes. "It's not safe."

Alexei's right and I know it. But still I stay by my brother's side. I rip off my cardigan and push it to his wound.

"We have to get to the embassy," I tell him.

"We have to get to a hospital!" Alexei shouts.

But I'm shaking my head. What was a wild theory five minutes ago is now unequivocal fact. "They thought Spence was him. That's why they killed him. And they're not gonna stop. They'll find him at the hospital, Alexei. They'll find him, and . . ."

Alexei searches the crowd, but for what I don't think either of us knows.

I think about another night in another crowd. I was stabbed, but now I know it was no coincidence, no accident. Maybe I wasn't simply in the wrong place at the wrong time. I was *stabbed*! And maybe Jamie was, too. Maybe he was shot. I can't even tell amid the darkness and the blood. Is the threat on some rooftop or just behind us, closing in?

"We have to get to the embassy," I say one more time, searching the crowd for Dominic. Dominic will know how to field dress the wound. He'll keep Jamie alive, keep me safe. He won't let Caroline's children die. Of that much I am certain.

We just have to find him and get to him and stay one step ahead of whatever or whoever is out here, hunting us.

"We should go into the tunnels," Alexei says, and maybe he's right, but at least among the crowd we are somewhat sheltered. We are in a forest of people, dodging among the trees. And I can't imagine that whoever is after us doesn't know about the tunnels — that they won't be able to follow us there, inside the darkness and the echoing chambers. And, besides, I'm finished hiding. If I'm going to die it's going to be in a place where I can see the stars.

"Grace," Alexei shouts. "Gracie!"

Jamie's eyes are closed, but he's still breathing.

We're running out of time.

I turn, searching the crowds for Noah or Lila or Megan, for someone on my grandfather's staff. We need a bulletproof car. We need fences and shelter and a fortress.

A palace.

I start pushing through the crowd, shouting, clawing my way toward the gates. The windows are right in front of me. I can see them, and even though I can't see her, I know she's up there, watching through that one-way glass.

"Ann!" I yell, as if she'll be able to hear me. I risk turning loose of my brother and wave with both arms, jumping up and down. "Help us! Help us!"

Alexei stares at me, dumbfounded. "Gracie, we have to go."

"We need help," I tell him.

"Yes, so we must . . ." But Alexei trails off as, slowly, the gates swing open.

I look at him and take up Jamie's arm. "Come on."

The guards recognize me. I was just here, they know. I was a personal guest of Princess Ann's, so one of the men rushes toward us.

"We need to see the princess," I say. "Now!"

But even I am a little surprised when the doors swing open, and the most wanted man in Adria and I drag an ambassador's unconscious grandson into the palace's halls.

Inside the palace walls there is a different kind of chaos.

Guards swarm around us. Two men take Jamie from Alexei and me, dragging him away. We are in a gleaming hallway and my brother is getting blood all over their good rug. I want to apologize, to ask for some paper towels so I might clean up the mess. But I'm too numb. I'm shaking, reaching out for Jamie.

I yell out his name, but my brother doesn't answer. His eyelids flutter and his legs go weak.

Princess Ann is before me now, gripping my arms.

"Grace!" she yells. "Look at me! Are you hurt?"

"Jamie's been shot. Or stabbed. I don't know. He's bleeding. He's lost a lot of blood."

"I know. But, Grace, are *you* okay? Were you hit?"

Was I? I wonder. I was stabbed and didn't realize it until the adrenaline wore off. Maybe . . . "I don't know. I don't think so."

"It's okay, Grace. You're with me now. You're going to be okay."

"I knew you were there," I say. "In the window. I knew you were watching. And that you'd help. And . . . Where are they taking Jamie?"

"These are my private guards, Grace. They can be trusted."

I want to breathe. I want it to be okay. But more than anything, I want to be back in the embassy, on US soil, safe and sound.

I just want Jamie to be safe.

"Someone shot Jamie," I mutter again, because it's only just now sinking in. "Or was he stabbed?" It's a big thing not to know, but a silly thing to wonder. Does it even matter? My brother might die either way.

Ann holds me steady. "I never should have let you leave."

"Why would anyone want to shoot Jamie?"

For a moment, it looks as if Ann might actually tell me, but she just grips me by the shoulders, steers me down a long hall.

"Dominic was with me," I say. "But then he wasn't."

"Yes. Dominic has always been protective of the women in your family. Now come. We have to get you away, Grace."

"Wait." I stop and look around. "I need to go with Jamie. Where's Alexei?"

"Don't worry about them."

"I need to see my brother. Take me to him."

People don't give orders to princesses. I watch Ann process this fact, see her start to speak, but before she can say a word, alarms sound. Ann gasps and jumps as the doors swing open and armed guards swarm the room, yelling and running. Only Dominic stands still among the chaos.

It takes me a moment to realize that he has a death grip on Alexei's arm and he's not smiling. The most wanted man in Adria is inside the palace, just feet away from the future queen. Maybe that's why Ann's face morphs from fear to confusion to anger.

"What's going on here?" she says.

"I'm sorry for the disturbance, Your Highness, but as you can see we have the fugitive in custody. You're safe now," Dominic reports.

Ann was safe before they burst through the doors, but I don't say so. I'm too relieved to see Alexei and Dominic, to know that they're both still okay.

Dominic tugs Alexei's arm and stares at me. "We're sorry to disturb you, ma'am. But don't worry. It's over. I'll escort your guests home, and I apologize again for this. Come on, Grace — we need to get you and your brother home. Now."

He gives Alexei's arm a shake, and before I can say anything, Dominic turns and I follow. With one quick glance back at Princess Ann, I rush toward the doors.

Outside, a van idles. There are no cameras, no cops. There's only Dominic and the palace guards.

"This boy's been injured!" someone yells in Adrian, but Dominic is already there, calmly directing the men who are carrying Jamie on a gurney, sliding it into the van. Alexei follows, but I stay in Dominic's arms, screaming without making a sound.

CHAPTER THIRTY-FIVE

Dominic's sleeves are rolled up and his hands are inside my brother's chest — they're *inside his chest*, I realize, and I think I'm going to be sick. But I can't stop looking as Jamie lies on the table in the formal dining room — the very place where just days ago Spence told Ms. Chancellor about his family, where Jamie and Grandpa passed looks between them as if *I* was the one who would never be okay again.

Chaos surrounds us.

I can hear Grandpa yelling in the hall.

"This is Ambassador William Blakely. I want a helicopter and I want it now! You tell the general I don't care who he has to get out of bed or dig up from the grave, there will be a chopper on the roof of this embassy within the hour. Do you hear me?"

"Maybe we *should* go to a hospital," I say, terrified I was wrong, that my foolishness might cost my brother his life.

But Dominic looks at me. "We can't secure the hospital, Grace Olivia. Not in time."

The embassy is my country — not Adria. The embassy is safe.

Bloody rags are thrown to the floor. People run in and out, bringing medical supplies from I-don't-know-where.

There should be doctors.

There should be nurses and bright lights and rooms so clean they stink with the smell of antiseptic.

This isn't some third-world country, and yet my brother lies on a dining room table. Saline bags hang from a chandelier. And I can hear marines running in the hallways, making sure the embassy is secure, trying to keep us safe.

Then my brother coughs. Blood runs from his lips, and I know it's too late. Jamie is anything but safe.

"Where's the blasted helicopter?" my grandfather keeps shouting.

"Grace, you shouldn't be here." Ms. Chancellor tries to touch me but I cringe and jerk away. "Grace, dear, come with me."

"I won't leave him," I say.

"He wouldn't want you to see him like this."

She means it wouldn't be good for me to see a second member of my family die right before my eyes. But I don't care. If Jamie dies, then that fact in itself will kill me. So I don't move an inch.

"Someone get me some light!" Dominic yells. "I need light!"

"Here." The flashlight is always in my pocket now. I take it out, hold it as steady as I can.

The lights are off in the dining room, as if that will help Jamie rest. Only a single spotlight shines down upon my brother's bloody chest. I want to whisper into his ear, tell him not to follow the light. But maybe Mom is at the end of it. Maybe I'm just jealous that I can't go, too.

"Will someone tell me what is happening now?"

"No." Dominic's tone tells me that it isn't up for debate. He's not my father, not my grandfather. He doesn't even work at the embassy. But my brother's blood is still all over his hands. I'm not going to complain.

"The army has a wonderful medical facility at their base in Germany. We'll get him there," Ms. Chancellor says. "If we can."

If.

I look at them then, Dominic and Ms. Chancellor — really look at them. At what it is they aren't saying.

"You should get some rest, dear," Ms. Chancellor says, but I pull away from her.

"Tell me. Now." I'm trying to be calm, to be cool. And that's what scares them. "Why is someone after my family? Why are they out to kill us?"

Ms. Chancellor and Dominic share a look. He says, "If it were up to me, I would have told her years ago."

"Tell me now," I say again, and wait for Ms. Chancellor to do just that.

"Grace, two hundred years ago, during the coup, palace guards abandoned their posts and threw open the gates. As you know, members of the Society went that night to try to salvage what they could. It was too late, though, to save the king and queen and princes, and the palace was bedlam. Looters and murderers, thieves . . . It was a nightmare, but sometimes chaos serves a purpose. And that night, among the chaos, one of the royal nursemaids was able to hide a very small baby in her arms —"

"Amelia lived," I say, and let the words wash over me. I look up at Ms. Chancellor. *The treasure.*"

"Yes, dear. When the Society came, they found the princess and her nurse. Of course, they had also gathered some records and artifacts and other items as well," Ms. Chancellor adds. "But Amelia was without a doubt the most valuable thing taken from the palace that night."

"Was she really lost?" I ask in disbelief.

Ms. Chancellor considers this and answers carefully. "Yes. In a sense."

"They lost a baby?"

"No. The elders *hid* a baby. There were four baby girls born to Society members that spring — all at about the same time. Their mothers brought them to the headquarters that night and the babies were wrapped in identical blankets. And then *five* Society members took daughters home, the idea being that no one would ever know exactly which child was Amelia."

"*Hush, little princess, wait and see. No one's gonna know that you are me,*" I sing. "*Princess.* Not *princes.* Jamie was right. I did always get the words wrong." I have to laugh a little. And then, desperately, I want to cry.

Ms. Chancellor shrugs, smiles a sad smile. "It's just a nursery rhyme. But all nursery rhymes begin with a kernel of truth."

"What does this have to do with my mother?" I ask, spinning on them. I'm tired of playing games.

"Now, Grace, you must understand that your mother was only interested in the history — the overwhelming historical significance of Amelia's story. She didn't know what she would find, or that it would lead to any of this."

"Tell me!"

"Amelia didn't just survive, Grace. She lived. She grew into adulthood and married and had a child of her own. And that child had children and so on and so on. And now it's too late to change what has happened — to change what your mother discovered."

"Tell me," I say, because I know there's more; I can see it in her eyes and feel it in my gut. I think, deep down, a part of me has always known it.

"Ms. Chancellor, tell me!" I demand, but before she can say a word, Alexei appears in the doorway and says, "The helicopter is here."

He and Dominic pick up Jamie's stretcher and rush him up the stairs to the embassy's roof. The wind is strong here. I can hear the flag flapping, the chain pinging against the metal pole. Overhead, the helicopter's blades keep whirling, not slowing down. There isn't a minute to lose, I know.

"Get in!" Dominic orders Alexei, who doesn't argue. He's sitting by Jamie's head like an anchor, refusing to let his best friend drift away. "Both of you," he tells me, but I look back at Ms. Chancellor.

"You have to go with him, dear," Ms. Chancellor says.

"Tell me!" I demand one final time.

The Scarred Man is the only one who'll meet my gaze. For years, I saw his face in my nightmares, the shadow in my dreams. Three years ago he came to my mother's shop, but that wasn't when this started. No. Our path was set ages ago, wrapped in a blanket and carried away. A secret hidden for centuries.

"Grace Olivia," the Scarred Man says, "you are the lost princess of Adria."

Before I can ask a question, say a word, Dominic pushes me into the chopper then follows, slamming the door.

I feel the helicopter rising, floating above the embassy. It's like this secret has been weighing us down for years and now, without those lies to tether us, my brother and I are floating free, weightless and directionless like balloons released into a strong wind.

The embassies recede. The great wall of Adria grows smaller and smaller. And smaller. It feels like maybe I've jumped again, but this time I do not fall; I just keep rising.

Behind us, the sun is coming up over Valancia, casting the city in its golden glow. Ahead of us, the blue waters of the Mediterranean stretch out to the edge of the earth.

I hold my brother's hand. I look into Alexei's eyes. And we keep flying.

Suspended somewhere in between.

ALLY CARTER is the *New York Times* bestselling author of *All Fall Down*, the first book in the Embassy Row series, as well as the Gallagher Girls and Heist Society series. Her books have been published all over the world, in over twenty languages. You can visit her online at www.allycarter.com.